A CATERED DOGGIE WEDDING

Books by Isis Crawford

A CATERED MURDER
A CATERED WEDDING
A CATERED CHRISTMAS
A CATERED VALENTINE'S DAY
A CATERED HALLOWEEN
A CATERED BIRTHDAY PARTY
A CATERED THANKSGIVING
A CATERED ST. PATRICK'S DAY
A CATERED CHRISTMAS COOKIE EXCHANGE
A CATERED FOURTH OF JULY
A CATERED MOTHER'S DAY
A CATERED TEA PARTY
A CATERED COSTUME PARTY
A CATERED CAT WEDDING
A CATERED NEW YEAR'S EVE
A CATERED BOOK CLUB MURDER
A CATERED DOGGIE WEDDING

Published by Kensington Publishing Corp.

A Mystery with Recipes

A CATERED DOGGIE WEDDING

ISIS CRAWFORD

Kensington Publishing Corp.
www.kensingtonbooks.com

KENSINGTON BOOKS are published by

Kensington Publishing Corp.
119 West 40th Street
New York, NY 10018

All Kensington titles, imprints and distributed lines are available at special quantity discounts for bulk purchases for sales promotion, premiums, fund-raising, educational or institutional use.

Special book excerpts or customized printings can also be created to fit specific needs. For details, write or phone the office of the Kensington Special Sales Manager: Kensington Publishing Corp., 119 West 40th Street, New York, NY, 10018. Attn. Special Sales Department. Phone: 1-800-221-2647.

The K and Teapot logo is a trademark of Kensington Publishing Corp.

Library of Congress Control Number: 2022931851

ISBN: 978-1-4967-3496-9
First Kensington Hardcover Edition: July 2022

ISBN: 978-1-4967-3499-0 (ebook)

10 9 8 7 6 5 4 3 2 1

Printed in the United States of America

For my dad, Harry Bonat, and for Anya,
who makes life interesting.

A CATERED DOGGIE WEDDING

Chapter 1

The whole thing started at eight in the evening of June 8. Maybe not exactly then, but close enough. The request had seemed so innocuous, both Libby and Bernie later agreed.

Who would have thought it would have ended with a body? Actually two. Certainly they hadn't. It's true there was the email Bernie had gotten later that evening. **Don't cater the wedding. You'll be sorry if you do.** That should have warned them something was afoot.

But it hadn't. Bernie had shown it to her sister, then deleted it. They both agreed it was ridiculous. Who would object to the wedding? Dog-hating trolls? Or maybe it was a joke. Or a competitor wanting the job? There were lots of possibilities. But the sisters were tired. It had been a long day—they'd catered a luncheon for the Longely Garden Club and a bridal shower for Mrs. Kimbell's niece—and it was late, so they'd blown the email off and gone to bed.

But honestly, as Bernie later confessed, even if they'd known what was going to happen, they would have taken the job, anyway. On principle. Because neither she nor her sister liked being told what to do. And there was the curiosity factor, not to mention the "helping someone out" factor. But they might have been more careful. Taken more precautions. Not that it probably would have made a difference when all was said and done.

Googie had shown up fifteen minutes early that morning, an unusual occurrence for their twenty-four-year-old, six-foot, five-inch counterman, and been extra helpful throughout the day.

"I have a favor to ask," he'd said as he'd put the half-full tub of A Taste of Heaven's famous freshly made cabbage, jicama, and pineapple coleslaw back in the cooler for the night.

"Ah," Libby replied, looking up from the tray of chocolate ginger cookies she was covering with plastic wrap to keep them fresh for the next day and thinking that now Googie's behavior made sense. He'd even cleaned out the mixers without being asked.

Googie closed the cooler's sliding glass door. "Well, not really a favor," he amended. "We'll pay."

"Be still my heart," Bernie remarked as she came out of the prep room. It was seven forty-five, and the shop was closing for the evening. Normally, they closed at seven in the summer, but tonight they'd stayed open later to accommodate one of their customers.

"Ha ha. Very funny," Googie shot back.

Bernie grinned. "I thought it was. Seriously, what do you need?"

"We need you to cater a wedding," Googie explained. "We thought we could do it by ourselves, but the wedding has gotten bigger. A lot bigger, actually."

"Oh my God! You and Jennie are getting married," Bernie shrieked, rushing to embrace him.

"Not exactly," Googie replied, smiling sheepishly as he took a step back. He wasn't a huggy, kissy kinda guy.

"Bertha and Ernie are." And he pointed through the opened door to the sidewalk, where his two eight-month-old golden retrievers were sitting. They wagged their tails in unison and woofed. His girlfriend, Jennie, grinned and waved.

"Ah, puppy love is a beautiful thing," Bernie observed.

Googie pressed an imaginary button. "Wrong choice. Try again."

"A shotgun wedding?"

Googie feigned outrage. "I'm shocked you would suggest something like that."

"I believe the phrase is *shocked and appalled*," Bernie said.

Googie gave her a blank look.

"*Casablanca*?" Bernie said.

Googie shook his head.

"Obviously, you're not a lover of old movies," Bernie told him.

"Westerns," Googie said. "I like Westerns."

"Me too," Bernie agreed, changing the subject. "Too bad about the puppies. I would have taken one."

Googie raised an eyebrow. "Would you really?"

"Yes," Bernie said at the same time her sister said, "No."

"In any case," Bernie continued, "they're adorable, and I'm sure the wedding will be, too."

Libby wasn't so sure about that. She remembered the cat wedding she and her sister had catered some years ago. That hadn't gone well. To say the least. But then again, cats weren't known for their ability to take directions.

"You're serious?" she asked, turning to face Googie.

"I'm serious," Googie assured her. "Jennie is opening up a doggie day-care center where Beerly There was."

Bernie whistled. "I bet Renee isn't happy," Bernie observed, Renee being the owner of the high-end dress store next door.

Googie frowned. "Talk about an understatement. She

tried to get a restraining order. Something about an unten-able atmosphere imperiling her business—whatever that means."

"It means she doesn't want dogs around," Bernie said. "Of course, she wasn't too happy about the restaurant, ei-ther," Bernie reflected. "I guess she should have read her lease more carefully."

"Meaning?"

"Meaning some commercial leases have exclusion clauses. Obviously, Renee's doesn't."

Googie's frown deepened. "I don't know about clauses, but I do know she's a . . ."

"Little tightly wound," Bernie said. She had been going to say *bitch* but had decided against it.

Googie laughed. "So you know her?" he asked.

"I do," Bernie replied, thinking about her last encounter with Renee. She'd bought a dress there last year and dis-covered a small rip in one of the seams when she'd gotten it home. *Not a problem*, Bernie had thought. At least it shouldn't have been, but when she'd returned the dress the next day, Renee had accused Bernie of doing it herself. They'd finally come to an agreement, but the incident had left a bad taste in Bernie's mouth, and she hadn't shopped there since.

Googie sighed. "I hope she calms down."

"Me too," Bernie said, even though she was pretty sure Renee wasn't going to. But Bernie didn't say that. What would be the point? The lease had already been signed; the damage done. "So when are you and Jennie getting mar-ried?" Bernie teased, changing the subject. "We could have a double wedding."

"Ha. Ha. Very funny," Googie replied.

"Maybe I should ask Jennie what she thinks," Bernie mused.

"Don't you dare," Googie cried, a look of panic on his face.

Bernie lifted her hand. "Peace. Just kidding."

"I hope so. Now, as I was saying," Googie went on before Bernie could say anything else, "Jennie thought the wedding would be a good way to advertise the opening of Woof Woof. We have Marcy Black as the florist and Denise Alvarez as the photographer, and we were hoping to have you guys as the caterers. We started with ten people, but now we're up to . . ." He paused for a minute to do a mental count. "Oh, maybe a hundred."

"A hundred?" Libby repeated.

"Maybe a few more if we count the wedding party," Googie allowed.

"Is the wedding party canine or human?" Bernie asked.

"Canine, of course," Googie replied, "but I was talking about their handlers."

"Finger foods," Libby said suddenly, thinking out loud about the menu. "Definitely finger foods."

"Pigs in a blanket. Dog-shaped crackers with a variety of cheeses. Melon strips cut into bone shapes and wrapped in prosciutto," Bernie suggested. "Maybe a paw print wedding cake?"

Googie beamed. "So that's a yes? You'll take the job?"

Libby answered for herself and her sister. "We will." And with that she and Bernie went outside to greet the bride and the groom.

Jennie squealed and clapped her hands when she heard the verdict. "Oh, thank you. Thank you. This is going to be amazing." She turned to the goldens. "Right, Bertha? Right, Ernie?"

Ernie and Bertha wagged their tails so hard, their rear ends wiggled from side to side. Then Bertha jumped up and gave Libby a big, wet dog smooch on the mouth.

"Eww. Dog germs," Libby cried, wiping her mouth with the back of her hand, while Bernie laughed.

"We're working on their manners," Jennie said, apologizing, while trying and failing to stop Ernie from ramming his nose into Bernie's crotch and sniffing. "I guess he likes you," Jennie said, grabbing the eighty-pound golden retriever's collar and pulling him back as he tried to dive between Bernie's legs.

"I guess he does," Bernie said, scratching Ernie's back. His fur felt soft against her fingers. "So where's the reception going to be held?"

"At Woof Woof. The same place as the wedding," Jennie said. "Want to see it?"

"Now?"

Jennie nodded. "The reno isn't done yet, we still have to do most of the build-out, but it'll give you an idea. The whole thing is going to be state of the art."

"Sure. Why not?" Bernie replied. "Just give us another twenty minutes to finish closing up, and we'll be right over."

Jennie hugged them both. "This is going to be perfect," she gushed. "Absolutely perfect."

Chapter 2

"We're going to be late," Libby observed. It had taken her and her sister a little longer to close the shop than they'd anticipated.

"Ten minutes," Bernie replied as she stopped for the light on Elmcrest.

Five motorcyclists roared by them, the noise taking over the street; then it faded as they receded into the distance. *Old guys looking to recapture their joyriding days*, Bernie thought as the light turned green. She wasn't in a rush to arrive at their destination. It was a lovely summer evening, and she was reveling in its embrace. The day had cooled off, and the breeze coming through Mathilda's opened windows brought with it the sweet scent of early June. It had been an unusually long, cold, and wet spring, and the trees had greened out and gotten their summer outfits on later than usual.

Limestone Plaza was a cute little cul-de-sac that butted up against an upscale residential neighborhood. Shops fronted the sidewalk. Behind them a meadow filled with dandelions and clover sloped down to a small creek where watercress grew. There was a New York–style steak house on one side of the road, as well as a fancy beauty salon and spa, a jewelry store, a wine shop, a yoga studio, and a small gift shop that specialized in organic handmade objects.

Woof Woof was located on the opposite side of the street, next to Renee's shop, the two places forming a triangle with the yoga studio and the beauty salon. Large cedar barrels filled with begonias and ivy demarcated the line between the sidewalk and the street, while wire baskets full of pink and purple impatiens hung from the lampposts. In the afternoon, the parking spaces were filled with doctors' wives' BMWs and Infinitis, but now the stores were closed, and the street was empty, the freshly painted white lines vivid against the blacktop. Only a handful of vehicles remained, and they belonged to the people dining at the steak house.

Bernie had just reached the cul-de-sac and was singing along to "Dancing in the Street" when she heard yelling intertwined with barking. The sounds grew louder as they got closer. "Ah, nothing like the sweet sound of conflict on a summer's eve," she remarked, paraphrasing a line from *Apocalypse Now*.

Libby turned toward her sister. "Do those voices belong to whom I think they do?" she asked.

Bernie pressed her lips together, gave the van a little more gas, and rounded the corner as she spoke. "That would be a yes."

"They're not exactly evenly matched," Libby commented as she watched Jennie and Renee facing off on the sidewalk.

"Definitely not," Bernie agreed. She put Renee at five feet, two inches tall and one hundred pounds, if that, while Jennie was five feet, eight inches tall and a fit 140 pounds.

"Very far from," Libby observed.

"My money's on Renee in a full-on catfight, though," Bernie added as she brought Mathilda to a stop in front of the two women. "What she lacks in height she makes up for in ferocity."

"Definitely," Libby said as Renee and Jennie stopped screaming at each other and faced the van.

"Are you two trying out for the new all girls Wrestle-Mania team?" Bernie asked as she exited Mathilda. "I understand they're looking for new recruits. I can see it now." Bernie lifted her hand and painted an imaginary banner in the sky. "The fashionista vs. the granolista. I bet it would be a cult hit on Netflix."

"Cute," Renee said.

Bernie gave her, her best smile. "I like to think I am."

"Thank God you're here," Jennie said at the same time Renee told Bernie she wasn't talking about her.

"See, she likes me," Bernie said, pointing to Jennie.

"She likes them, too," Renee said, nodding to the goldens. "It wasn't intended as a compliment."

Bertha and Ernie barked and wagged their tails.

"How can anyone not like them?" Jennie demanded.

"Yeah," Bernie said, raising her voice to be heard over the dogs. "Inquiring minds want to know."

Renee glared at her. "Oh joy," she said. "Just what we need."

"A charming woman with an excellent fashion sense?" Bernie chirped, because sometimes she couldn't help herself.

Renee snorted and patted her curly red hair into place. "I would love someone like that . . . if they were here. Unfortunately, they're not."

"Is that any way to treat an old customer?" Bernie asked as she reflected that if Renee fell off a boat, she'd sink under the weight of all the jewelry she was wearing. "Tell me," she asked Renee, referring to the necklaces and bracelets she had on, "do you take off all those necklaces and bracelets every night?"

"I'd go broke if I had customers like you," Renee retorted, ignoring Bernie's question.

"I hear that's what you're doing," Bernie shot back as Ernie and Bertha charged toward her, their tails going back and forth like metronomes.

Renee glowered. "I don't know where you're getting your news from, but you should find a new source."

"I think my source is pretty accurate," Bernie lied, because there was no source. She'd made her comment up.

"And who would that be?" Renee demanded.

"I'm not at liberty to say," Bernie answered. As she spoke, she reflected that Renee had lost more weight. She wasn't quite skin and bones, but she was getting there. Her cheekbones looked sharp enough to slice bread. For a moment, Bernie wondered if Renee was sick.

Renee put her hands on her hips. "What are you doing here, anyway?"

"Sightseeing," Bernie replied.

"Our job," Libby said. She wanted to say something cutting and witty, but nothing came to mind. It would later, of course. Probably at two in the morning. That's the way it always seemed to work with her.

"What job?" Renee demanded. Then an expression of horror crossed her face as it hit her. She turned her head and narrowed her eyes. "Are you going to have some sort of event here, Jennifer?"

Jennie straightened her shoulders and stuck out her chin. "As a matter of fact, I am." She had to yell to be heard over Bertha and Ernie's barking.

"And what would that be?"

"A wedding."

Renee lifted an eyebrow. "You're getting married here? In your place?" Her tone was incredulous. "What an . . . interesting choice."

"I'm not getting married." Jennie pointed to the dogs. "They are. On Sunday morning."

"This Sunday?" Renee squeaked.

"No," Jennie replied. "Two weeks from this coming one. It's not like it's going to interfere with you or anything."

"That's when I'm having my Missoni trunk show," Renee cried. "You have to change it."

"I can't," Jennifer told her.

"Of course you can," Renee insisted.

"No, I can't. I already put down payments for the florist, the photographer, and the invitations."

"So cancel them."

"I can't. I'll lose my money."

Renee rolled her eyes. "Working close to the margins, are we? How many people are you inviting?"

"About one hundred," Jennie answered. "More or less."

Renee looked as if she was going to faint. "Are you serious?"

"It's a way to advertise Woof Woof's opening."

"When is your trunk show?" Bernie asked Renee.

"That Sunday at noon."

"The wedding is in the morning," Jennie said. "The two events won't interfere with each other. See, no problem. Everything is going to be fine."

"No. It will not be," Renee countered. Then she pointed to the large mound of dog poop on the ground. "What about that?"

"What about it?" Jennie asked.

"That's what I'm talking about. Are you just going to leave it there?"

"Hardly. For your information, I was about to clean it up when you started screaming at me."

"Right," Renee shot back.

"Are you calling me a liar?" Jennie demanded.

"You said it. I didn't," Renee replied.

Two splotches of color appeared on Jennie's cheeks. She was about to take a step toward Renee, but Bernie stepped between the two women before she could.

"I don't understand your problem, Renee," she said as she scratched Ernie's big blocky head. He barked and leaned against her.

"My problem, Bernie, is that she shouldn't be here," Renee replied, using a tone usually reserved for speaking to two-year-olds.

"I have as much right to be here as you," Jennie countered. Bertha and Ernie woofed in agreement.

"No, you don't," Renee snapped.

"The landlord thinks I do." Jennie pointed to the goldens. "So do they."

Renee rolled her eyes again. "You don't get it, do you?"

"There's nothing to get," Jennie said.

Renee went on. "I'm trying to do you a favor. Ruffo is just using you to make me leave. He wants to empty the place out."

Jennie shrugged. "I'll take my chances."

"Fine, but then he'll do the same thing to you. You're throwing money in the garbage. How much are you spending on the reno anyway?"

"Enough," Jennie said as she swatted at a mosquito. "But if he wanted to empty out this strip mall, why rent to me at all? Why not leave the space empty? It makes no sense."

"I'll tell you why. He just heard the rumors about Syntech coming in and building a campus here," Renee said. "Listen," she repeated, "I'm trying to help you."

"Sure you are." Jennie pointed to the brick neocolonial

building in back of them. "I know the branch manager, and he said they're remodeling. Why would they be doing that if Syntech was coming in?"

Renee shrugged. "Have it your own way."

"You just don't want me here!"

"You're right," Renee said. "I don't. What do you think one of my customers is going to say when she steps in poop in her Manolos? I'll tell you. She's not going to want to come back."

"She's not going to step in poop," Jennie protested.

"Even if she doesn't, she'll hear the dogs barking on the other side of the wall, she'll smell them, and she'll hear them when they're in the backyard."

Jennie frowned. "Some people like dogs."

"I'm sure they do, but I'm trying to sell three-thousand-dollar dresses here. You think that's easy?"

"I wouldn't know, but I don't see what that has to do with my dogs."

"It's about atmosphere, not that you'd get it."

"You're right. I don't," Jennie told her. "Like I don't get spending all that money on a piece of clothing when you could be using it to do good."

And that was the point at which Ernie broke free from Jennie's restraining hand and licked Renee's Chanel skirt.

Unprepared for the assault, Renee stumbled backward. Her heel caught in a crack in the concrete path, and she slipped and sat down in Ernie's poop.

Which was when Libby and Bernie did the unforgivable.

They started to laugh.

Chapter 3

"I couldn't help it," Bernie told Brandon as she drank a wheat beer. "I laughed until I cried. Literally."

"Me too," Libby said to Marvin, raising her voice slightly so she could be heard over the whir of the overhead fans, the buzz of customers' voices, and the sports announcer on the TV.

The sisters were sitting at the bar at RJ's, having a beer with their beaus, as their mom would have called Brandon and Marvin, while regaling them with their latest adventure.

"And then what happened?" Brandon asked after he'd scanned the bar for anyone wanting a refill.

Usually, the big barn of a place was empty on a summer's night, but for some reason, this evening RJ's was full, the patrons' laughter rising and falling like waves in the ocean while the neon beer signs decorating the walls pulsed in time to an unknown rhythm. The Longely softball team was congregated at the far end of the bar, clinking bottles to celebrate their surprise victory of the season, while a noisy game of darts was underway in the backroom, and the pool table had been taken over by two overdressed couples up from New York City, who were spending more time arguing than playing.

"Renee turned red in the face," Bernie said after taking another sip of her beer. "I'm talking bright red. Crimson, really." She stifled a yawn. It had been a very long day.

"I was convinced we were going to have to call nine-one-one," Libby interjected. "I thought Renee was going to have a stroke."

"It didn't help that Bertha and Ernie ran over and started licking Renee's face," Bernie added.

"They were probably just trying to cheer her up," Marvin posited as he grabbed a handful of peanuts out of the bowl in front of him and began tossing them in his mouth one at a time. "Although I'm sure Renee didn't see it that way."

"No, she didn't," Libby agreed, giggling at the memory. "She started shrieking like someone was trying to kill her."

"Which made Ernie and Bertha lick all the harder." Bernie emptied her glass, then fished out the orange slice in it, ate it, deposited the rind on her napkin, and asked Brandon for another wheat beer before continuing. "On a totally different note, is it true that Syntech is moving in here?" Bernie asked, referring to the company that was tagged to become the next Google.

"That's TBD," Brandon said as he placed her glass in front of her.

Bernie raised an eyebrow. "Meaning?"

"To be decided," Brandon told her. "Why are you asking?"

Bernie told him as she held the glass up and studied it before taking a sip. The golden color. The tiny bubbles. They always reminded her of summer.

"So Renee was lying?" Libby asked. She was always

amazed by how much Brandon knew about what was going on in Longely.

"I'd say exaggerating," Brandon replied.

"I don't envy you guys having to deal with her," Marvin said, giving his full attention to the conversation instead of half watching the Mets on the TV above the bar. Then he explained. "A week after her aunt's funeral, she came into the office, waving our bill in her hand, accusing us of double billing her, yelling she was going to the police."

"And had you?" Brandon kidded.

"Yeah. We charged her for two caskets instead of one."

"So what happened?" Libby asked.

"Nothing. My father told her to go ahead, at which point she stormed out, but before she did, I thought she was going to slap him. She came this close." Marvin indicated an inch with his thumb and index finger. "She told him she'd see him in court instead."

"She slapped Bernie's hand away when she tried to help her up," Libby recalled after taking a sip of her shandy. She'd loved the beer and lemonade combination since she'd had her first one in a London pub when she was a teenager. Libby took another sip of her drink and put the glass down on RJ's burnished copper counter. "She told Jennie that she was done," Libby added, remembering the scene.

Brandon raised an eyebrow. "Done?"

"Done," Bernie answered. "As in 'You'll never work in this town again' kind of done."

"Good thing she didn't have a gun on her," Libby added. "Because if she had, I think she would have used it."

"Let's not overdramatize," Bernie told her sister.

"I'm not," Libby insisted. "She was that mad."

"For heaven's sake, it was just a skirt," Brandon remarked, wiping a glass with the towel he always had slung over his shoulder.

"A three-thousand-dollar Chanel skirt, to be exact," Bernie said. "That's not just a skirt. That's an investment."

"Who is Chanel, and why does a skirt from there cost so much?" Brandon asked.

"Tell me you're kidding," Bernie replied, studying Brandon's face. She couldn't tell if he was teasing her or not.

Brandon grinned. "Nope. I'm not."

"How can you not know who Chanel is?"

"How can you not know who Fitzmagic is?" Brandon countered.

Bernie scrunched up her face. "Fitzmagic?"

"Ryan Fitzpatrick. NFL. Miami Dolphins," Brandon elucidated.

"I don't do football," Bernie protested.

"Exactly. And I don't do fashion," Brandon replied.

"Obviously," Bernie said, indicating Brandon's T-shirt with a nod of her head.

Brandon pulled at his shirt. "What's wrong with this?"

"It's camo."

"And the problem is?"

Bernie sighed her long-suffering sigh. "I can't explain if you don't get it."

"You're saying I'm sartorially challenged, Bernie?"

Bernie raised her glass in a mock toast. "You said it. I didn't."

"What about Marvin?" Brandon asked.

"What about me?" Marvin squawked.

"Look at what you're wearing," Brandon replied.

Marvin glanced down at his khaki shorts and blue polo shirt. "What's wrong with what I'm wearing?" he demanded.

"Black socks and sandals?" Brandon replied. "Even I know better than that."

Marvin frowned. "I don't see the problem."

"The problem is the combo makes you look like an old man," Bernie told him.

"I do not," Marvin said indignantly. "Do I?" he asked Libby.

Libby patted him on the arm. "Definitely not," she lied.

"See," Marvin told Bernie.

She shrugged. "Have it your way."

"How about we get back to what happened with Renee and Jennie?" Marvin suggested, anxious to get the spotlight off himself.

Libby answered. "There isn't much more to tell," she replied, picking up the story where she'd left off. "Renee got up and told Jennie she'd make sure that anyone who had anything to do with the wedding would be blacklisted, and then she went inside her shop and slammed the door."

"And we left and came here," Bernie said.

Marvin ate the last peanut in the bowl, reflecting as he did that this wasn't the way to lose the twenty pounds he needed to. "And Jennie?"

Libby answered, "Jennie went home after she cleaned up the poop."

"So you didn't see the inside of Beerly There?" Brandon asked.

Bernie shook her head. "Nope. Why?"

Brandon shrugged. "No reason, really. I was just wondering how they're going to reconfigure the place, given the fireplace and all."

"You were there?" Marvin asked, indicating as he did that he could use another beer.

"Just once," Brandon said. He gave Marvin another Pabst. "The service was terrible, the beer was skunked, and the burger tasted like cardboard."

Bernie laughed. "Don't give us your real opinion."

"Which is what happens when someone who likes t
cook decides that opening a restaurant will be fun," Libby
editorialized, putting the word *fun* in finger quotes, as
Brandon headed off to wait on a couple of the softballers
at the far end of the bar.

"If you ask me, it sounds like amateur night at the O.K.
Corral," Marvin noted. He'd been watching old Westerns,
too, on Brandon's recommendation.

"Restaurants are not fun," Bernie declared, riffing off
her sister's train of thought. "They are the absolute opposite. But then, I imagine running a dress shop would be
pretty stressful, too."

"But not as stressful," Libby objected. "You don't have
to throw your product out if you can't sell it in a couple of
days."

"But you have to put it on sale, and if you don't sell it,
you've laid out a ton of money, which you can't get back,"
Bernie countered before turning to Marvin. "Which is not
a problem you have in the funeral business."

"No, but we have other issues," Marvin replied. "Like
competing with the big guys over pricing. Coffins have
gotten really expensive, and we don't do enough business
to buy in volume, like the chains do."

"I guess it would be bad form to do a twofer," Brandon
reflected, having returned from down the bar. "You know,
two people in one casket."

"It's been done," Marvin said. "You'd be surprised what
happens in the funeral business." Then he changed the
subject before Libby could ask him what he was talking
about. "So when are you guys going to get to see the inside
of Beerly There?" he asked Bernie and Libby.

"What *was* Beerly There," Bernie corrected. "Tomorrow morning. We're going to see it tomorrow morning. At
least that's the plan."

"Good luck," Brandon said.

"Yeah, let's hope Renee isn't there," Bernie said. "I could use a little less drama."

"That's not her real name, you know," Brandon told them.

"You're kidding," Libby said.

Brandon shook his head. "No, I am not. It's Hilda Hickenloop."

Bernie whistled. "Wow. Decidedly unsexy."

"I can see why she doesn't want to use it," Libby observed. "It certainly lacks a certain je ne sais quoi."

"You can say that again," Bernie agreed.

Libby did.

"How do you know that?" Bernie asked Brandon.

"Her brother told me."

"I didn't know she had a brother," Libby said, not that there was any reason she should know.

"That's because she and John are estranged," Brandon replied. "Have been for a while now." And he went down the bar to serve the couples that had been playing pool.

Chapter 4

"What are you going to do?" Googie asked when he ambled into work the next morning.

Libby looked up from the corn and cheddar cheese muffins she was arranging in the display case. "What am I going to do about what? The email Bernie got last night? The one I assume Renee sent about not catering the wedding? Ignore it, of course."

"Yeah, Jennie got one of those, too. Ridiculous. *Don't cater the wedding. You'll be sorry if you do.*" Googie snorted. "Give me a break." Then he walked around the counter, stowed his backpack under the counter, and straightened up before continuing to speak. "No, I'm talking about the van."

"Mathilda?"

"Do you have another van?"

"Why?" Libby's voice went up slightly. "What's wrong with her?"

"I'm guessing you haven't been outside yet," Googie said.

"No, I haven't," Libby replied. She hadn't even looked outside. She'd overslept and been racing around like a crazy person, trying to catch up, ever since. "Should I?"

"I'll tell you one thing. You're not going to be happy when you do," Googie predicted as Amber came barreling through the door. Today her hair was a bright Kelly green, and she was wearing deep purple eye shadow and a pale pink lipstick, which matched the pink-and-white-checked gingham sundress and neon pink Converse sneakers she was sporting.

"That sucks about the van," she said after she'd started taking the chairs off the four tabletops and putting them on the floor.

"What's wrong with Mathilda?" Libby repeated, anxiety tickling at her throat.

"She hasn't been outside yet," Googie explained to Amber as he started making the coffee. "She doesn't know."

"Bummer," Amber told Googie. "I hope you don't have deliveries to make today," she said, turning to Libby.

This day is not starting off well, Libby decided as she closed the display case and hurried outside. She walked down the sidewalk to the small blacktopped parking lot that abutted the entrance to the family's flat located over the store. She hoped that Googie and Amber were exaggerating, but she knew that they weren't.

"Holy crap," she cried when she saw what her employees had been talking about.

"That's what I said, too, when I saw it," Googie remarked. He'd followed Libby out of the shop, as had Amber.

"Who would do that?" Amber asked as a slight breeze ruffled her hair. "That's such a dick move."

"I have a pretty good idea," Libby answered, her voice grim, as a flush of anger surged through her. She took a deep breath and tried to calm herself. After all, she told herself, it could be worse. This was just annoying. Then she told herself that again and walked over to the door that led to the Simmonses' flat, opened it, and yelled upstairs for Bernie to come down.

"Why?" her father shouted back. He was sitting in his favorite chair in the living room, petting the cat, and watching the local news. "What's wrong?"

"Come and see," Libby answered. "And bring Bernie."

A moment later, Sean and her sister were standing in front of Mathilda. The van shimmered in the morning sun, last night's rain having washed all the dust away. It looked good. Well, as good as a ten-year-old van with over one hundred thousand miles on it could look. Except for the tires. They didn't look so great. They looked as if they had melted.

Bernie and her dad stood there for a moment, contemplating the damage.

"That's not good," Sean observed, referring to the four slashed tires.

"Nine hundred dollars not good," Bernie said. Van tires were expensive.

Googie rubbed his eyes. He'd been up late calming down Jennie after her scene with Renee. "Those tires are, like, pancake flat. I didn't think they could get like that."

"Neither did I," Amber said. "It looks like whoever did this sucked all the air out of them. Is that even possible?"

"Evidently it is," Sean said. He'd never seen tires like that, either, which was saying a lot considering his thirty-five-year career in law enforcement. He walked over and inspected the damage. Bernie and Libby joined him. Upon close examination, they could see that each tire had multiple slashes in it.

"One thing is clear," Sean said after he'd completed his inspection. "Whoever did this took their time and did it right." There'd be no patching these. Hopefully, they could still use the old rims.

"Too bad they didn't do it wrong," Amber said.

Bernie retied the sleeveless sky-blue polka-dotted wrap-around dress she'd hurriedly thrown on. "I'm going to kill her. Slowly," she declared.

"I take it you mean Renee?" Sean asked. He'd heard the Beerly There doggie day-care story this morning over breakfast, while he'd been eating the multigrain blueberry pancakes Bernie had made and sipping iced coffee with a touch of cream in it.

"Who else?" Bernie replied.

"You don't know that she did this," Sean pointed out.

"Yeah, Dad, I do."

"No, you don't, Bernie. You suspect it, but you can't prove it," Sean countered. "At least not yet. There's a big difference between the two, as you well know."

"Semantics," Bernie replied.

"Hardly," Sean told his daughter, giving her "the look." "We don't know what happened, because we can't see what happened."

And here it was, the comment Bernie had been waiting for. What should she do? Ignore it? Say something? While she was deciding, she pushed a lock of wet hair behind her ear. She had just washed it and had been in the midst of drying it when her dad had told her she needed to get downstairs ASAP.

"Okay. You were right," she told her dad after a minute had gone by.

"About what, Bernie?" Sean asked, all pretend innocence.

"Are you going to make me say it?"

"Yes, Bernie. I am." And Sean crossed his arms over his chest and waited for the apology. These days he'd take his victories, however small, where he could find them.

"Fine, Dad. We should have installed the security cameras, like you said. Satisfied?"

"Yes, because if we had, we'd know who did this."

"You don't have to rub it in," Bernie protested.

"Hey," Sean replied as he began massaging the knuckles on his right hand. He was always a little stiff in the morning, and the dampness from last night's rain didn't help. "You were the one who brought the whole thing up."

"I just said what you were thinking," Bernie countered.

"How do you know what I was thinking?" Sean demanded. "Can you read my mind?"

"No, but I can read the expression on your face."

Sean didn't say anything, because his daughter was correct. That was exactly what he'd been thinking. They'd had three break-ins on the block in the past year and a half, and Sean had suggested installing surveillance cameras outside the store and in the parking lot. His daughters had agreed in a lukewarm kinda way, but despite a certain amount of nagging on his part—okay, a lot of nagging on his part—they'd never gotten around to doing it.

"It could be worse," Libby chimed in, trying to inject a positive note into the proceedings.

"Things could always be worse," Bernie retorted as she bent down to inspect the tires one more time, thinking as she did about the amount of money it was going to cost to replace them. "This must have happened between two and six thirty in the morning," she guessed, standing up as she did the math. "Libby and I got back from RJ's around one thirty . . ."

"Two," Libby corrected.

"One forty-five," Bernie said. "We were in bed by two, and we got up at six thirty." They'd both overslept by half an hour. In the summer the sisters opened the shop later and closed earlier.

Sean mulled over Bernie's timeline while he tucked the hem of his polo shirt into his Bermuda shorts. "I thought I heard something outside round four," he reflected after a moment had passed. "But I put it down to Dan taking one of his nocturnal strolls." Dan, their neighbor, had been walking the neighborhood somewhere between two and five in the morning ever since his wife's death three months ago.

"We should talk to him," Bernie said.

Sean nodded. "I will, not that I think he saw anything. If he had, he would have called the police. Or me."

"True," Libby said.

Sean frowned. "I should have gotten out of bed and looked."

"And you would have seen Renee if you had," Bernie insisted.

"Perhaps," Sean allowed.

"Definitely," Bernie said.

"There's the email," Libby said. "What about that?"

Googie shifted his weight from one leg to the other. "I checked it out. So did Jennie. It's a dead end. It wasn't sent from Renee's account. Whoever sent it either went to the library and used one of their computers or bought a TracFone and used that, making it impossible to trace." He frowned. "At least that's what Jennie said, and she's pretty good at that type of stuff. She used to work in IT."

"So much for that," Sean commented. He indicated the

van's tires with a jerk of his head. "I'm sorry, Bernie, but I really don't see Renee for this."

"Because?" Bernie prompted.

"Because my gut tells me she didn't do it." Sean went on to explain. "She's not a hands-on kind of person. For God's sake, she goes to the Mobil on Dell because they'll check the air in her tires and put gas in her tank. She hates getting her hands dirty."

"Then maybe she got someone to do it for her," Libby suggested.

"Good point," Sean agreed, immediately thinking of Ivan, Renee's current live-in. Last year the twenty-five-year-old had shattered the windows on Renee's neighbor's SUV with a nine iron after the neighbor had complained to the town's code inspector about the height of a privacy fence Ivan was installing. Evidently, he hadn't been happy when the inspector had come around and made him take it down, in addition to levying a fine.

"I'd forgotten about that," Bernie was saying when Googie's cell rang.

He fished it out of his pocket and answered it.

"It's Jennie," he said when he was done talking. "The florist and the photographer called."

"Let me guess. Their vehicles got hit, too," Bernie said from reading the expression on Googie's face.

Googie made a gun with his index finger and thumb and pulled the trigger. "Give the girl a prize. To be accurate, Marcy's van was keyed, and Denise woke up to a noose nailed to her door. Jennie wants to know if you could talk to them. You know, try to reassure them, see if they know what's going on."

Bernie and Libby exchanged glances. Libby spoke first.

"I guess we could, but maybe they should call the police," she suggested. "We're getting serious here."

"Jennie doesn't want the story to appear in the local paper," Googie explained.

Bernie nodded. Reported crimes appeared in the Crime Beat column of the *Longely Sentinel*, as well as in the neighborhood watch list.

"She doesn't think it's a good way to start off a new business," Googie continued. "It doesn't exactly inspire a vote of confidence."

"So no publicity is *good* publicity?" Libby asked.

"In this case," Googie replied. "Anyway, Jennie thinks the police will just take her report and file it."

"What makes you say that?" Sean asked, even though he was pretty sure he knew the answer. He was just curious to hear what Googie was going to tell him.

"Well, there was that story in the paper about how they're short staffed."

Sean nodded encouragingly.

"Plus, she's had a few issues with them in the past," Googie replied.

"Like what?" Libby asked.

"Parking tickets." Googie shooed a fly away. "She didn't pay them."

"How much?" Sean inquired.

"One thousand dollars, more or less."

Sean whistled. "Not too shabby."

"And the cops weren't very nice when she got into a fight with her neighbor over Bertha and Ernie," Googie continued. "I mean, it wasn't her fault that the dogs saw something at five thirty in the morning and started barking."

"Fair enough," Bernie said. She turned to her sister. "Yes or no? In or out?"

"In," Libby said. "If Dad lets us borrow his car, that is. Otherwise, we're not going anywhere for a while. So, Dad. What's it going to be?"

Sean raised one eyebrow and then the other. "Us? Who's us?"

Bernie pointed to her sister. "Me and her, obviously."

"It's not obvious to me. You can use the car, but only if I drive," Sean said.

Bernie suppressed a groan. This was what she'd feared. Her dad was a horrible driver. When he was a cop, he used to go too fast, but now that he was a civilian, he went too slow. He called it balancing things out. Bernie called it making everyone on the road nuts.

"Take it or leave it," Sean told her.

"Don't you think you're going a bit overboard with the car thing?" Bernie asked.

"Not with my baby, I don't," her dad replied. The vehicle in question was his pride and joy, and he wasn't going to let anyone else drive it. For any reason. Period.

Libby patted her sister on the shoulder. "It's okay, Bernie," she said. "You go with Dad, and I'll call the garage and arrange for a tow."

Bernie gave Libby the evil eye, but Libby pretended not to see it.

"After all," Libby said, continuing with her charade, "someone has to be here for the morning rush."

"Fine." Bernie knew when she was beaten. She turned to Googie and Amber. "You two. Playtime is over. Time to get to work."

Googie bowed, and Amber curtsied.

"Your wish is my command, my lady," Googie said.

"As it should be," Bernie replied.

"You know . . . ," Googie said, then stopped.

"What?" Libby prompted.

He shook his head. "Never mind."

"Are you sure?" Bernie asked.

Googie nodded. "I'm positive."

Then he, Amber, and Libby turned and walked into A Little Taste of Heaven, while Sean went back upstairs to get his keys, and Bernie contemplated Mathilda's ruined tires. She and Libby definitely had to get those security cameras up and running by the end of the week.

Chapter 5

Sean had just passed the Citgo station on Dell Street when Jennie called Bernie to tell her that she'd just been contacted by her landlord, as well. Evidently, Ruffo had woken up this morning to see WOOF WOOF HAS TO GO written on his driveway in white paint.

"He's pretty pissed."

"Did he call the cops?" Bernie asked.

"Yeah. They took a statement, and that was that. I was wondering . . ."

"If we could swing by and talk to him, too? Not a problem," Bernie told her.

"What's not a problem?" Sean asked after Bernie had hung up.

She explained.

"Well, I will say that whoever is doing this has had a busy night," Sean observed as he stopped at a red light. "Whoever is behind this is quite energetic, not to mention knowing all the players."

"I hadn't thought of that," Bernie allowed.

"The other interesting thing," Sean mused as the light turned green, "the thing that makes this a little more alarming than your average stupid stunt, is that whoever did this targeted everyone at their homes instead of their businesses."

"Why is that alarming?" Bernie asked.

"It's alarming because it adds an element of menace. Implicit menace, as in 'I know where you live' kind of menace," Sean explained, taking a right and heading to Ruffo's place.

"We're going in the wrong direction," Bernie pointed out.

Sean gave her the look. "Not if we're going to talk to Ruffo."

"We are?"

"Yes, Bernie, we are."

"What happened to Denise and Marcy?"

"And Ivan," Sean added. "All in good time, my dear. All in good time." Then Sean stopped speaking and concentrated on his driving. There was a lot more traffic than he thought there would be at this time of the day.

"I see you called in the heavy artillery," Ruffo said to Bernie when he answered the door ten minutes later.

Sean laughed. "Nice to know that's what I am."

"Lookin' good," Ruffo told him. "That extra fifteen pounds suits you."

Sean patted his belly. "The same for you, Bob," Sean joked. Ruffo was one of the guys he'd hung out with at the gym before he'd stopped going. Then he pointed to Ruffo's driveway. "You certainly don't need glasses to see that." The block letters were thick and took up the entire space. "Nice penmanship."

Ruffo moved a dirt clod off his porch's step with the side of his foot. "I've always said that neatness counts," he commented as he walked down the stairs.

Sean snorted. "I wonder if whoever did this used a stencil."

"Yeah. I gotta tell you that's my question, too," Ruffo said. "Let's stake out the craft stores and find out." He grinned and hitched up his cargo shorts. "It sure makes you wonder about people these days. Everyone seems to have gone nuts."

Sean studied the letters for a moment. Whoever had done this had taken their time and done it properly. Like with the van. This wasn't some quick tag job. "I don't suppose you have a security camera?"

"If I had, we wouldn't be having this conversation." Ruffo shook his head at himself. "I keep on meaning to get one, but it's one of those things I never seem to get around to."

Sean shot a look at Bernie. "Tell me about it. How about your neighbors? They have security cameras?"

Ruffo shook his head again. "Nah. I already called and asked them. And no, no one saw or heard anything," he told Sean, answering Bernie's father's unanswered question. "No one with insomnia on this block."

"You think Renee did this?" Bernie asked him.

Ruffo took a minute to frame his response. "Given what Jennie told me and from what I heard from Dino—he owns the Chop House—she's the logical subject, but somehow . . ."

"You can't see her for it," Sean said as Ruffo's voice trailed away.

"Neither can my dad," Bernie informed Ruffo, "but you weren't there. You didn't see how angry she got." And she told him what had happened.

Ruffo grinned. "Sorry I missed it. She does love that skirt." Then he readjusted the brim of his baseball hat. Sean and Bernie had caught him before he took off on his runabout to do a little fishing. "In truth, I'm not sure. One part of me says, 'Yes, she did it,' and the other part of me says, 'No, not a chance in hell.' Calling the cops, yes. Doing this kind of stuff, no."

"What about Ivan?" Sean asked Ruffo. "Can you see him for this?"

"That putz?" Ruffo responded. "Absolutely. What does she see in him, anyway?"

"I hear he's got a—" Bernie began, but Sean put up his hand.

"Stop," he said before Bernie could finish. "I don't want to know."

"I was going to say a good sense of humor," Bernie told him.

"Sure you were," Sean said to her.

Ruffo smiled. "You were always a delicate soul, Sean."

"Ha ha," Sean said before getting back to the matter at hand. "Bernie said Renee told her that you'd rented the space out to Jennie because you want to get rid of her."

Ruffo snorted. "Renee said that when I rented the space out to Beerly There, too."

"Is it true?" Sean inquired.

"No. She's paranoid. Why would I shoot myself in the foot? Retail is down. I told Renee that if she knew of someone who wanted to move in there, someone in the apparel business, I'd be glad to talk to them."

"I take it she didn't," Bernie said.

"Let's just say if she did, she didn't tell me." Ruffo lifted his hands and turned them outward for emphasis, then dropped them. "These days I have to take the tenants I can get. It's a big space, and there aren't that many people who want something that large. Retail is down, in case you haven't heard, and buying online is in." He leaned forward. "Frankly, I think—no, I know—that Renee's having trouble making her rent. She's already asked me for a reduction."

"And you refused," Sean said.

Russo lifted his hands again. "Hey, I got expenses, just like everyone else. My bank isn't giving me a free pass. It's not saying, 'Hey, Bob, old buddy, take a couple of months off, dude! Have a vacation. Go to Maui. Have a good time.' I'll tell you one thing, though," he continued. "I'm tired of dealing with everything, and this nonsense is just the icing on the cake."

He scratched behind his ear and reseated his hat on his head. "It's making me reconsider leasing the space out to this Jennie. I wasn't so happy about doing it in the first place. She doesn't have a great credit rating, to put it mildly. But with this."

He grimaced. "I don't need this kind of aggravation at my age. I have enough as it is with my wife. Thank God, she's at her sister's and isn't coming back until next week. She would have . . . Well, I don't want to say what she would have if she saw the driveway. She's been after me to sell the strip mall for the past couple of years so we can move down to Florida and be with her sister." He wrinkled his nose. "I think I'd rather shoot myself. But this is just the excuse she needs."

"We'll find out who did it," Bernie promised.

Ruffo turned to Sean. "Can I count on what she says?" he asked him.

"She's my daughter," Sean responded. "When she says something, she means it."

"And you, Sean?" Ruffo asked.

Sean pointed to himself. "What about me?"

"Are you involved in finding out who did this, too?"

"What the hell do you think I'm doing here?" Sean demanded.

"Playing chauffeur?" Ruffo replied.

"Yeah, that's it," Sean told him.

Ruffo leaned over and pulled a deadly nightshade vine off the laurel hedge. "Damn things," he muttered. "Once they start, you can't get rid of them."

"Like so many other things in life," Sean commented.

"Waxing philosophical in your old age, I see," Ruffo observed.

Bernie brushed a moth away. "You know, Jennie has all her money wrapped up in this."

Ruffo shrugged. "Why tell me? That's her problem, not mine. Time for her to put on her big girl pants. Business is business. If she wants charity, she should go to the Salvation Army. And now, if you don't mind, I have a date with some perch."

"Those your fishing clothes?" Sean asked.

"Why?" Ruffo inquired.

"No reason. They're just a lot neater than mine," Sean said, taking in Ruffo's khaki shorts, polo shirt, and docksiders. "Of course," he reflected, "I use mine for painting, too."

Ruffo laughed. "I guess I'm more careful than you are when it comes to that."

"Except for the spot of paint on your docksiders," Sean commented.

Ruffo looked down at the two white spots on the top of the docksider on his left foot. "Impressive. I see your eyesight is still pretty good."

Then as Bernie and Sean watched, he walked over to his Dodge Ram, got in, started the truck up, zoomed out of his driveway, and drove away.

Chapter 6

"Charming man," Bernie commented after she and her dad had gotten back into Sean's vehicle.

Her dad chuckled and started his car. "He really has a heart of gold."

"Seriously, Dad?" Bernie asked.

"More like a heart of lead," Sean said as he backed down the driveway and hung a left onto Plainsville Road.

"Ivan is in the other direction," Bernie pointed out.

"I know, but the florist and photographer are this way," Sean said.

Bernie frowned. "I thought you wanted to talk to Ivan first."

"I did, but I've changed my mind."

"But Marcy Black and Denise Alvarez—"

Sean cut her off. "I know who they are," he told his daughter, irritation in his voice. "I might be old, but I'm not senile yet."

Bernie stopped fiddling with the radio. "I never said you were. I just want to know why you changed your mind."

"Simple," Sean answered. "Because the more you know, the better the questions you can ask," he replied as he headed toward the photographer's place. It was one of the rules he'd lived by in his law enforcement career.

Bernie wanted to say, "It would have been nice if you'd said that in the first place," but she knew better. Instead, she said, "Speaking of knowing things, do you know that Renee isn't Renee's real name?"

"As a matter of fact, I do," Sean told her as the light he had stopped at turned green.

"Why didn't you tell me?"

"Because you never asked," Sean replied.

"But I didn't know enough to ask," Bernie protested.

"Which is what I was saying before."

Bernie laughed. "You were, weren't you?"

They rode in silence for the next couple of minutes, Sean concentrating on the traffic, which was always heavy this time of year, with people going to and from their second homes.

"This whole thing is just weird," Bernie said as the driver behind Sean honked at him to speed up.

"Agreed," Sean replied, purposely slowing down.

"I mean, why all this drama?" Bernie asked as the other driver whipped around him and gave him the finger.

"That is the question, isn't it?" Sean replied as he returned the favor.

"Jeez, Dad."

"Jeez, Dad, what?"

"Nothing," Bernie said, catching herself before she commented on her dad's driving. There was no point. Commenting only made things worse. "I wonder if there's something else going on," Bernie declared instead as she glanced at the text from Libby that had just appeared on her cell phone, telling her she had to stop at the Elwood Dairy on her way home and pick up some more butter.

"Hopefully, we'll get some answers when we talk to Marcy and Denise," Sean replied.

But they didn't. Their stories were the same. Both women had woken up, gotten dressed, eaten breakfast, and then gone outside. Denise had found a noose nailed to her front door, and Marcy had found her van keyed.

And then there were the notes. They were identical. Both notes were on computer paper and featured sketches of dogs in the upper right-hand corner. The words *walk away from the wedding* were printed in the center of each page in sixteen-point Helvetica type. Both women were as puzzled as Bernie and her dad were.

"Are you photographing another wedding by any chance?" Bernie asked Denise after Denise had shown her the note and Sean had carefully placed it in a sandwich bag.

"You mean like a dog wedding? Sure, because they're so common. I've got a beagle one coming up next week."

"No need to be sarcastic," Bernie replied. "Just asking on the off chance that you were."

Denise pointed to the note she'd just handed Sean. "What else could it have to do with?" she snapped. "Marcy's car was vandalized. You just told me your tires were slashed." She indicated the Escalade parked in her driveway. "Frankly, I'm thankful for the noose. This isn't even my car. It's my parents. They're lending it to me." She shuddered. "They'd have a fit if anything happened to it. But the noose is creepy," she allowed.

"Yes, it is," Bernie agreed.

Denise bit her lower lip. "Like horror movie creepy." Her face collapsed. She looked as if she was going to cry. "I mean, I walked out, and there it was."

"Not the way you want to start the day," Sean said in a soothing voice.

"No, it isn't," Denise replied.

"I don't suppose you happened to see anything?" Sean continued. "Or anybody?"

"No, and neither did the neighbors," Denise replied. "I already asked."

"Did you report it to the police?"

"Yes, I did," Denise replied. "Even though Jennie told me not to."

"And what did the police say?" Sean asked.

"Nothing. Jennie was correct. I shouldn't have bothered. They wrote the report up and left. I got the impression they weren't going to do anything." Denise sighed and tugged up her bra strap. It had slipped out from under her black sleeveless T-shirt. "But realistically, I don't know if there's anything they can do."

"Maybe they can't, but we will," Bernie promised.

Sean patted Denise on the shoulder. "We'll find out who did this," he told her.

"I'm not sure I want to do the wedding now," Denise said, ignoring Sean's assurances. "I mean, whoever did this knows where I live."

Sean gave his daughter an "I told you so" glance.

A couple of minutes later they headed back to Sean's car. Marcy said the same thing when they caught up with her. She had just opened up her shop and was putting bunches of yellow roses in the front window when they stopped by.

"I didn't sign up for this," she said as they trooped outside so Marcy could show Bernie and Sean her damaged vehicle and the accompanying note that went with it.

Sean took the note and put it in a separate plastic baggie. He was hoping that he could persuade his friend Clyde to run both notes through the crime lab for prints. Back in the old days it wouldn't have been a problem, but today, with all the budget cuts, Lucy, the current chief, was keeping an eagle eye on expenses, not that he hadn't always been a micromanager.

Marcy ran her hand through her hair. She'd bleached and buzzed it, which emphasized her full lips, an effect she played up with bright red lipstick and purple eyeliner. Then she offered some advice on Woof Woof. "That place has always had bad luck. If I were Jennie, I'd smudge the place. Every business that's gone in there has closed for one reason or another." And with that Marcy reentered her shop, and Sean and Bernie got back in Sean's car and headed over to talk to Ivan and Renee.

"Is what Marcy said true?" Bernie asked her dad.

"Pretty much," Sean said as he remembered the place's history.

"Funny how some places are like that," Bernie observed as she watched the clouds massing in the sky. A tongue of lightning flickered on the other side of the Palisades.

"It looks as if the weather forecaster was correct," Sean noted as he made a right at the stone pillars that marked the beginning of the Riverside Estates.

When the area had been developed in the 1950s, it had been earmarked for young executives moving out of New York City. Then the development had been touted as the ultimate in luxury living, but time had taken its toll. Most of the houses Bernie passed needed a new coat of paint, their hedges needed trimming, and the access roads needed to be patched. As Sean drove by, the words that came to Bernie's mind were *tired* and *drab*. Renee's house was no different. The large black numbers tacked on the entrance to the white ranch were skewed, and the foundation shrubs looked long past their prime. Bernie was surprised. She'd expected better.

"What the hell are you doing here?" Renee demanded of Bernie and Sean when she stepped out the front door. They hadn't even had a chance to ring the doorbell. Renee had seen them coming through the picture window in her living room.

"Yeah," Ivan echoed. He was right behind her.

Bernie put him between twenty-five and thirty. He was a good-looking guy in a surfer dude kinda way. He had shaggy blond hair, a tan, blinding white teeth, and a body that looked as if he spent a fair amount of time working out at the gym.

"What do you want?" Ivan demanded, puffing out his chest and flexing his biceps.

"Nice pet you got there, Renee," Sean observed. "But then you always did have a certain flair. Where'd you pick him up? LA? Venice Beach?"

Ivan took a step forward, but Renee put out her arm and blocked him. "Don't," she told him. "He's just trying to get you upset."

"So where were you guys last night?" Bernie inquired.

Renee snorted. "Why should we tell you?"

"Why shouldn't you?" Bernie replied.

"How about because it's none of your business?" Renee told her.

"We're making it ours," Bernie answered.

Sean took a step forward. "We just wondered if either of you were out having fun," Sean said.

"What do you mean by fun?" Ivan demanded.

"You know," Sean answered, "keying cars, flattening tires, graffitiing driveways. That kind of fun."

"You're not a cop anymore," Renee answered. "You're just an old man. We don't have to answer you."

"Yeah," Ivan repeated. "We don't have to answer."

"Are you her parrot, Ivan?" Sean asked.

Renee pointed to Sean's vehicle. "Get out," she said. "Get out of here, before I call the real cops."

"Are you sure you wouldn't like to have a conversation?" Sean inquired.

"I've never been more positive of anything in my life," Renee shot back. "In fact, I'm going to call Chief Broadbent right now and tell him you're harassing Ivan and me."

"By all means, call Lucy," Sean replied. "I'll look forward to his visit."

Renee sniffed. "Come, Ivan," she said. "Let's finish our breakfast."

"Enjoy," Sean told her.

"I don't need your permission," Renee shot back.

"No, you don't," Sean agreed equably. "Unlike your boyfriend here needing yours." Sean smiled and addressed Ivan directly. "Tell me, Ivan, do you always do what your girlfriend says? Because I'm here to tell you it's a bad idea. It won't stop her from kicking you to the curb when you're arrested for criminal mischief. I can guarantee it."

"Don't," Renee cried, grabbing a fistful of the back of Ivan's shirt as he lunged forward. "He's trying to bait you."

Ivan stopped. His chest was heaving, and he'd made his hands into fists. "You're lucky you're an old man," he told Sean when he'd gotten control of himself after a moment. "Otherwise, Renee would be calling an ambulance for you right about now."

Sean grinned. "It's nice to know age has some advantages." He held up his hands in a gesture of surrender. "Hey, I was just trying to help you out here, buddy. You know, give you a piece of friendly advice."

"Thanks for the effort, but Ivan and I have no idea what

you're talking about," Renee replied before Ivan could speak.

"I think you do," Sean warned.

Renee laughed. "I like a man with a rich imagination," she said. And with that she motioned for Ivan to come inside.

"I just bet you do," Sean couldn't resist saying as Ivan glared at him. "Have you told Ivan your real name yet?" he asked her.

Renee froze.

Ivan turned toward her. "What's he talking about?" he asked.

"Tell him," Sean urged.

Renee threw him a hate-filled look. "It's Hilda."

"Hilda what?" Sean asked.

"Hilda Hickenloop. I changed it a long time ago. Satisfied?" she asked Sean.

"Here's my question," Sean said, ignoring Renee and addressing his next comment to Ivan. "How can you trust someone who lies about their name?"

"You really are an ass," Renee told Sean.

Sean gave a slight bow. "So I've been told," he replied as Renee turned and stomped inside.

"Is your name really Hilda Hickenloop?" Bernie and Sean could hear Ivan saying right before Renee slammed her front door shut. The noise echoed in the quiet of the summer morning and set off the neighborhood dogs barking.

"I thought I was going to play bad cop and you were going to play good cop," Bernie said to her dad as they headed toward the dairy to pick up the butter Libby had requested.

"That *was* me playing good cop," Sean replied.

"What's your bad cop like?"

Sean shook his head. "Believe me, you don't want to know."

Bernie had a feeling he was right.

"The thing is," Sean continued, "Renee knows she doesn't have to talk to us, so she won't. It's not like on the TV. We have no legal right to compel."

"I know, Dad." Bernie frowned. She hated when her dad said the obvious. "Does Renee really know Lucy?"

"More or less. Her sister is friends with Lucy's wife. Or at least she used to be."

"How do you know that?" Bernie asked as she watched the driver in back of Sean whip around him.

Sean shrugged and continued driving thirty miles an hour in a forty-mile-an-hour zone. "I still hear things, you know."

"I didn't say you didn't," Bernie told him. She waited until they were safely through the intersection at Ferndale and Main before asking her next question. "I'm sorry, but I still don't see the point of what we . . . you did with Ivan, Dad."

"Sowing seeds of discord."

Bernie wrinkled her nose in puzzlement. "Seeds of discord?"

Sean nodded. "That's what I just said. You know, like the apple of discord."

"You mean the one in Greek mythology, where the goddess of strife threw an apple into a feast, where Athena, Hera, and Aphrodite were sitting, and caused them to start fighting."

Sean beamed. "Exactly." It was times like these that he thought that his daughters' liberal arts educations hadn't been a waste of money, after all. "Maybe if Ivan thinks Renee will rat him out, he'll start talking."

"What happened to your gut telling you Renee didn't do this?"

Sean laughed. "I still think she didn't, literally speaking. Ivan, on the other hand . . ." Sean shrugged his shoulders. "To my mind, he's the most obvious suspect." He paused for a moment, then mused, "But why three different approaches? Why not key all three vehicles? Why didn't you guys get a note?"

"You really think what you did will work?" Bernie asked.

"You mean with Ivan?"

Bernie nodded.

"I hope so. Like I said, always go for the weak link," Sean told her. "Anyway, we don't have anything else going on at the moment. I mean, you can never tell what will spark a reaction." He cleared his throat. "Besides, I like to think of what I did with Ivan as a variation on the butterfly effect. Maybe the seed I planted will grow and bring about a change."

Bernie shook her head.

"Why are you shaking your head?" Sean asked.

"I don't think that's what the butterfly effect is, Dad," Bernie replied.

"It's close enough," Sean told her.

Bernie was about to argue the point when the driver in the Toyota behind her dad leaned on his horn and Sean stuck his head out the window and yelled at him to go around. As Bernie gripped the strap above the window, she reflected that she couldn't wait till the van was fixed.

Chapter 7

The next day dawned bright and clear. "It's going to be a nice day," Libby announced as she and her sister left their flat and went down the stairs.

"As soon as I have my coffee, it will be," Bernie remarked while she opened the door to the outside and stepped out onto the street.

She took a deep breath. At six thirty in the morning, the air smelled of summer. A tug hooted on the Hudson, a slight breeze carrying the sound inland. Bernie waved to Mrs. Gardner, her neighbor across the street. Mrs. Gardner waved back, collected her paper, and went inside as Bernie and Libby walked toward the shop's small parking lot. Only two vehicles and the van could fit in it. The lot didn't solve the parking problem, but it was still better than nothing. As Bernie walked, she ran her hand along the laurel hedge bordering the space between the house and the sidewalk, dislodging an orb-weaver spider.

"Sorry about that," she told the spider as she watched it scurry away. Bernie was nervous about the van, even though logically she knew Mathilda was okay. She knew this for two reasons: one, Brandon had come over yesterday and installed two videocams aimed at the parking lot before he'd gone to work at RJ's; and two, Libby had had a car alarm put in Mathilda when she was getting her new tires.

"She's fine," Libby said when she saw the van, the relief evident in her voice. She'd been concerned, as well.

"Let's hope yesterday was the end of it," Bernie said as Libby unlocked the shop door and held it for her sister. It took Bernie a moment to notice the note lying on the floor when she stepped inside. "Or maybe not," she said, referring to her last comment.

"Maybe it's a flyer," Libby said, trying to be optimistic. Bernie snorted.

"Okay. Well, it could be worse. At least they just shoved it under the door and didn't tie it to a rock and throw it through the window," Libby observed as she picked the note up and read it.

"We need another couple of cameras," Bernie said after Libby showed her the note.

She handed it back to her sister, who turned around and went back upstairs to show it to her dad. He was right where she'd left him, sitting in his chair, petting the cat, and watching the local morning news.

"What?" he asked, his eyes still glued to the screen.

Libby gave him the note. "This," she said.

Sean put on his reading glasses and studied the piece of paper. "This looks like the same typeface and the same computer paper as the ones from the other day," he commented. Then he read the message out loud. "Next time will be worse." He handed the note back to Libby. "Whoever is doing this is certainly persistent, isn't he? Or she." Sean didn't want to be sexist.

"So it would seem," Libby agreed.

Her dad sighed. It had been such a nice morning, too,

up till now. Quiet. Peaceful. Unlike their meeting with Lucy last night. Nothing like being told to back off by the chief of police of the town you lived in. Or else, the "or else" being unspecified. Not that Sean or his daughters had broken any rules. At least not yet. Sean took off his glasses and hung them on the neck of his polo shirt before speaking. "I wonder if Ruffo got one, too."

"Probably," Bernie said as she entered the flat. "Marcy and Denise did," Bernie informed her dad as she handed him a cup of coffee and a raspberry cornmeal muffin. "They just called to let me know. They're definitely freaked," Bernie added. "It took me a little while to calm them down."

"So is Jennie," Googie reported as he stepped inside the flat a minute later. "She's worried that this whole thing is going to go kaput, that she's going to lose every cent she has."

Bernie, Libby, and Sean turned around. They hadn't heard Googie come up the stairs.

"Is everything all right?" Libby asked.

"What's going on?" Bernie inquired, alarmed. "Did something break? Please, God, don't let the cooler be on the fritz again. I don't think I can take much more."

Googie shook his head. "No. Everything is fine downstairs."

"Then why are you here?" Libby asked, thinking of the display cases that still had to be filled, the coffee that had to be made, and the chairs that had to be taken off the tabletops.

Googie looked down at the floor, then back up at everyone. "Amber said I had to tell you."

"Tell us what?" Bernie asked.

"About where the notes come from."

"Where do they come from?" Sean asked as he read the text from Ruffo that had just popped up on his cell. Evidently, he must have gotten a note, too, because the text said, **You promised you'd take care of this.** "What about them? Spit it out," he commanded when Googie remained silent.

"I should have said something, only . . . only I'm not sure . . . It's probably nothing."

"What?" Sean snapped. He was losing his patience.

"What I heard," Googie said. "It's just that I figured she would tell you. I don't know why she hasn't."

"Jennie?" Bernie guessed.

Googie nodded.

Bernie studied Googie's face. He seemed genuinely upset. "Why don't you start from the beginning?" she suggested gently.

Googie nodded again. After a moment of silence, Googie did just that. "I heard her . . . Jennie arguing on the phone this morning. She had her cell on speaker. That's how come I could hear."

Bernie nodded encouragingly. "Who was she arguing with?" Berne asked when Googie didn't say anything else.

"Liam, Liam Nelson," Googie replied. "He's her ex-boyfriend."

"And?" Libby prodded as the cat jumped off her dad's lap and onto the windowsill to watch a robin that had landed on the lower branch of the Japanese maple in front of the shop.

Googie swallowed. "It's complicated."

Sean snorted. "It always is."

"So what makes you think Liam had anything to do with all the stuff that happened yesterday?" Bernie asked.

"I think Jennie thinks he does," Googie said. "I mean, she said as much to him."

"What did she say exactly?" Sean asked.

"That she'd kill him if he didn't stop."

Bernie, Libby, and Sean exchanged looks.

"That's pretty explicit," Libby said.

"Stop what?" Sean asked.

"I didn't hear. She walked out of the room." Googie shifted his weight from his right to his left leg and back again. "I know what it sounds like, but she talks that way all the time," Googie said, an earnest expression on his face. "It doesn't mean anything."

"I'm sure you're right," Libby said.

"Why do you think she was referring to what happened yesterday?" Sean asked Googie. "She could have been referring to something else."

Googie brightened. "That's what I told Amber. But you know how nannyish she is." He cleared his throat as he turned to the door. "I guess I should get back to work." And with that he left.

"What do you think, Dad?" Bernie asked after she heard the downstairs door close.

"That Googie is pretty light on his feet for a big guy."

"Besides that," Bernie told him.

Sean shrugged. "I'm not sure. If that's the case, why didn't Jennie say anything to you?"

"Good point, Dad," Libby agreed. "Maybe Googie is just jealous."

"Maybe. He could be. On the other hand, it might be worth having a chat with this Liam. It's not as if you have anything to lose."

"No, we don't," Libby agreed. "Now all we have to do is find him."

"Maybe Googie can help you with that," Sean suggested. Then he reached for the remote and changed the channel. There was a program on a famous bank robbery that happened in Longely thirty years ago that he wanted to watch.

"Maybe he can," Libby agreed.

Her dad, who'd been first on the scene of the robbery, grunted an acknowledgment. The FBI had swooped in and taken over the case, but they'd never solved it, and he was curious to see if any new avenues of inquiry had opened up. Sean was sipping his coffee and waiting for the program to start as Libby and Bernie went downstairs to finish opening the shop and to talk to Googie.

As it turned out, for once their father was mistaken. Googie couldn't help them.

Chapter 8

"Funny you should mention Liam," Brandon said when he called later in the day and Bernie was telling him about her conversation with Googie. "He was in here at RJ's a couple of hours ago for a quick beer and burger, and yes," he continued before Bernie could say anything else, "I do happen to know where he was headed off to. At least where he told Mike he was heading off to. I might even be persuaded to tell you if you're really, really nice to me."

Bernie laughed. "Define *nice*."

Brandon did.

"Interesting," Bernie told him as she snugged her phone against her ear and started refilling the saltshakers and pepper mills she'd collected from the shop's tables.

"I'll take that as a yes," Brandon replied, raising his voice so he could be heard over the television playing in the background.

Bernie screwed the top back on one of the pepper mills she'd just filled. "That depends on your intel."

"My intel is always good," Brandon huffed, mock outrage in his voice. Then he told Bernie what he'd overheard. "Of course," he added, "Liam might have left the site by now."

*   *   *

But he hadn't.

Half an hour later, Libby pointed to the white truck with the words LIAM NELSON CONSTRUCTION, WE DO IT ALL written across its side. "Looks as if Brandon was right," she commented as her sister ignored the sign that warned DANGER—HARD HATS ONLY and pulled through the gate into the construction site of the new Core Eatery that was going up off Route 29.

"I guess everyone's knocked off for the day," Bernie observed, looking at the mostly empty building site. She'd expected a beehive of activity.

"Apparently," Libby agreed, studying the building. It was in its beginning stages and reminded her of the structures she had built with her dad's old Erector Set when she was a kid. She said as much to her sister while Mathilda bounced over the dirt, trailing a plume of dust behind her.

"I remember," Bernie said, smiling at the memory. She zigzagged to avoid two large piles of building material in front of her and headed left toward Liam's rig, which was parked off to the side of the site, next to three other trucks, a bulldozer, and a small crane.

"You should have parked on the street," Libby said to Bernie, thinking of the van's shocks after her head hit the roof when her sister drove over a particularly deep rut. A new set of tires was enough of an expense for the week, Libby reflected. They didn't need to put shocks on the shop's credit card, as well. Plus, she was beginning to feel like a James Bond martini—shaken, not stirred. "I'm getting whiplash."

Bernie snorted. "Such a delicate flower."

"I'm serious," Libby retorted.

"Does the word *hypochondriac* mean anything to you?" Bernie asked.

"Funny," Libby said as the van bounced over another rut. "I'm driving out of here," Libby added when her sister didn't answer.

"Be my guest," Bernie replied.

Two minutes later, they were at Liam's truck, and Bernie parked next to it. "Here goes nothing," she said as she and her sister exited the van a moment later, Libby coughing from the dust in the air the van had kicked up.

"I hope not," Libby said.

"It's a figure of speech," Bernie replied.

"I know what it is," Libby rejoined. "Glad I'm not wearing open-toed shoes," Libby commented, making a pointed observation about her sister's choice of footwear as she avoided a piece of rebar lying on the ground. "It's lucky we don't have to go that far."

Bernie looked down at her open-toed, high-heeled Chanel sandals. Her sister was correct. She shouldn't have worn them—what had she been thinking?—but she wasn't going to give Libby the satisfaction of saying so. Instead, she pretended not to have heard her comment, and concentrated on where she was stepping. Fortunately, by now the sisters were within hailing distance of their prey.

"Liam," Bernie yelled over the sound of an electric saw.

The man fitting the description Brandon had given Bernie turned from contemplating the steel beam in front of him. Dressed in a neon green T-shirt and jeans, he was very tall and on the rangy side, with a pronounced jaw and wide-set brown eyes. *He looks just like Googie*, Bernie reflected. *Guess Jennie has a definite type*, Bernie thought. *But then who doesn't?*

"Yes," Liam replied. He tipped his hard hat back slightly and frowned at the two women. "Do I know you?"

"Not really," Libby said.

"Is what your truck says true? Can you do everything?"

Bernie asked, indicating Liam's vehicle with a nod of her head.

"It says it, doesn't it? What do you want, anyway?" Then Liam added, "You shouldn't be here without a hard hat. This is a construction site."

"So we noticed," Bernie said.

Liam squinted at them. "Are you from the office? Because if you are, I've already told Donna I called in my hours. You guys should get your act together."

Obviously, he hasn't noticed the van, Bernie decided as she told him that they were from the office at the same time that Libby told him that they weren't.

Liam put his hands on his hips. "Which is it?" he demanded.

"Actually," Bernie confessed, "we want to speak to you about Jennie."

Liam's eyes narrowed. "I might have known. Tell her I've said everything I have to say." He pointed to the street. "Now, if you two don't mind leaving, I need to get back to work."

"This will just take a minute," Bernie told him.

"Nothing that involves her ever takes a minute," Liam noted. Bernie watched as Liam clenched, then unclenched his hands. They looked huge. "You do know she's nuts, right?"

Bernie put on her best sympathetic smile and turned to her sister. "Well, she did seem very upset, didn't she, Libby?"

"Oh, yes," Libby answered, playing along. "I'd say the word *hysterical* comes to mind."

Liam nodded. His body relaxed. "Exactly. Thank you. She was screaming at me this morning, telling me I'm sending threatening notes, telling me to back off. I ask her what notes, and she goes even crazier on me. I thought I was going to have to call the cops. And now she sends you two."

Neither Bernie nor Libby corrected his assumption.

"Not a good way to start the day," Bernie observed.

"No, it wasn't," Liam agreed. He looked them up and down. "What do you want? Exactly?"

"A conversation," Libby said.

"Just five minutes of your time," Bernie told him.

"We have nothing to talk about," Liam said. "Absolutely nothing. I already told you that."

"Why does Jennie think you're involved in this?" Bernie asked, ignoring Liam's response. She could see he wanted to tell his side of the story.

"Which I'm not," Liam replied.

"So tell us why she thinks you are," Libby urged.

"Like I said, because she's batshit crazy." Liam looked at his watch and back at Bernie. "And now it's time for you to go."

"We will," Bernie assured him. "I can see you're really stressed, and I certainly don't want to add to that. It's hard dealing with crazies. I know. I get it. My ex sounds like Jennie," Bernie lied. "He was always going off about something or other."

Liam shook his head ruefully. "Then you know."

"I do," Bernie told him, oozing fake empathy.

Liam sighed. "Jennie and I did not have a good breakup. I mean, it was really bad. I literally threw her out of my house. You don't need to know the details."

Bernie and Libby nodded encouragingly.

"So when she found out I was supposed to help Tom with the job—"

Libby interrupted. "Who is Tom?"

"Tom Bannon, the guy who's doing the build-out for Jennie's doggie day care. So she freaked. I didn't know it was her project, or believe me, I never would have said yes to the job. She's a real piece of work," Liam repeated. He frowned and adjusted his hard hat. "And I don't say that about a lot of people. I feel bad for Googie. I really do. I don't know him that well, but I don't think he has a clue about what he's gotten himself into."

Bernie nodded. She was about to ask Liam another question—for a guy who hadn't wanted to talk, he was turning out to be a chatty Cathy—when her cell rang. She stepped away to answer it. "We gotta go," she told Libby after she'd heard what her father had to say.

"What's going on?" Libby asked as they started walking back to the van.

"That was Dad," Bernie informed her. "He called to tell me Clyde just called him."

"And?"

"Someone just took a shot at Denise as she was going into her house."

"Denise?" Libby echoed, momentarily drawing a blank on the name.

"Denise, the photographer who's doing Bertha and Ernie's wedding photos."

Libby put her hand to her mouth. "Oh my God. Is she okay?"

"She's fine. Whoever did it missed. Either that or it was a warning shot."

"Well, whatever it was, at least we know that Liam didn't do it," Libby said, turning and looking at him. He was taking a drink from his water bottle and had gone back to studying the steel beam. "I guess we can cross him off our list."

"For the moment. Of course," Bernie kidded, "he could have a twin brother."

"Or a doppelgänger."

"Or be a time traveler from the multiverse."

The sisters laughed as a truck lumbered by them, kicking up dust as it went.

"I suppose we should go talk to Denise," Libby said after she'd stopped coughing.

"I suppose we should," Bernie reluctantly agreed, watching the rest of her day's plans disappear. "Maybe she saw something." Then she added, "Although Clyde told Dad she didn't."

"You know," Libby said after a minute had gone by, "this is not going in a good direction."

"Ya think?" Bernie agreed as she brushed dust off the front of her mint-green shirtdress.

"Only when I have to," Libby replied.

Bernie laughed. "You said it. I didn't."

Chapter 9

A Little Taste of Heaven had closed for the evening. It was one of those warm summer nights, and Bernie had gone for a walk and gotten to thinking about what had happened to Denise. Not that there was much to think about. Not really. As Bernie had expected, Denise hadn't seen anything. She'd been going into her house when she'd heard a noise. A crack. At first, she'd thought it was a car backfiring, and it was only when she'd noticed the hole in her door that she realized what had happened.

According to Denise, by the time she had turned around, the street was empty. No cars. No people. Just the neighbor's tabby cat staring at her. At least that was what Denise had told Bernie, and there was no reason to think that Denise was lying. Had the shooter meant to miss Denise, or was he or she simply a bad shot? There were other possibilities, as well. Two in fact. Both were a little far-fetched, considering what was going on, but worth entertaining, Bernie thought.

Maybe the shot hadn't been intended for Denise at all. Perhaps the shot had been an accident. Maybe someone had been doing something stupid, like firing into the air, although Bernie had to concede that the trajectory of the bullet made that unlikely. Then her dad had pointed out another possibility.

"Maybe Denise was the shooter. After all, she could be trying to deflect suspicion from herself."

"But why would she do something like that?" Bernie had countered. "She wasn't a suspect in the first place."

"Maybe she should be," her father had replied.

Maybe her dad was right, Bernie reflected, but the question still remained, Why do this at all? A drive-by shooting? That was something you'd expect from a rival gang in a drug deal gone wrong. But for a real estate deal? A possible lease dispute? Not that people hadn't been killed for less.

And there was this. Did the person who was doing this object to the wedding itself or to the doggie day care? Or was, as Sherlock Holmes would have said, something else afoot? But if so, what? Who else besides Renee would have a motive? There was Liam, but she and Libby had been speaking to Jennie's ex when the shot had been fired. Although Liam could have hired someone. But once again Bernie asked herself, *Why do that*? There was something going on that neither she, her sister, nor her dad was seeing.

She was puzzling over what that could possibly be as she was walking back. She was a block away from home when her neighbor flagged her down. Bernie suppressed a groan. Mrs. Van Chester, the neighborhood gossip, always had a lot to say. This evening she wanted to discuss the upcoming September block party, the new planters the town board had okayed last month, her dad's health, where her dad had driven off to earlier in the evening, her new hair color, and last but not least, the couple across the street, who seemed to be having a spate of martial disagreements at one o'clock in the morning. Thirty minutes later, Bernie managed to extricate herself and continue on her way. She was almost home when Googie called and asked her to hurry over to Woof Woof's new site.

"Jennie needs you," he said.

"Why?" Bernie asked him, thinking as she did this that Googie sounded concerned. "What's going on now?"

"I don't know exactly," Googie replied. "I couldn't make sense of what Jennie was saying. She sounded hysterical. The only thing I got out of her was that the police are there."

Bernie groaned.

"I know," Googie said. "I'm on my way, but I won't get there for at least an hour, probably more. I'm in Scarsdale, helping my cousin Andy out with his car. I know it's a big ask, but considering what's been going on with Bertha and Ernie's wedding, I thought—"

"Don't worry. We'll go," Bernie said, cutting him off.

"Thanks," Googie told her. "I owe you."

"Yes, you do. Big-time. But don't worry. I'll collect," Bernie replied.

Googie laughed and hung up as Bernie opened the door to the flat and went upstairs.

"What now?" Libby inquired when Bernie told her about Googie's phone call. She'd been about to meet Marvin down by the Hudson and go for an evening stroll along its banks.

"I don't know," Bernie answered. "I guess we'll find out."

"All I can say is this better be good," Libby told her sister as she called Marvin and informed him about the change in their plans.

"Would it help if I told you I like your dress?" Bernie

asked after her sister had hung up. It was a pale blue floral-print, knee-length cotton sundress. "Where'd you get it?" she asked, because it looked familiar.

Libby grinned. "From the donation bag."

"I knew I'd seen it before!" Bernie exclaimed.

"You should, Bernie. It's yours."

Bernie hit her forehead with the palm of her hand. Maybe her sister was right. Maybe she did have too many clothes.

"I didn't have time to do laundry," Libby explained.

"Keep it," Bernie told her. "It looks good on you."

"I might just do that," Libby replied as she grabbed the van's keys and headed out the door.

Traffic was light that time of night, and Libby made good time. Fifteen minutes later, the sisters arrived at the scene. As they pulled into the cul-de-sac, they could see the parking strip was empty except for two police cars with their red lights flashing, beacons in the dark. The cops were leaning against their vehicles, talking to each other over the squawk of their radios, while Jennie was standing on the sidewalk next to what had once been Beerly There, holding Bertha's and Ernie's leashes.

"Thank God," Jennie cried after Bernie and Libby had parked the van and gotten out. The goldens woofed and wagged their tails as the sisters approached. "I'm not lying. I'm not," Jennie exclaimed as the goldens barked louder, jumped on Bernie and Libby, and licked their faces. Jennie pointed to the dogs. "They saw him, too." Bernie didn't make the obvious comment, as Jennie stuck out her jaw. "I saw him. I did. He was dead. He was," she insisted as both patrolmen stopped talking to each other and walked over.

Bernie put both cops in their twenties. One had brown

hair, and the other was blond, but outside of that, they could have been twins. Same height. Same weight. Same hazel eyes.

The cop on the right indicated Jennie with a nod of his head. "Is she your friend?" he asked.

"Yes, Officer Price," Bernie responded, reading his name off the bar attached to his uniform in the light the street-lamp provided. She could have explained that Jennie was a customer, but it was late, and she was tired, and it seemed to Bernie that right now simple was best.

"You should take her home," Price said. "She's had a little too much to drink. I would run her in if it wasn't for these two." And he pointed to Bertha and Ernie, who were now wagging their tails at him. "I don't want them to go to the shelter."

"I had one beer," Jennie protested. "One beer."

The officer on the left started slapping his hand against his thigh. "Right," he said.

"It's true, Officer Hanson," Jennie protested.

"Maybe the aliens beamed him up," Hanson taunted. "Maybe that's where he's gone. Or maybe he's turned into a zombie like on *The Walking Dead* and is waiting to eat your brains."

"I'm serious," Jennie responded, her cheeks coloring. "He was in his car, sitting behind the wheel, and there was blood running down his head."

"He could have scratched himself," Hanson continued. "Maybe he took himself off to the hospital to get it looked at. Have you thought of that?"

"It wasn't a scratch," Jennie protested. "There was a hole in his forehead."

Hanson rolled his eyes. "Are you sure you didn't have something else with your beer? Like drop a tab of LSD? Do some Special K?"

Jennie's cheeks turned redder. "I know what I saw. And for your information, I don't do drugs."

Hanson snorted. "Let's get out of here," he said to Price.

Price nodded and told Jennie to call 911 if the guy showed up. "Have fun," he said to Bernie and Libby.

"Who are we talking about, anyway?" Libby asked him as he turned to leave. "Who's missing?"

"Tom, Tom Bannon, and he's not missing," Price answered.

"You don't know that," Jennie argued.

"Yeah I do, and if you're smart, you'll let this drop." Price started to walk away. After two steps, he stopped and turned around. "Hey," he said, looking at Bernie and Libby, "I thought you guys looked familiar. You run A Little Taste of Heaven. My wife goes in there all the time to buy your blueberry corn muffins."

"Send her in and we'll give her some. Our treat," Bernie told him.

Hanson smiled for the first time. "My son likes your brownies, the ones with the cinnamon and walnuts. So do I," he confessed.

"My sister's offer goes for you, too," Libby told him.

Price grinned. "Bribing an officer of the law, are we?"

"We are," Libby replied.

"Works for me," Hanson said. Then he and Price turned, walked over to their squad cars, got in them, and drove away.

"Tell me what happened," Bernie said to Jennie once the police cars' taillights were no longer visible and as she and Libby continued to pet Bertha and Ernie. She wanted to hear if Jennie would mention Liam or not.

"Tom Bannon is the contractor who is working on the build-out," Jennie explained.

"We know who he is," Libby said, indicating her sister and herself.

"Okay then. So we were meeting because he wanted me to decide about the framing for the door that leads out to the backyard. It's one of those double door jobbies, the kind where you can open the top but keep the door closed."

"Makes sense," Bernie said. "Go on."

Jennie hesitated for a moment before continuing. "Tom wasn't here when I arrived. I mean, I didn't see his truck here. I assumed he was late."

"You didn't go inside your place?" Libby asked.

Jennie shook her head. "I couldn't. I forgot my keys. That's why I was waiting outside. After ten minutes or so, I called Tom. I thought maybe I'd gotten the time wrong," she explained. "And that's when I heard the phone ringing." She pointed to the end of the parking strip. "It was coming from the car parked at the end of the strip. I saw the car when I drove in, but I didn't think much about it. I've noticed that sometimes people leave their cars here overnight. And then I walked over and saw what was inside." Jennie shuddered at the memory.

"Tom was in the front seat, behind the steering wheel, and there was blood running down his face. A lot of blood. I totally freaked and grabbed the dogs, got in my car, and drove over to the first house I could find on Mot and banged on their door." Jennie swallowed and rubbed her hands together. "But no one answered. I tried the next two or three other houses—I don't remember how many—but they didn't answer, either. They probably thought I was crazy. Anyway, I finally found a gas station, and the guy behind the counter called Googie, and he called the police. By the time I got back, the car was gone."

"I'm confused," Bernie said. "Why didn't you call the police right away?"

"I couldn't. My phone died," Jennie said.

"But you called Bannon," Libby pointed out.

"I ran out of power. The bar was on red when I called him. My phone is really old and doesn't hold a charge anymore." Jennie started to cry. "I don't understand. Tom was there when I left. He was," she insisted. She put up her hand. "I swear to God he was. I don't know. Maybe I'm going crazy."

"Is there any chance you made a mistake?" Bernie asked. "Maybe the policeman was right. Maybe Tom Bannon wasn't that badly injured. Maybe he drove himself to the hospital."

Jennie shook her head. "He was dead."

"How can you be so sure?" Libby asked. "Did you feel for his pulse?"

Jennie shook her head. "I just know, that's all."

"Have you ever seen a dead person?" Libby asked.

"My uncle," Jennie told her. "I went to the wake." She put her hands to her head and dropped them. "What am I going to do now?" she wailed.

"About what?" Bernie asked.

"Finishing the doggie day care so we can have the wedding, of course," Jennie said.

"Of course," Bernie said. "Maybe you should make sure that Tom is . . ."

"Dead," Jennie said.

"I was going to say out of commission before you go hunting for someone else," Bernie told her. Then she walked over to Woof Woof's door and tried it. The door was locked, just as Jennie had said it was. "I take it the police didn't look inside?" Bernie asked.

Jennie shook her head.

"Figured," Bernie said. Then, with Jennie watching, she went back to the van, rummaged around in the glove compartment, and came out with a flat-edged screwdriver. "This should do it," she said.

"Do what?" Jennie asked Bernie as Bernie headed back to the door.

"Open the door. See if Bannon is inside," Bernie told her. "You should really get a better lock," Bernie told Jennie as she popped it and entered. Libby, Jennie, and the dogs followed.

Quite a bit of work had already been done, Bernie decided, looking around. Things were definitely in the home stretch constructionwise. The bar, the dark wood paneling, and the small kitchen in the back were gone.

"It looks nice," Libby commented as she took in the gates that would be used to separate the big and little dog spaces, the entryway/reception area, the mural on the far left wall, and the dog beds and food bowls stacked up along the walls. "Airy."

Jennie beamed, while Bertha and Ernie ran around investigating all the place's nooks and crevices.

"Do you see anything out of place here?" Bernie asked Jennie. "Anything missing? Or anything here that wasn't here before?"

After taking ten minutes to look around, Jennie shook her head. "Nothing. Everything looks like the last time I was here."

"Which was?" Libby asked.

"The other day," Jennie replied.

"Bannon left his tools and supplies," Bernie commented, pointing to the toolbox nestled among the tarps, the boxes filled with light fixtures, the large white pail of joint compound, and the paint trays, paint cans, and brushes.

"Meaning?" Jennie asked.

"Meaning it looks as if he wasn't through with the job," Bernie replied.

"Obviously," Jennie retorted as Bernie headed for the back door.

It was locked, as well, so Bernie unlocked it and stepped outside into what Beerly There had used as an outdoor eating and drinking area. Now the tables and chairs were gone, replaced by three doghouses, a large wading pool, and several doggie cots.

"I'm putting some canvas shades up for the wedding," Jennie said, pointing to the left side of the yard. "It'll help with the sun. And these"—she pointed to the doghouse, cots, and pool—"will be stored away on the big day."

"That should work," Bernie said absentmindedly as she took a look around. Then she peeked inside the doghouses. No Tom Bannon. Not that she'd expected him to be in one of them. She just wanted to make sure. She straightened up and glanced at her watch. An hour had gone by since Jennie claimed she'd seen a dead Tom Bannon in his vehicle. "Try calling him again," Bernie said to Jennie. "Maybe he's like Lazarus and has risen from the dead."

"I can't," Jennie told her. "Remember?"

"Right," Bernie said, and she handed Jennie her phone. When there was no answer, Jennie left a message and hung up.

After she handed Bernie her phone back, Bernie and Libby tried the hospitals and ER rooms. Nothing. Bernie was just about to try the urgent care facilities when Googie called and told her he was going to be later than he had thought. When Jennie heard that, she reached out and took Bernie's hands in hers.

"Do you think you could give me and the pups a lift home?" she asked. "I feel like I'm going to crash. I think I'm too shaky to drive."

"Of course," Libby said. She'd been just about to suggest that herself.

On the way to Jennie's house, they stopped at Tom Bannon's place. The lights were out. Bernie parked in the driveway, and Jennie jumped out and rang his doorbell. No one answered. She tried once more, then gave it up.

"See," Jennie said when she got back in Mathilda. "I told you."

"The fact that he's not home doesn't mean anything," Libby observed. "There could be lots of reasons why he's not here. Family emergency. He could have gotten into an accident."

"You think I made all of this up, don't you?" Jennie demanded of Libby.

"I didn't say that," Libby protested.

"No, but you thought it," Jennie told her. "Just like the cops."

"Well, you have to admit the situation is a little . . . odd," Bernie answered for her sister.

"I'll give you that," Jennie answered after a few minutes. "I mean, if it wasn't for the other stuff going on . . ." Jennie's voice faded out. She looked as if she was going to start crying again. Then she swallowed and rallied. "But you're wrong," she said. "I mean, what would I have to gain by doing something like this?"

"I don't know. What would you have to gain?" Bernie asked.

Jennie grimaced. "Seriously?"

"Yes, seriously," Bernie responded.

"Nothing, absolutely nothing," Jennie replied. Then she turned and stared out the window, watching the evening breeze ruffle the leaves of the maple trees. It looked as if a cold front was moving in, pushing rain clouds in front of it.

Chapter 10

The next day, after A Taste of Heaven's morning rush had subsided, Libby and Bernie called the hospitals again. They started with the local ones and branched out to the ones down in Westchester and New York City. Just in case. But no one by the name of Tom Bannon had been treated in the ER or been admitted to any of the facilities. Not that the sisters were surprised by the results.

"I didn't know that Tom Bannon had a sister," Googie commented after Bernie had finished talking to the admitting desk at Mount Sinai.

Bernie grinned. "He could have one," she said. "If they knew I was me, they'd just tell me about HIPAA laws and hang up."

"I wonder if he does have a sister," Googie mused while he finished preparing Mrs. Daysun's to-go order of three gazpacho soups, two lobster rolls, and two strawberry tarts. She was going to pick up the order in ten minutes. "You know, I could be his brother if you want me to make some calls."

"Bernie and I might take you up on that," Libby said as she measured out the beans for another pot of coffee. "Does he?"

"Bannon have a brother? Damned if I know," Googie replied as he carefully packed Mrs. Daysun's order in the picnic basket she had supplied, and nestled three cold packs between the food and the wicker.

"Well, what do you know about Bannon?" Libby asked after she'd finished making the coffee.

"Not much," Googie said after a moment's thought. "I remember hearing that he was divorced—one of those early marriage six-month deals—but that's about it."

"And he knows Liam."

Googie nodded.

"What do you know about Liam?"

"I know he and Jennie had a really bad breakup and that he's with someone else now—actually several some-one elses—and that he plays a mean game of pool."

"Anything else?" Libby inquired.

Googie carefully closed the top of the wicker basket. "Just that sometimes he and Bannon work together. That's about it."

"And Jennie?" Bernie asked Googie as she looked over the rest of the day's orders. "How's she doing this morning? Because she wasn't in great shape last night."

"She's doing better," Googie replied. "Much, much better. When I left, she was on the phone with Peter G."

"The contractor?" Libby asked.

Googie nodded. "I think he's taking over for Bannon."

"So, still no Tom?" Bernie asked.

"Nope," Googie said as Mrs. Daysun walked into the store. "She hasn't gotten a phone call, a text, an email, anything."

"We should drive by Bannon's house again and see if he's there," Bernie suggested after Mrs. Daysun had paid and left. "Maybe he's back from where he's gone."

"Like the grave," Libby said.

Bernie snorted. "Cute. Very cute."

"I guess it wouldn't hurt to take a quick gander round his house," Libby said. "Just to double-check."

Which is what they did twenty minutes later.

Libby pulled into Bannon's driveway and parked. The sisters got out at the same time, with Libby heading toward the unattached garage and Bernie crossing the lawn on her way to the house. It was a large pale blue Colonial that had been divided into two flats, and according to the sign on the lawn, the upper one was for rent. The grass was still wet from last night's rain showers, and Bernie could feel water droplets against her feet and ankles.

"No car in here," Libby announced after she cupped her hands over her eyes and looked through the garage window.

Bernie grunted and rang the doorbell. No one answered. She tried two more times and got the same result.

"I wonder if Bannon is living with anyone," Libby mused as she joined Bernie on the wraparound porch. The sofa and coffee table on it looked as if they'd seen better days. "I mean, he could be at his girlfriend's house."

"He could if he has one," her sister said as she opened the mailbox labeled with Bannon's name. There were two letters and a bunch of flyers from yesterday. "Nothing here is addressed to anyone else—not that that means anything." She held the letters up to the light. One of the letters was from an insurance company, and the other one was a proffer from a heating company. "Nothing of interest," Bernie noted as she slid the mail back in the mailbox.

Next, she and Libby walked around to the backyard. There was nothing to see except a vegetable garden that needed some serious weeding and a small wooden toolshed that was listing to the right. The door was ajar, and Libby stepped in and took a quick look around. All she saw was a push mower with rusty blades, a couple of shovels, and a large bag of mulch covered with cobwebs. Obviously, Bannon didn't take his gardening seriously.

"Nothing here, either," Libby noted, closing the shed door.

As Libby and Bernie were coming back around the house, a woman in a white Kia pulled into the driveway of the house on the right-hand side and began unloading her groceries out of the trunk of her car.

"Maybe she knows something," Libby said to Bernie.

"The secret to the universe?" Bernie asked.

"I was thinking more about how to teleport to another dimension," her sister replied.

"Yes?" the woman said when Bernie and Libby got close enough.

She looked tired, Bernie reflected. Washed out. Her blond hair needed a good brushing, and her face was bare of makeup. A little mascara and eyebrow liner would make a big difference, Bernie decided as she asked the woman if she'd seen Tom Bannon this morning or yesterday.

She shook her head. "Sorry," she said. "Usually, he's gone by now."

"Do you know if he lives with anyone?" Bernie asked.

"He doesn't," the woman replied. "Why? What's going on? Is anything wrong?"

"There might be." And Bernie introduced herself and her sister and explained the situation.

The woman shifted the paper bag of groceries she was carrying from her left to her right hip. "Well, I don't know if this is relevant or not, but I did hear him having an argument with someone early yesterday morning," she said. "At least I heard shouting."

Bernie lifted an eyebrow. This sounded more promising.

"Do you know who he was arguing with and what it was about?"

The woman shook her head. "I was in my bedroom, getting dressed," she explained. "The only reason I heard anything was that I had the windows opened to air the place out."

"Do you think Bannon was arguing with a man or a woman?" asked Libby.

"A woman. I think," the woman said after a slight hesitation. "Or maybe a younger guy. Honestly, I'm not sure. I was listening to a podcast, so I really wasn't paying that much attention. Sorry I can't be more helpful." And she grabbed another bag of groceries out of the trunk of her car and started toward her house.

"At least we know Bannon was alive yesterday morning, so I guess that's progress," Libby noted as she and her sister got ready to canvass the block. "I wonder who he was arguing with."

"Good question," Bernie said as she walked up to the neighboring house on the left and rang the bell.

No one answered. No one answered at the house next door to that one, either. As it turned out, most of the people on the block weren't home, and the ones who were hadn't seen Tom Bannon and didn't know anything about any argument.

"So much for that," Libby said as they headed back to A Little Taste of Heaven.

The rest of the day passed uneventfully. There were no more incidents, a fact Libby and Bernie were profoundly thankful for.

Chapter 11

It was nine thirty at night, and Marvin was sitting between Bernie and Libby at the bar at RJ's, nursing a summer wheat ale and discussing Tom Bannon's disappearance with Brandon and the sisters.

"Do you think Jennie was telling the truth about what she saw?" Marvin asked them.

"I don't see why she shouldn't have," Libby replied.

"She was really upset," Bernie added, remembering Jennie's reaction. "At least she appeared to be. So either she was telling the truth or she's an excellent liar or she was hallucinating."

"Which of the three is it?" Brandon asked.

Bernie ran her finger around the rim of the glass holding her gin and tonic while she spoke. "I don't know. I can't decide."

Marvin stretched. "So then, what do you think happened to Tom Bannon?" he asked. "Could he have been playing a practical joke on Jennie?"

"That would be quite the joke," Libby observed.

Marvin thought of something else. "Or what if he's in cahoots with the person who has been causing everyone all the trouble you and Bernie were telling us about?" Marvin posited.

Libby rubbed her arms. The air-conditioning was cranked up too high for her liking. "Why would he be?"

Marvin allowed as how he didn't know.

"Which leads us back to the question, what does this person or persons have against Jennie?" Brandon said.

Bernie shook her head. "At this point"—she gestured to herself and her sister—"we don't have a clue. The only thing we do know is that Bannon wasn't home this morning. Or this evening. We stopped by on our way over here to check."

"If he was, that would give the phrase *dead man walking* new meaning," Brandon noted as he scanned the bar for anyone who needed another drink. No one did. "Assuming he was dead, of course."

"It could be the beginning of a zombie apocalypse," Marvin observed.

"That wouldn't be good for your business," Libby said.

Marvin laughed. "No, it most definitely would not be," he agreed.

Brandon turned to Bernie and Libby. "What does your dad say?" he asked.

"He said that ordinarily he would say that Jennie was either nuts or pulling some kind of stunt, but considering the other stuff . . ." Bernie ate a pretzel out of the bowl in front of her. "He doesn't know what to think."

"Me either," Brandon said as he poured himself a glass of water. "I don't know if this is relevant or not, but Bannon's gotten himself in trouble before—at least that's what he told me. He got in deep with the loan sharks. That's why he moved here from Cali. He used to come in here a couple of times a month," Brandon explained, seeing the looks on everyone's faces, "but I haven't seen him lately."

Everyone was silent for a moment while they listened to the weather forecast on the TV. Then Brandon spoke again.

"How much time did Jennie say elapsed between the time she left to make her phone call and the time she returned?" he asked.

"She didn't," Libby answered. "But I'm figuring fifteen minutes max." She looked at her sister. "What do you think, Bernie?"

"Maybe twenty, but certainly no more."

"Well, that would be enough time for someone to drive Tom Bannon's car away," Marvin pointed out. "Maybe they'd just finished shooting Tom Bannon when Jennie arrived, and they hid in the back and waited till Jennie left and then stashed him somewhere."

"Plausible," Brandon said.

"Very," Bernie agreed.

"Maybe he owed more money to someone," Libby suggested, running with the scenario Marvin had suggested, "and they tracked him down . . ."

"To Longely," Marvin said, finishing Libby's sentence for her.

"Except why kill someone who owes you money?" Bernie objected. "Why not kneecap him instead?"

"Maybe they wanted to make him an object lesson," Marvin suggested.

"Then why hide the body?" Bernie countered. "Why not leave it out in the open for everyone to see?"

"Good point. The logic doesn't work," Libby said. "Besides," she added, "you're assuming that the Bannon thing isn't related to what's going on with Ernie and Bertha's wedding. I find that difficult to believe."

Marvin yawned. It had been a long day. "That's true. And then there's the fact that all of this is based on Jennie telling the truth about seeing Bannon's body," he said.

"I know." Bernie finished off her gin and tonic. "But why would she lie?"

"That is the question, isn't it?" Marvin replied. He took another sip of his ale. He was about to take a third sip when his phone rang. "Business," he announced as his caller ID flashed across his screen.

Libby watched Marvin as he got up and stepped outside to take the call. The bar wasn't jammed, but it was still noisy enough what with the TV going to make it hard to hear. "You don't look happy," Libby commented when Marvin came back in.

"I'm not," Marvin replied before he reached over, grabbed his glass, and downed the best of his drink. "I have to go."

"Runaway corpse?" Libby asked.

"Not exactly," Marvin said, and he told them what the caretaker had told him.

"College kids," Brandon said, proffering his opinion when Marvin was done talking.

"Possibly." Marvin frowned. "Or stoned high school kids doing God knows what. Last month a couple of art students stole Johnson's skull out of his mausoleum. Claimed they wanted to sketch it."

"I remember," Bernie said. It had been a banner head-line in the local paper because Johnson was one of the town founders.

"What happened to the kids?" Libby asked Marvin.

"They got twenty hours of community service." Marvin frowned. "They should have gotten more if you ask me." He ran his finger around the rim of his empty glass. "I don't understand what fascination these kids have with messing around with graves."

Libby and Bernie looked at each other.

"Are you thinking what I'm thinking?" Bernie asked her sister.

"What are you thinking?" Marvin asked Bernie before Libby could reply.

"Yes, what?" Brandon asked. "Inquiring minds want to know."

"I'm thinking maybe that's where Tom Bannon is," Bernie replied.

Marvin laughed. "You're kidding, right?"

"No, I'm serious," Bernie said. "Kinda."

"So you're saying this isn't some random kid vandal thing, Bernie?"

"It could be, Marvin. Or not."

Marvin shook his head. "That's a pretty big stretch."

"Maybe not," Brandon suggested.

Bernie, Libby, and Marvin turned toward him.

"How so?" Marvin asked.

"I realize this is a little bit out there, but I think Bannon is some sort of distant relation to the person you just buried," Brandon told them.

"Mrs. Vanderchild?" Bernie asked.

Brandon refilled the bowl in front of Libby with pretzels before nodding. "I'm pretty sure. I remember overhearing him saying he tried to borrow money from her, but she turned him down. Called him a shirttail relative."

"So what?" Libby said.

"All I'm saying is there might be a connection," Brandon replied.

"Let me get this straight," Marvin said. "So you're telling me that this Bannon guy disappears . . ."

"We think," Libby said.

"He's assumed dead, and someone in the funeral party is connected to him in some way and decides to bury him in Mrs. Vanderchild's grave?" Marvin asked, an incredulous expression on his face. "Is that what you're saying?"

Brandon shrugged. "Yeah. Pretty much."

"Anyone could know about the funeral," Bernie pointed out. "It was in the local paper."

Marvin was forced to admit that was true.

"We should look," Bernie said. "Just in case."

"And it's a nice night for a drive," Brandon observed.

"Well, that makes all the difference," Marvin said sarcastically.

"You're going out there, anyway," Bernie said.

"There's a big difference between tiding up a grave and digging one up," Marvin said. "Do you have any idea how much work what you're suggesting is?"

"I never said dig up," Bernie told him "Brandon did."

"I don't care," Marvin snapped.

Libby reached out and put her hand on Marvin's shoulder. "You don't have to do this."

"Yeah, he does," Bernie replied. "What if he's right?"

"What if you're not?" Libby shot back.

"To dig up, or not to dig up, that is the question," Brandon mused in his best Shakespearean voice.

"Is it?" Marvin asked Brandon.

"Yes, it is," Brandon replied, looking around the bar again to make sure his customers didn't need anything. "So, Marvin, what's it going to be?"

Marvin didn't say anything.

"Let me put it this way," Brandon continued. "Better that you figure out what's going on now than someone else does later. This is something you want to get ahead of."

"I guess," Marvin conceded unenthusiastically. All he wanted to do was go home, watch a little TV, and go to sleep. "I suppose I'd better make sure."

Brandon grinned and rubbed his hands together. "Now that we have that settled, how about making this a little more interesting?"

"What do you have in mind?" Bernie asked.

Brandon leaned forward. "Bernie, you think Marvin will find Tom Bannon's body and, Libby, you think he won't, correct?"

"I think it's possible," Bernie said.

"Good enough," Brandon said. His smile grew. "How about the loser pays for a steak dinner at Luigi's?" Luigi's was a very expensive, very good steak house located in Rye, New York. "For all of us. And your dad."

"You, Marvin, and my dad win whoever loses," Bernie objected.

Brandon took a drink from his bottle of water. "Exactly."

"Seems fair to me," Marvin replied.

"What the hell," Libby said. She turned to her sister. "I'm going to enjoy watching you pay."

"I wouldn't count on that if I were you," Bernie replied. "Besides, who can resist a midnight drive through the cemetery on a balmy summer night?"

"That's what I say," Brandon told Bernie as Libby made a face. "You know, that was my old make-out place when I was in high school," he reminisced. "Brings back fond memories."

"Brandon, don't you think of anything else besides sex?" Bernie chided.

"I think of food," Brandon declared. He turned to Marvin. "I mean, what else is there, right?"

Marvin raised his hands. "I plead the Fifth."

"And, of course, there are the ghosts that walk among the headstones of Willowwood," Brandon teased. "They're always fun to see. Something to tell your grandchildren about."

"Funny," said Libby.

Brandon looked at Marvin. "Tell her the stories."

"He's lying, Libby," Marvin told her. "There are no stories." Which wasn't true. There were lots of stories. Some of them were even true. So people said.

Libby sighed. "I guess we should go."

"I guess we should," Marvin said. He stood up. "Time to head out."

"Wish I could come," Brandon commented.

"We'll let you know what we find," Bernie assured him as she slung her tote over her shoulder.

Brandon laughed. "You'd better."

Fifteen minutes later, Bernie, Libby, and Marvin arrived at Willowwood. The cemetery was located on the outskirts of Longely. Created in the 1890s as a park/cemetery, it was designed by the same person who had designed Central Park.

"Why are we going in this way?" Libby asked as they drove through the north gate. The stone angel guarding it looked at them with appraising eyes as they went in.

"Because the old part is full up," Marvin explained. "They haven't buried anyone there in five years."

"I did not know that," Bernie said. She liked the old part better. Unlike the newer part, it had towering oak and maple trees, ornamental lampposts, benches, and large mausoleums and monuments, while the new part was bereft of headstones and statues. In the new part, groves of trees dominated the hilly landscape, and the grave markers, pieces of granite lying flat in the ground, were nestled among them.

That should have made things better for Libby, but it didn't. She knew it was silly, but the space seemed empty, waiting to be filled by creatures of the night. To make things worse, a breeze had come up and set the birch and the maple tree limbs dancing, making shadows on the road, which seemed to clutch at Marvin's car as it traveled through them. Marvin drove slowly with his brights on because it was hard to see under the waning moon.

The caretaker was waiting for them when they arrived. "I'm sorry to bother you, but I figured I'd better call considering . . . ," he told Marvin as he indicated the freshly dug grave in front of him with his flashlight.

The beam revealed a soda can, a bag from Wendy's, and a couple of Snickers wrappers on top of the grave.

"Looks as if someone was having a picnic," Marvin said as he took in the shovel marks and divots on the mound of dirt. They certainly hadn't been there before, and then there were the roses. They had been neatly bunched together but were now scattered on the grave site and the ground.

"I don't remember the flowers being this way, either," the caretaker continued. He scratched his cheek. "Although I could be wrong."

"No, you're not," Marvin told him.

The caretaker nodded. "That's what I thought. And with what happened a couple of months ago . . . We don't need another headline like that." His voice faded away, then came back stronger. "Not to mention Ms. Vanderchild being who she is." The caretaker shrugged. "I just figured you'd want to get a head start fixing whatever needs to be fixed."

"This is Ms. Vanderchild's mother's grave," Marvin explained to Libby and Bernie before either of the sisters could ask who Ms. Vanderchild was. "She's rather . . ."

"Difficult," said the caretaker, who had witnessed the scene earlier in the afternoon when Ms. Vanderchild had thrown a fit because the canopy over her mother's coffin had been white with a green border instead of white with a blue border.

That's one way of putting it, Marvin thought. *Entitled*, *spoiled*, and *powerful* were other words that came to his mind. "She's on the board of directors," Marvin said. He sighed, remembering Ms. Vanderchild threatening to blackball him for the canopy. He didn't think she could forbid his funeral home from burying anyone at Willowwood, but he didn't want to take that chance. The legal bills alone would kill the business, never mind what his dad would say.

Libby bit at a cuticle while she studied the grave. She had a feeling someone was watching them. "Do you think Bannon is in there?" she asked Marvin, trying to distract herself from the feeling.

"Who's Bannon?" the caretaker asked at the same time that Marvin said, "I hope not."

Bernie was the one who elucidated.

The caretaker snorted when she was done. "My, my, that would certainly be something, wouldn't it?" he observed.

"*Something* is one way to put it," Marvin replied grimly, thoughts of possible headlines dancing in his head. The funeral home hadn't made the front page of the local paper in the sixty years it had been in business, and he intended to keep it that way. He took a deep breath, said a short pray to the gods, and asked the caretaker for a shovel. "Let's find out, shall we?" he said as he carefully gathered up the roses and put them to one side.

Then he and the caretaker began to dig. He just hoped this was going to turn out to be a waste of time.

Chapter 12

For the next ten minutes, Bernie and Libby stood in front of a large maple tree, waved away mosquitoes, and watched Marvin and the caretaker digging. Libby was wishing she'd brought insect repellent with her when she thought she heard something. Smelled something, too. *Men's cologne?* she wondered. *Maybe Old Spice?* Libby sniffed again. *No. Something else.* She just couldn't put a name to it right then and there.

"Are either of you wearing cologne?" she asked Marvin and the caretaker.

"No," they both said together.

"Why?" Marvin wanted to know as he paused to wipe the sweat from his forehead with his forearm. He wasn't happy. Even though the digging was easy, he was convinced this was going to turn out to be a colossal waste of time.

"I thought I smelled it," Libby replied as she caught a glimpse of something moving out of the corner of her eye. Either that or she was imagining things. She nudged Bernie with her elbow. "I thought I saw something under the trees."

Bernie laughed. "It's probably a deer." There were a lot of them living at Willowwood.

"No, it definitely wasn't a deer," Libby replied.

"Then maybe it's Tom Bannon," Bernie couldn't resist saying. Teasing her sister was always fun. "Maybe he got tired of lying in a grave and decided to take a walk," she suggested.

"Ha ha, very funny, Bernie."

"I thought so," Bernie answered. She was about to tell Libby that maybe she'd seen the ghost of Willowwood— something she'd just made up—when she smelled a whiff of aftershave.

"You saw something, didn't you?" Libby said, reading the expression on her sister's face. "And it wasn't a deer."

"Smelled something," Bernie corrected, "and no, it wasn't a deer."

"Because deer don't wear aftershave."

"At least they don't wear Eternity by Calvin Klein," Bernie declared, the name of the scent having come to her.

Libby raised an eyebrow. "I'm impressed by your olfactory prowess."

"And I'm impressed by your vocabulary."

"Thank you."

"Joe wore it."

"I remember him." Libby laughed. "Wasn't he the one who stole your car when you lived in Oakland?"

"Borrowed, and I don't want to talk about it," Bernie huffed. She scanned the trees and saw a flash of color over to the right. Maybe. Or were her eyes playing tricks on her? There was only one way to find out.

Marvin watched Bernie walk toward the nearby cluster of white birch. "Where are you going?" he called after her.

"Into the arms of the unknown," Bernie replied as she stepped into the grove. It was dark in there. All the light was cut off by the leaf canopy. She stopped and called to her sister. "Coming?" she asked Libby as she took her phone out of her tote and turned on the flashlight. The white trunks looked skeletal in the light.

Libby nodded, even though her heart was still hammering in her chest. Which she knew was ridiculous. "There's a perfectly rational explanation, isn't there?"

"Grave robbers," Bernie said as she smelled another whiff of Eternity, then wondered if eternity had an odor.

"You're not helping," Libby told her sister as Marvin watched Libby and Bernie disappear into the trees, the beam of light from Bernie's phone marking their progress.

"Where do they think they're going?" the caretaker asked Marvin.

"No idea," he replied as he returned to digging. The sooner he got done with this, the happier he'd be.

While Marvin and the caretaker were continuing their excavation project, Bernie was playing the light from her phone over the ground and the trees. She could hear a rustling noise up ahead of her but decided that was probably the leaves on the trees. A twig snapped behind her, and she jumped.

"Gotcha," Libby said.

"Not funny," Bernie observed as she continued walking.

"I thought it was," Libby told her. "Now you know how I feel." After all, fair was fair.

Bernie grunted and stepped over a large rock in her path. So far there was nothing here that she could see that pertained to Tom Bannon's whereabouts, but then she reminded herself that coming out here had been a long shot, anyway. And on that note, she continued walking straight ahead. Ten feet later, she stopped in front of a large downed branch. Should she walk to the right or the left? *Right*, she decided. She was about to go that way when she caught the faint smell of men's aftershave again. It seemed to be coming from the left, so she went that way instead. With every step she took, the scent seemed to be getting stronger. Then the wind shifted, and she lost the scent.

"Do you smell anything?" Bernie asked Libby.

Libby shook her head. "Maybe we should go back and see how Marvin is doing," she suggested. This wasn't getting them anywhere.

"Let's give it a few more minutes," Bernie said as she studied the trees surrounding her. *Looming* was the word that came to mind.

"Because we seem to have reached a dead end here," Libby observed.

Both literally and figuratively, Bernie thought. Although it pained her deeply to admit it, this time her sister was correct. For once. She was about to tell her that when she caught a faint whiff of aftershave again. Where was it coming from? Her eyes swept the grove. There was nothing here. Then she looked up and saw a white something in the crook of the birch tree to the left of her. High up. About twenty feet, she estimated. She squinted. A paper bag? No. A sneaker? Yes. Her first thought was that someone had thrown it up there, but then she took another look. There was an ankle attached to the sneaker. She poked Libby in her side with her elbow.

"What?" Libby asked as Bernie put a finger to her lips and pointed to the crook in the tree. Libby looked. At first, she couldn't see what Bernie was pointing to, and then she could. "Oh my God," she cried.

"So much for the element of surprise," Bernie told her sister.

"It's not as if he didn't know we were there," she replied as Bernie ordered the person in the tree to come down. "He can see us."

There was no response.

"We see you," Bernie said.

Still nothing.

"Don't make me come up and get you," Bernie threatened.

The person in the tree snorted.

"Don't think I can?" Bernie asked.

Another snort ensued.

Bernie put her hands on her hips. "Okay. If that's the way you want it," Bernie told the person up in the tree. "Then let's try this. If your butt isn't on the ground in the next two seconds, I'm calling the cops."

There was a moment of silence; then a voice from up above them floated down. "Chillax. I don't see why you're making such a big deal about this, anyway."

The voice sounded young and male to Bernie. *A teenager*, she guessed. "How old are you?" she asked when he was down on the ground. "Fifteen?"

"Sixteen," the boy said sullenly, looking at the ground and shuffling his feet from side to side.

Bernie gave him a gentle push. "Let's go."

"Hey, hands off," he snapped as he walked in front of her with the unconscious grace of a natural athlete, stepping over small tree branches and rocks without breaking stride.

"Look what we found," Bernie called out once she, Libby, and their captive were within sight of Marvin and the caretaker.

Marvin stopped digging. His eyes widened. "Mike?"

The kid hunched his shoulders. "Yeah," he muttered.

Marvin could see smudges of dirt on the teenager's forehead and cheeks in the light provided by Bernie's phone. "What are you doing here?" he asked.

"Why do you care?" Mike replied.

Bernie pointed to the teenager. "You know him?" she asked Marvin.

Marvin leaned his shovel against the caretaker's truck. His back was killing him. "Of course I know him. He's Ms. Vanderchild's mother's grandson."

"The woman you just buried?" Libby asked.

"The very same," Marvin replied.

Mike scowled. "How'd you find me, anyway?" he asked Bernie and Libby.

Libby replied, "Let's just say that next time you decide to do something like this, go easy on the aftershave."

"And wear black," Bernie added. "A red shirt and white sneakers leave something to be desired in the concealment department."

"Let's dispense with the fashion advice, shall we?" the caretaker told Bernie. Then he addressed the teenager. "What I want to know is exactly what you were doing messing around with your grandmother's grave."

Mike shrugged. "Maybe I like to play in the dirt."

"We will call the cops," Bernie said, repeating her threat.

Mike folded his hands across his chest. "Do what you want."

The caretaker was reaching for his phone when Marvin raised his hand. "Wait. I think I know," he said, remembering the argument he'd overheard earlier in the day, before the funeral. "Mike, did you bury Poppy in the grave?"

"So what if I did?" Mike challenged.

"Who the hell is Poppy?" the caretaker demanded.

"She's my grandmother's dog," Mike replied. "My nana wanted to be buried with her."

"You killed your grandmother's dog?" Bernie asked, horrified.

Mike took a step back. "What do you think I am? Of course not. I buried Poppy's ashes. That's what my nana wanted. She wanted Poppy in the Summerlands with her, but my mom wouldn't do it. She said it was illegal."

"Your mom was right," Marvin told him. "It is illegal to bury dogs and people together."

"That's stupid," Mike said.

Marvin nodded. "I agree, but I didn't make the rules."

"So you decided to take matters into your own hands?" Libby asked Mike.

Mike nodded. "I figured it was the least I could do for my nana after everything she did for me. I was in the middle of putting everything back the way it was when I heard this guy"—Mike motioned to the caretaker—"coming, so I hid." He looked down at the ground, then back up at Marvin and swallowed. "Are you going to tell my mom?" he asked him, suddenly sounding like a little kid.

"No, I'm not," Marvin told him. "I don't think she has to know as long as you fix this." And Marvin gestured to the grave site. *Why get the kid in trouble?* he thought. And, anyway, the kid had done something nice. Who wouldn't want their pet with them in the afterlife?

Mike grinned. He ran over to Marvin and gave him a big hug. "Thank you. Thank you so much, and I know my nana thanks you, too."

Marvin nodded and handed him his shovel. "And don't forget to put the roses back the way you found them."

"See, Bernie?" Libby couldn't resist saying once they were back in Marvin's car. "I told you."

"I never said this wasn't a long shot," Bernie replied. She was calculating how much dinner at Luigi's was going to cost her when Marvin spoke.

"So what do you think happened to Tom Bannon?" he asked her.

"Not a clue," Bernie replied. "I hope he's off having a good time."

Unfortunately, that didn't turn out to be the case.

Chapter 13

Marvin had almost reached the stone angel guarding the north gate when Libby put her hand on Marvin's arm and pointed out the window. "What's that?" she asked.

"What's what?" Marvin responded, glancing around. He couldn't see anything in the dark besides the outline of a copse of pine trees.

"Over to the side," Libby told him. "On the left. I thought I saw something moving."

"Tom Bannon's ghost?" Bernie quipped from the back seat.

"Ha ha," her sister responded. "Very funny. I'm serious."

"So am I," Bernie said as she followed her sister's glance. Like Marvin, she couldn't see anything, either. "What kind of something?"

"I don't know, Bernie," Libby replied. "If I knew, I would tell you. It was some kind of animal. Maybe something like a puma."

"We don't have pumas in Longely," Bernie commented as she peered into the darkness. "This isn't Wyoming."

"So you say, Miss Know-It-All."

"I do know it all," Bernie told her sister as she continued scanning the darkness. At first, she didn't see anything, and then she saw a pale smudge against the dark. "I think it's a dog, Libby. A dog with a plumy tail. Maybe a golden. Wait. I see another tail."

"Are you sure?" Libby asked.

Bernie leaned forward and scanned the area. "Pretty sure. No. I'm positive. The size and shape are right. Definitely two dogs. Two goldens." She saw a flash. "Maybe wearing reflective collars."

"Jennie's goldens were wearing reflective collars when we saw them," Libby noted.

"Lots of dogs wear reflective collars," Marvin observed, not liking the direction the conversation was going in. "And there are lots of goldens around. They're a very popular breed."

"Agreed," Bernie said.

"There's no reason those two dogs—if they are what you say they are—are hers," Marvin added.

"I didn't say they were," Libby countered.

"Let's find out," Bernie suggested.

"Let's not," Marvin countered. This was what he'd been afraid of.

Libby was about to pat Marvin's arm and tell him she thought Bernie was wrong when she remembered something. "Jennie lives around here, doesn't she?" she asked Bernie.

"Yes, she does. Three blocks away, on Hawley Avenue, I believe," Bernie said as she watched the two retrievers cresting the hill and disappearing from view. "I wonder where they're going."

"Hopefully home," Marvin said.

"Then they're going in the wrong direction," Bernie pointed out.

"She's right," Libby told Marvin. "I wonder if Jennie knows they're gone," she mused.

"I'm guessing not," Bernie replied. "She doesn't strike me as the type of person to let her pets go gallivanting around. I should call her and let her know." And she dug her phone out of her tote and made the call. Jennie didn't answer, so Bernie called Googie. When he didn't answer, Bernie left a voicemail. Then she texted both of them—just to be sure, she explained to Libby—and hung up, at which point Libby tapped Marvin on the shoulder.

"No," he said.

"How can you say no when you don't even know what I was going to say?" Libby asked him.

Marvin snorted. "It doesn't take a mind reader to figure out what you want," he replied. "You want to find the goldens and take them back home." He grimaced. "I'm sure they'll find their way home on their own."

"You don't know that," Libby protested. "They could get lost."

"Or hit by a car," Bernie added from the back seat.

"Or stolen and sold to an animal testing site," Libby said. The local paper had had an article about that a few weeks ago. Evidently, labs used goldens for cardiac research. "How would you feel then? You'd never forgive yourself."

"Yes, I would," Marvin lied. But Libby was right. He would feel awful. He just wasn't going to admit it.

"This shouldn't take that long," Bernie coaxed.

"You have no idea how long it's going to take," Marvin replied peevishly, making one last attempt to postpone the inevitable.

"Please do this, Marvin," Libby begged. "As a favor to me."

"We're wasting time," Bernie noted. "The longer we wait, the farther away Bertha and Ernie are getting, and the harder finding them will be."

Marvin sighed. He couldn't argue with the logic, even though he wanted to. Then Bernie supplied the final kicker.

"If you don't want to," she said to Marvin, "we'll get out and track the pups on foot."

Marvin took his hands off the wheel in a gesture of surrender, then quickly put them back on. "Fine. You win. Enough with the guilt," he told Bernie as he turned the car around. "Which way?" he asked, hoping to find the pups as quickly as possible.

Bernie pointed to a narrow dark slash off to the left.

"That's not a road," Marvin protested, following Bernie's finger. "That's a dirt path."

"It's the same thing," Bernie said.

"No, it isn't," Marvin grumbled as he left the road he'd been on. "It isn't at all." At least he wasn't driving the hearse, he reflected, because he'd never get it up the incline.

"It's close enough," Bernie said.

The path she'd indicated was intended for maintenance vehicles only. It snaked its way up a steep thirty-degree incline, through a grove of pine trees, and down the other side of the hill, ran parallel to a small creek that meandered through the cemetery, and ended up at the maintenance shed on the other side of the property.

Bernie and Libby kept a lookout for the goldens as they started up the hill, but they didn't spot anything moving except a large male raccoon waddling across the road a couple of yards ahead of them, followed shortly thereafter by a cat stalking something in the long grass.

"All I can say is that my car had better not slide down the hill," Marvin grumbled as he gave his vehicle more gas. "Any luck?" he asked the sisters as he tried to keep from going off the path and onto the grass.

"No," Libby and Bernie said together.

"I don't see them," Libby added.

For the next ten minutes, Libby, Bernie, and Marvin rode in silence as they concentrated on keeping a lookout for the goldens, but they didn't see anything except two more cats out hunting.

"Can we go back now?" Marvin asked when they reached the pine trees.

"Let's give it another five minutes," Bernie said as they entered the grove. The trees blocked what little light there was, and the smell of pine filled the air. Bernie took a deep breath and then another. The aroma reminded her of the time she'd lived next to a pine grove in Diamond Heights, a neighborhood in San Francisco. "Please."

"Fine." Marvin slowed down to five miles an hour, then to three.

"Can you go any slower?" Bernie asked.

Libby turned and faced her sister. "Do you want to drive?" she snapped.

Bernie allowed as how she didn't.

"Fine," Libby replied. "Then leave Marvin alone."

"I'm doing the best I can," Marvin added, thinking that the last thing he needed was to get into an accident, an easy thing to do, since the path he was following twisted and turned, making it difficult to navigate in the dark even with his headlights illuminating the tree trunks. A few minutes later, Marvin let out a sigh of relief. They were almost out of the grove. He could see the grass ahead when Bernie thought she heard something.

"Is that a bark?" she asked, coming to attention.

Libby listened. "I don't hear anything."

"Neither do I," Marvin agreed.

"Stop the car," Bernie ordered.

Marvin killed the engine.

For a moment, the three of them sat there listening to the rustle of the branches in the wind and the hoot of a tug on the river as they strained to hear the sound of a dog. Then Bernie heard it again. A bark. She opened the window and leaned her head out. She hadn't been mistaken. There it was, somewhere in the distance.

"I think it's coming from down the hill and over to the right," Bernie said.

Marvin and Libby listened, too.

"By Jove, I think you're right," Libby replied a moment later.

"Let's do this," Marvin said as he started his vehicle back up. A minute later, they were out of the grove of trees. "I don't see anything, do you?" he asked, stopping again. The panorama from the top of the hill offered an unobstructed view. He couldn't see anything except grass and another road off to the right, which led to a second, smaller maintenance shed, where the lawn mowers were kept. Then he heard two barks and a woof.

"That way," Libby said, indicating the direction the sound was coming from. "The barks are coming from that way."

Marvin nodded. He rode the brake as he slowly inched his way down the hill. "Thank God," he said, breathing a big sigh of relief, when he reached the road.

The barking got louder, and Marvin followed the sound. Rounding the bend in the road, he saw the corner of the maintenance shed.

"Looks like you were right, Bernie," Marvin said, spotting a sliver of a car's taillight.

"I always am," Bernie replied smugly.

Libby rolled her eyes. "Seriously?"

"Well, I am," Bernie told her as they got close enough to get a good look.

Chapter 14

Marvin stopped his car along the side of the road, and he, Bernie, and Libby jumped out. As the three of them advanced on the vehicle parked alongside the maintenance shed, Bertha and Ernie ran toward them, their tails frantically wagging. This, Bernie reflected, was in marked contrast to their owner, who stood rooted to the spot in her T-shirt, shorts, and bright yellow Crocs, looking as if she'd just gotten out of bed. The phrase *caught like a deer in the headlights* went through Bernie's mind as she studied the expression on Jennie's face.

"Fancy meeting you here," Bernie said as she watched Jennie swallow. Then she followed Jennie's eyes as they slid to the blue Toyota and back again. Bernie couldn't believe what she was seeing. "Is that Tom Bannon I see sitting in the passenger seat?" she asked, even though she already knew the answer to her question.

Jennie gulped and nodded.

"A dead Tom Bannon?" Bernie inquired, just to make sure.

Jennie gave a short nod.

Now it was Libby's turn. "And this is the vehicle he was

in when you last saw him?" she asked, continuing with Bernie's line of questioning.

Jennie nodded for the third time, took a step back, and hugged herself. "I know what this looks like," she replied, her voice ragged with desperation. "But it's not. I got a call to come here. I did." She stuck her chin out, emphasizing her statement. "You have to believe me."

"I didn't say you didn't," Bernie remarked at the same time Libby told Jennie her story was pretty hard to swallow.

Jennie pointed toward the Toyota, while Bertha jumped up, placed her paws on Bernie's shoulders, and licked her cheek. "The police are going to think I did this," she continued as Marvin walked over to get a closer look at what was inside the vehicle.

"No kidding," Bernie replied.

"Killed Bannon?" Libby asked Jennie.

"No, Libby. Played basketball with him," Bernie snapped. Libby ignored her sister. "Did you?" she asked Jennie.

"No, of course not," Jennie spluttered. "What kind of person do you think I am, Libby? And no, don't you answer, either," she said to Marvin, who'd just opened his mouth to say something.

"I was just going to say Bannon looks a little worse for wear," Marvin commented in a mild voice as he peered inside the vehicle. Rigor had passed, and Bannon's head was leaning forward, his chin lolling on his chest. The blood on his T-shirt had dried and looked black in the light supplied by the shed's spotlight.

"Bernie, Libby, you have to help me, you have to," Jennie pleaded as Marvin took a step back.

"Where was Bannon sitting when you last saw him?" Bernie asked her.

"In the car. His car."

"Where in the car?" Bernie demanded.

"In the driver's seat, of course," Jennie answered, puzzled. "I already told you that. I thought he was sitting in his car, waiting for me. He was supposed to be. That's why I went over to Woof Woof in the first place. I was supposed to meet him there."

"So, between when you saw Bannon last and now, someone moved him from the driver's to the passenger's seat," Bernie recapped.

"Duh. Yes. Obviously, someone moved him," Jennie replied as Ernie nudged her hand with his nose. She gave the golden an absentminded pat. "It's not like he moved himself over."

Bernie continued with her thought. "Maybe he was alive when you saw him."

"He wasn't," Jennie cried. "How many times do I have to say that!"

"As many as it takes," Bernie told her. Then she thought for another moment and said, "Moving Bannon wouldn't be easy to do. He wasn't a small guy."

"No, he wasn't," Jennie agreed. "He is—excuse me, was—just a little smaller than George is."

"George?" Libby asked.

"Yes, George. Googie. You know. The person that works for you," Jennie told her.

"Right." For a moment Libby had forgotten that George was Googie's first name. "Speaking of which, where is he?" Libby asked.

"He's at a friend's bachelor party." And Jennie supplied the location.

"And before that?" Bernie asked.

"He was working for you, and then he went over to his mom's house to cut the grass. Why?"

"Just curious." Bernie let out the breath she didn't know she'd been holding. Not that she thought he was involved in this, but experience had taught her it was good to check.

"You don't think he's mixed up in whatever this is?" Marvin asked Bernie.

"No, I don't think Googie is," Bernie replied. "Just making sure."

Jennie sniffed, "Of course he isn't. That's ridiculous."

"Not really," Libby told her.

Jennie turned and faced her. "How do you figure that?"

"Well, figuring two people are involved in this," Libby pointed out. "So if you are . . ."

"I'm not," Jennie exclaimed.

Libby held up her hand. "Let me finish."

"Sorry," Jennie murmured.

Libby continued. "If you are—hypothetically speaking—then it makes sense that Googie would be, too."

"I'm still not following the whole two-person thing. How do you get that?" Marvin asked her.

Libby broke it down for him. "For openers, it probably took two people to move Bannon from the driver's to the passenger's seat, since he's not exactly a lightweight."

"Deadweight, to be exact," Bernie quipped. "Too soon?" she asked, taking in the expressions on everyone's faces.

"Definitely too soon," Libby replied. "And then," she continued, "someone had to have driven Bannon's Toyota to the cemetery." Libby pointed to Jennie's black Kia, with a DOG MAMA sticker on its bumper. It was parked in front of the maintenance shed. "Obviously, that person wasn't Jennie."

"She could have driven Bannon over earlier," Marvin objected.

"I could have, but I didn't," Jennie answered. "If I had, the last thing I would do is come back here."

"I don't know," Marvin told her. "Maybe you thought you forgot something in the Toyota. Like your wallet. Something like that." Then, looking at Jennie's quivering lower lip and shaking hands, Marvin decided he was wrong. She really did seem genuinely upset. On the other hand, she could be acting. His gut told him she wasn't, but what if she was a pathological liar? He'd been fooled before.

Marvin was quiet for a minute; then something else occurred to him. "Okay, so someone had to drive the Toyota here, agreed?"

"Agreed," Bernie and Libby said.

"Which means whoever did either got a lift back or"—he held up his hand to emphasize the point—"or he or she could have walked back from here. It's not that far from Elmcrest Avenue, and they could have gotten a bus from there. So the two-person thing doesn't necessarily apply."

"I suppose," Bernie allowed. What Marvin had just said was true. Whoever did this could have caught a bus. Although most people around here didn't use mass transportation. They had cars.

Marvin gestured in the direction of the north gate. "Too bad management never fixed the cameras at the entrance. We might have seen the driver if they had. Of course, there is another explanation," Marvin continued. He swatted at a moth flitting around his head. "It is pretty far-fetched, though," he conceded. "It's really out there."

"Bannon is a zombie," Bernie said.

"Ha ha," Marvin said.

"Tell us," Libby urged.

"You'll laugh," Marvin replied.

"No, we won't, Marvin," Libby assured him.

"Your sister will."

"She won't." Libby held up her hand. "We swear. Right, Bernie?"

"Right," Bernie said.

Marvin nodded. He hesitated.

"Please," Bernie said. "Pretty please with a cherry on top."

Marvin smiled. "In that case." A cloud scudded across the moon's face while Marvin took a moment to gather his thoughts. Then he spoke. "Well, here goes nothing," he said as he fended off the two golden retrievers, one of whom was leaning against his right leg, while the other was licking his calf. "What if Tom Bannon wasn't really dead when Jennie saw him?"

"That's nuts," Jennie said.

"It's pretty out there," Marvin agreed.

"It's absurd. How can you come up with something like that?" Jennie told him. "There was all this blood all over the place. I saw it."

Marvin held up his hand. "Let me finish."

Jennie crossed her arms over her chest and shifted her weight from her right to her left leg. "Go on."

Marvin did. "What if the blood was ketchup or that stuff they use in plays and movies?"

"Karo syrup and red food dye?" Bernie asked.

"Yes," Marvin said. "What if that's what you saw, Jennie? What if Bannon was just pretending to be dead, and then later, after he drove away, someone killed him?"

"Why on earth would he do that?" Jennie asked.

Marvin shrugged. "Pretend to be dead?"

"Yes," Jennie said.

Marvin unwrapped a piece of gum and began to chew. "I don't know. A practical joke?"

"That would be some joke," Libby said.

"Or," Marvin went on, "maybe the loan sharks were after him again, and he figured he'd fake his own death and get out of town."

"Even if what you say is true," Bernie said, "what would give him the idea to do that? It isn't something that would occur to me."

"That's because you don't do the makeup for the Longely Rep," Marvin told her, a smug tone in his voice.

"Bannon does?" Libby asked. "Did," she said, correcting herself.

Marvin nodded. "I overheard one of Mrs. Vanderchild's nieces say the company was hiring him to do *The Wizard of Oz* and that he had a possible gig in September out in Hollywood."

"That's pretty impressive," Libby said.

"Yeah, it is. Evidently, the niece is playing the Wicked Witch in the production, and someone asked her if she was going to do her own makeup, and she said, 'No. The company has stopped cheaping out and has hired Bannon.'"

"Do you remember the niece's name by any chance?" Bernie asked.

"I think it was something like Nicole or Keri. I can look it up in the book if you want."

Bernie smiled. "That would be great."

Jennie frowned. She'd just thought of something, too. "Okay, Marvin, answer me this. What if I hadn't left when I did? What if I'd waited there? What if my phone was charged, so I could call the police? Bannon didn't know that it wouldn't be. He couldn't have, unless he could tell the future."

"Good point," Bernie said as she smoothed down her skirt. She nodded in the direction of Tom Bannon's corpse. "And speaking of TB, what do we do now?"

"We could leave and let one of the maintenance crew discover him in the morning," Jennie suggested.

Libby frowned. "That wouldn't be right."

"Why not?" Jennie demanded. "He's dead already. What difference will a couple of hours make?"

"A lot. We need to call the police immediately," Marvin said, thinking of the ramifications if they didn't and it was discovered that they hadn't.

"You can't. They'll arrest me," Jennie cried.

"Not necessarily," Marvin said, even though he thought that would be the case.

"Yes, necessarily," Jennie cried.

"I think we should call Dad and see what he has to say," Libby suggested.

"I think you're right," Bernie told her, even though she knew what her father was going to say. She was taking her cell out of her tote when she saw lights cresting the hill. "Crap," she said as the lights drew closer. "It's the police."

Everyone turned and watched the black-and-white cruiser come to a stop in front of them. A policewoman got out. Bertha and Ernie started to run over to her, but before they could, Jennie grabbed the dogs by their collars and attached their leashes.

"Hello," the officer said, her hand on her weapon.

"Hello," Libby and Bernie replied.

"What do we have here?" the officer asked.

"Would you believe a group of friends getting together for a summer evening revelry?" Bernie answered.

"Really? Because that's not what the dispatcher said,"

the officer noted as she made her way over to the blue Toyota. The dogs barked out hellos as she bent over and looked in the vehicle's windows. Then she straightened up and drew her weapon. "I need everyone to get down on the ground," she instructed. "I need you to do it now."

Chapter 15

"So what do you think?" Clyde asked Sean as Clyde stretched his legs out.

It was the following evening, and he, Sean, Bernie, and Libby were sitting on a park bench by the Hudson River, throwing handfuls of frozen corn to a family of ducks and enjoying the cool breeze coming off the water as they watched the sun set and discussed what had happened at Willowwood the night before.

"I don't know," Sean told his friend Clyde as a couple pushing a stroller walked by them.

Bernie unscrewed the top of her thermos and took a sip of the iced tea she'd brought along. "Well, I know what I think. I think someone is trying to frame Jennie for Tom Bannon's murder," she declared.

Sean turned to his other daughter. "Is that what you think, too, Libby?"

She nodded. "Yeah, I do. How else can you explain the calls?"

"Good question," Sean said.

"First, Jennie gets a call to go down to Willowwood and check out the car, and then someone calls the police and tells them that there's a vehicle down there with a dead body," Libby went on. "If that doesn't sound like a setup, I don't know what does."

Sean threw another handful of corn into the water and watched the ducks dive for the kernels. "*If* Jennie got the call. We just have her word to go on."

"I believe her," Bernie said.

"Did she tell you what the caller said, specifically?" Sean asked.

"She did," Libby replied. "The caller said that there was something down behind the main shed at Willowwood she needed to see and that she should hurry up and go in through the north gate, or she'd miss it."

"And you think she was telling the truth?" Sean asked.

"Yeah, Dad, I do," Bernie replied.

Sean turned toward Bernie, "Let me ask you a question. Would you have gone if you had gotten a call like that?" he asked her.

"Yes, given the circumstances," Bernie told him.

"You hesitated a minute."

Bernie stuck her chin out. "What if I did?"

"Which means you're lying,"

"No, Dad. It means I'm not sure. It is a stretch."

"Fair enough," Sean said. His daughter's answer would do for the moment. He turned his attention back to the scene in front of him. "Male or female?" Sean asked as he watched the sky turn red. What was that saying . . . ? *Red sky in the morning, sailors take warning. Red sky at night, sailors' delight*? He wished he hadn't sold his boat. He'd be out on the water now if he hadn't.

"Male or female what?" Bernie asked while she reached up and readjusted her ponytail.

"Jennie's caller."

"I asked that, too," Bernie told her dad. "She said it was hard to tell. There was too much background noise."

Clyde snorted.

Bernie turned to him. "So you don't believe Jennie, either?"

"Do pigs fly? The whole thing is too neat for me."

Bernie frowned. "I can see where you'd say that."

"You're just trying to get on my good side, aren't you?" Clyde told Bernie, but he was smiling when he said it.

"Nah," Bernie said, but she was smiling, too. "I don't suppose you know who made the call?"

"Nope. It was anonymous, like Jennie said," Clyde responded.

"One point in her favor," Bernie pointed out.

Her dad shook his head. "Not necessarily. Not if this is a scheme she's in on. This could just be another part of the setup."

"That's ridiculous," Bernie told him.

"Did you trace it?" Libby asked Clyde.

"The call?" Clyde asked.

"Yes," Libby answered.

Clyde shook his head. He stopped himself from saying, "Obviously not." If they had been able to, they wouldn't be having this conversation. Instead, he said, "According to Ripley, the call came from a burner phone."

"Is that who's assigned to the case?" Sean asked.

Clyde nodded. "Lucy wouldn't give it to me." Lucy was the Longely chief of police. "He said I was too close to you."

"I wouldn't have, either," Sean confessed. It wasn't often that he agreed with Lucy about anything. Then he turned to his daughters. "At least Lucy didn't arrest you, too."

"True," Libby agreed. She thought about Googie's forgetting to add water to the coffee and forgetting to put the mayo back in the cooler and said, "Googie's pretty upset about what happened with Jennie last night."

"I would be, too, if my girlfriend was arrested," Bernie noted.

"For murder," Sean noted. "We're not talking parking tickets here."

Clyde corrected Bernie. "Jennie wasn't arrested. She was brought in for questioning and released."

Sean threw his last handful of corn to the ducks, then took a sip of his watermelon-cucumber cooler. Bernie and Libby were correct. Normally, he was a gin and tonic kinda guy, but this was good. "If I were investigating, she would be my primary suspect," Sean pointed out as he screwed the lid back on his thermos.

"She's Ripley's," Clyde informed them after he took a bite of the blueberry corn muffin Bernie had asked him to try. It was tasty. Very tasty. The blueberries added just the right amount of tartness, counterbalancing the corn's sweetness. "In fact, she's the only suspect. I think the DA is getting ready to bring the case in front of the grand jury and ask for an indictment."

Bernie shook her head. "I repeat what I said before. I think she was framed."

"If she was, it's a pretty good frame," Clyde noted.

"Yes, it is," Libby agreed. "Too bad you guys couldn't trace the call."

Clyde nodded. "For her, absolutely. Why would anyone frame her? Who would want to frame her?"

Bernie watched a white moth hover around the streetlight. "Googie thinks it was her ex-boyfriend."

"The obvious answer," Sean said. "At least it was when I was head of the Longely PD."

"He was out of town, visiting his mom," Bernie noted. "We checked."

"At least that's what his friend says," Libby added. They had stopped by Liam's earlier in the day and had had a chat with a woman called Yolanda.

Clyde shook his head. "Back to Jennie again."

Bernie turned to face Clyde. "Why would Jennie kill Bannon? What's her motive?"

"I don't know," Clyde admitted.

"Exactly," Bernie said.

"But that doesn't mean it's not there," Clyde added.

"Okay. Even if it is there, and I'm not saying it is," Bernie continued, "why would Jennie do it the way she did? Talk about attracting attention to yourself. It makes no sense."

"People do strange things all the time," Sean weighed in as he finished his muffin and brushed the crumbs into the palm of his hand and threw them to the ducks. "Inexplicable things."

Bernie hesitated for a moment. Then she said, "You think the person that shot at Denise and keyed Marcy's van and flattened our tires . . ."

"And warned us not to get involved," Libby added.

"Is the same person who killed Bannon?" Bernie said, finishing her thought.

"I expect so," Sean replied. He turned to Clyde. "Don't you?"

"It's likely," Clyde allowed. "I don't believe in coincidence, and neither does your dad, Bernie."

But Bernie already knew that. Actually, neither did she. She paused for a moment, then said, "Here's an idea. Maybe Jennie stirred something up when she rented Woof Woof."

"So you're saying Bannon is collateral damage?" Sean asked, to clarify.

"He could be," Bernie replied.

"Anything is possible," Clyde observed.

"True," Sean said, thinking back to his cases. "Maybe he saw something he shouldn't have when he was doing construction."

"Like what?" Clyde asked. "Empty beer cans?"

The question hung in the air. No one answered, because no one had an answer. Instead, the four of them sat there quietly for the next five minutes as Clyde threw his last handful of corn to the ducks.

"Did you know you're not supposed to feed bread to ducks?" Clyde said as he, Sean, Bernie, and Libby watched the ducks eat the corn, look for more and, when they couldn't find any more, quack in protest and paddle away. By now, the sun was sinking below the horizon, and the sky was turning dark. "Who knew? All these years I've been doing it wrong."

The sun had finished setting when Libby said, "Googie asked us to investigate the Tom Bannon thing."

"Of course he did," Clyde replied.

"I don't suppose we could speak to Ripley?" Bernie asked.

Clyde laughed. "That doesn't even merit an answer."

Bernie brushed a kernel of corn off her lap. "Figured it was worth a try. By the way, Jennie asked us, too," Bernie added.

Libby frowned. "She didn't ask me."

"I forgot to tell you. She called when you were taking a shower," Bernie informed her sister.

"So what are you going to do?" Sean asked his daughters, although he could guess the answer.

"Investigate," Bernie replied. "I don't see that we have much choice, do you?"

"How do you get that?" Sean asked. "You always have a choice."

"That's true, but Googie will never forgive us if we don't," Libby explained.

Which was also true, Sean thought. "And if Jennie wasn't Googie's girlfriend, then what?"

"We still would," Bernie said, speaking for herself and her sister, "because we don't think Jennie did it."

"Ah, the naivete of youth," Clyde said.

"What happened to everyone is innocent until proven guilty?" Bernie protested.

Clyde grinned. "I prefer the opposite—everyone is guilty until proven innocent."

"That's terrible," Libby said.

"No, that's experience," Clyde told her.

For once Bernie had no reply.

Chapter 16

The next morning Marvin came through with the information he had promised Libby and Bernie the night before. The woman he had overheard talking at the calling hours for Ms. Vanderchild's mother's funeral was Nicole, Nicole Vanderchild. She worked as a salesgirl for a shop called Save the Planet, which was located in the Marketplace Mall.

"Not that far," Bernie noted as she sliced tomatoes for the blueberry, tomato, and mozzarella salad they were featuring for lunch.

Libby stopped pitting the cherries for the cold cherry soup they were serving for dinner and looked up. "You think it'll be worth it?"

"Talking to Nicole?" Bernie asked her sister.

Libby nodded, her hands stained red with cherry juice.

Bernie shrugged. "I hope so. At this juncture any crumb of information would help."

By the time Bernie and Libby set off, it had gotten hotter. The sky was hazy, the flowers were wilting in the heat, and the humidity made it feel ten degrees warmer than it was. The route Bernie chose ran parallel to the Hudson.

The kayakers were already out on the river, groups paddling close to the shore, while terns squawked as they circled overhead, and tugs guided freighters down the Hudson to the city.

Twenty minutes later, Bernie and Libby arrived at their destination. At eleven, people hadn't sought refuge from the heat in the mall's cavernous embrace, and the parking lot was empty. Bernie parked directly across from the entrance, and she and Libby hurried inside. After a few inquiries, they found Nicole having an early lunch in a largely empty food court. She was sipping an iced coffee, eating a meatball sub, and texting on her cell phone, while a few of the sparrows that had decided life was better inside than out darted around the tabletops, looking for crumbs.

A petite twentysomething, Nicole had braided her hair in two pigtails, which emphasized her large gray-green eyes and oval face. Bernie noted that she was wearing what Save the Planet was featuring this week: a mint-green–colored T-shirt with a large daisy printed underneath a logo that said SAVE THE PLANET, navy blue cargo shorts, and a pair of white canvas sneakers.

She looked up when Bernie and Libby slid into the seats across from her. "Do I know you?" she asked, startled.

"No, you don't," Bernie said, putting on her most benign expression.

Libby smiled and leaned forward. "But we need to talk to you," she said.

An alarmed expression crossed Nicole's face. "About what?"

"Using your employee discount to sell clothes to your friends," Bernie improvised, guessing at the reason for Nicole's expression, as she remembered what she'd done when she worked retail at the mall her senior year of high school. Of course, it could be that Nicole had something to do with Bannon's death, but she doubted it.

Nicole swallowed. "It was just once, and that wasn't my fault." She was about to say something else when she took another look at Bernie's vintage sundress and Libby's light pink Izod polo shirt and said, "You're not from management, are you?"

Bernie smiled pleasantly. "We could be."

"But you're not," Nicole said.

Libby nodded. "You're right. We're not."

Nicole's expression turned sullen. She went back to looking at her phone.

"We won't tell management," Bernie said. She paused. "Unless . . ."

Nicole looked up, the alarmed expression back. "Unless what?"

"You don't help us," Bernie told her.

"You're blackmailing me?" Nicole squeaked. "Is that what you're trying to do?"

Bernie corrected her. "Will do."

"We just want to know about Tom Bannon," Libby explained before her sister could say anything else. She had no idea why her sister had started off the way she had.

Nicole's expression changed. "I just heard about it on the news," she said, blinking back tears. "That's so awful."

"It is," Libby agreed.

"He was going to do your makeup, right?" Bernie asked.

Nicole's smile lit up her face as she remembered. "I'm playing the Wicked Witch in *The Wizard of Oz*," she replied, all animosity momentarily forgotten.

Bernie offered her congratulations.

"It's my first big role," Nicole said proudly.

Libby leaned forward. "So was Tom any good in the makeup department?" she asked.

"Good!" Nicole exclaimed. "Tom was great. He was

going to Hollywood. He told me he'd see if he could get me some bit parts when he got there. You know, walk-ons. Stuff like that. We were even planning on rooming together." Her face fell. "I can't believe someone would kill him. Why would anyone do something like that?"

"That's what we're trying to find out," Libby said.

"Do you think he was capable of faking his own death?" Bernie asked.

"That's ridiculous," Nicole scoffed. "Why would he want to do that? I told you. He was making plans to go off to Hollywood."

"Okay," Bernie said. "Then do you know anyone who didn't like him? Anyone who had a beef with him?"

Nicole shook her head. "He was a sweet guy, a really sweet guy."

"I heard he had a gambling problem," Libby said.

"He did," Nicole told her. "But that was a long time ago in Cali. He doesn't . . . didn't . . . do that anymore."

"It's a hard habit to shake," Bernie noted.

Nicole stuck out her chin. "He would have told me. We had a deal."

Bernie wanted to say that in her experience, things didn't always work out that way, but she didn't. There was no point. Instead, she went on to the next item on her and Libby's agenda. "Did Bannon have a girlfriend?"

"Yeah," Nicole replied, "he did."

Bernie cocked her head and waited.

"They broke up a year ago," Nicole informed her.

"On good terms?" Bernie asked.

Nicole nodded. "Absolutely. She wanted kids, and he didn't. Well, Vanessa found someone who did, because she got married to this other dude and is living in Washington State. At least she was the last time I talked to her." She took a last bite of her meatball sub and pushed the wrapper away with the tips of her fingers. Bernie noticed that Nicole's nails were bitten down to the quick. "Actually, now that I think of it, I don't think Tom's been serious about anyone else since then."

So much for that lead, Bernie thought as Nicole glanced at her phone.

"I have to go soon," she announced. "My lunch break is almost over."

"Can you think of anything that could help us?" Libby asked Nicole. "Anything at all."

Nicole scrunched her face while she thought. "I don't know if this is anything," she said two minutes later. "It probably isn't, but a little while ago, right before . . ." Her lower lip quivered. "You know . . . he was showing me the apartment he wanted to rent in Hollywood. I mean, it was really nice, and I asked him how we could afford it, and he said, 'Not to worry. I have a little trick up my sleeve.' So I asked him if he was gambling again, and he said no. This was much more of a sure thing and that he'd tell me about it in time, but not now." She sniffled. "And now he never will."

"Any idea of what Bannon was talking about?" Bernie asked.

Nicole shook her head. Bernie could see the tears in her eyes. "I asked him a couple of times, but he always changed the subject."

"And when did this happen?" Libby asked.

Nicole cocked her head. "The conversation?"

Libby nodded.

Nicole thought for a moment, then counted back the weeks on her fingers. Bernie and Libby exchanged looks when she told them. It was around the same time that Bannon had started working on the reno for Woof Woof. It might mean something, or it might mean nothing at all.

Impossible to say at the moment.

Nicole got up. "And now I really have to go."

"Well, if you think of anything . . . ," Bernie told Nicole as Nicole walked over to the large silver metal trash can and stowed her tray in the slot above it.

"I'll let you know," Nicole said, finishing Bernie's sentence for her. Then she hurried off to her job, and Libby and Bernie walked back to their van.

"You think Bannon stopped gambling?" Libby asked Bernie as the mall door to the outside swung open.

"Nicole seems convinced," Bernie observed as she hurried across the asphalt. Hot air flowed out of the van when she opened Mathilda's door.

"Yeah. But what do you think?" Libby asked Bernie as she climbed inside Mathilda.

"I think Dad is right," Bernie replied as she started the van up. "I think Bannon merits a closer look."

Chapter 17

On the way back to the shop, Bernie and Libby stopped at Bannon's flat again. Bernie pulled into Bannon's driveway, parked the van, and she and Libby got out. Two squirrels were playing tag on the elm tree by the curb, while a crow pecked for worms in the grass. The house was shuttered; an UPPER FLAT FOR RENT sign was still planted on the unmown, clover-strewn front lawn. There was also a FOR RENT sign on the house across the street.

Nothing had changed since the last time Bernie and Libby had visited. The stairs leading to the porch creaked as Bernie and Libby walked up them. The porch floor was still painted an industrial gray, the paint bubbling up from the wooden planking, and the old sofa, its stuffing tumbling out in white tuffs, still sat next to the double doors that led to the upper and lower flats. Empty crushed Pabst beer cans on the rickety wicker coffee table in front of the sofa testified that someone had been sitting there recently, drinking and watching the world go by.

When Bernie and Libby reached the mailboxes, Libby suddenly turned and scanned the street.

"What's the matter?" Bernie asked.

Libby shook her head. "Nothing," she lied, not wanting to talk about the feeling that had suddenly come over her. A feeling she couldn't explain.

She turned back and checked the mailbox labeled with Bannon's name. The only things in it this time were a couple of flyers promising low vehicle insurance rates, a utility bill, proffers from a heating and an insurance company, and a promo for a new Chinese restaurant. She closed the top of the mailbox and scanned the street again. Just to make sure. No one was there, she told herself. Just a motley collection of vehicles baking in the sun. She was imagining things. So then why did she feel as if someone was watching her? She'd felt that way at Willowwood the other night, and she'd been right. The kid had been watching them. So maybe she was right now. Or maybe she wasn't.

While Libby was second-guessing herself, Bernie tried the door next to Bannon's mailbox. She expected it to be locked, but it wasn't. The doorknob turned, and the door swung open. Bernie bit her lip. *Interesting.* Had Bannon stepped out for a moment, expected to come back, and been intercepted? she wondered. Or had someone come in to look around—like they were doing—and not bothered to lock the door on their way out? Bernie studied the lock and the door. Neither one showed evidence of being forced open, but the lock was old, and it wouldn't take much to open it, Bernie reflected. She suspected she could have popped it open with a credit card if she'd needed to.

"The cops could have come in for a quick look-see," Bernie suggested before her sister could say anything.

"Doubtful," Libby replied. "This place would be festooned in yellow crime scene tape if they had," she pointed out.

"Like a gift gone bad," Bernie observed. Then she extended her arm and gestured toward the waiting door. "Shall we?" she asked Libby.

"Have you stopped to think that maybe the person who opened the door could still be in there?" Libby observed.

"Or maybe Bannon forgot to lock it," Bernie said.

"Or maybe he didn't," Libby countered.

"Let's find out," Bernie said, and she stepped inside. She spent a minute listening. Silence. No footsteps. No sound of the rear door closing. She cupped her hands and yelled, "Yoo-hoo. Is anyone home?"

No one answered.

"Ready or not, here we come," Bernie sang out.

Still nothing.

Bernie turned back to her sister. "See, Libby. No one's here."

"They could be hiding," her sister replied.

"Or beaming up to Mars. There's only one way to find out," Bernie told her, taking another step into the narrow hallway. After all, they couldn't stand here all day. They had other things to do.

"I can think of other ways to find out," Libby grumbled as she followed her sister inside.

The large three-bedroom, one-bathroom flat smelled stuffy, the odors of old food and dirty clothes predominating. It was hotter inside than outside, the heat having built up in Bannon's absence.

"I guess he didn't need a lot of the stuff he brought with him," Libby reflected, referring to the unpacked cartons piled up in the hallway.

"Either that or he knew he was going to move again," Bernie replied, thinking of what Nicole had told them.

She and Libby went through the cartons quickly. All the boxes were labeled and contained the contents that were listed on the cardboard flaps. When the sisters were done, they walked into the dining room.

"I wonder what Bannon was building," Bernie mused as she looked at the small band saw on the dining-room table, the planks of pine, and the sawdust on the floor, which contrasted with the wainscoting on the walls, the mullioned windows, and the dark wood floor.

"If I had to guess, I'd say some sort of shelving," Libby answered as she stepped into the living room and glanced around. "But that doesn't make sense in light of what Nicole said."

"Maybe they were for Jennie's place?" Bernie mused.

"Maybe," Libby said. "But then why build them here? Why not build them at Woof Woof? There is certainly enough room there."

Bernie grunted. Libby had a valid point. "So something for here, but not shelves."

"Like what?"

"I don't have a clue," Bernie replied.

"Neither do I," Libby said as she studied the cheap put-it-together-yourself sofa and coffee table, the TV, the game console, the working Pac-Man machine, and the basketful of unfolded laundry perched on the seat of a black leather armchair that had seen better days.

"Very cool," Bernie said, looking at the machine. She'd wanted one of those since she'd seen it in a local antique store three years ago. She started moving toward it, but Libby pulled her back.

"We don't have time, Bernie."

"I just want to see if it works," Bernie protested. As it turned out, it did. "I mean, maybe there's a clue in it that will solve the case," Bernie said after she'd played a round.

Libby snorted, picked up a sketchbook lying on the coffee table, and began thumbing through it. "Look at these," she said after she was done.

Bernie stopped playing and looked. The pencil drawings ranged from architectural renderings to portraits of everyday life to sketches of underground cities and tunnels to a couple of quick sketches of costumes for *The Wizard of Oz*. Bannon's crisp signature adorned the bottom of each page.

"He was really good," Bernie said admiringly as she studied Bannon's sketch of the elm tree outside the window. It was the last sketch in the book. Two other pages had been removed and were on the table, semi-hidden by the Entertainment section of the *Longely Sentinel*. "I wonder if he was going to frame these," Bernie said, picking them up.

"They would look nice hanging on a wall," Libby observed as she studied the drawings. The first one was of another tree with a twisted trunk, while the second one showed a squat brick building undergoing renovation. "What a waste of talent," she reflected, putting the sketch pad back where she'd found it. Then she and her sister walked into the kitchen. "He was really a talented artist."

"Lot of good it did him," Bernie observed, looking around the small space. One of the counters was taken up with a large collection of theatrical makeup and the carrying case the items were going to go into, while the other counter had a paper bag from one of the local grocery stores sitting on it.

Bernie went over and peered in. There was a pint of moldy strawberries, a bunch of browning bananas, a loaf of whole wheat bread, a jar of organic peanut butter, and a roll of paper towels. Bannon hadn't unpacked his groceries. Had something happened, or had he forgotten?

Bernie was just about to ask Libby what she thought when Libby said, "Look at this."

Bernie turned. Her sister was holding out an opened letter. It was from a rental agent in Hollywood, telling Bannon that the sublet they'd talked about was his if he wanted it, and if that was the case, could he please send payment through PayPal or Venmo?

"I guess Nicole was telling the truth," Libby observed as she put the letter back on the pile of mail where she'd found it. "Bannon was going to Hollywood in September."

"Evidently," Bernie said as she read a scrawled note written on the back of an old envelope. *Call Denise.* The two words were underlined three times, and there were three exclamation points next to them. Bernie waved the note in the air. "I wonder if this Denise Alvarez."

"The photographer Jennie is working with?" Libby asked.

Bernie nodded. "We should ask," she said as she tucked the note into the pocket of her skirt and started toward the bedrooms. Two of them were furnished with mattresses on the floor and gave no sign of being inhabited, while the third bedroom—obviously Bannon's—contained a chest of drawers, a nightstand, and a futon. It didn't take long for Bernie and her sister to go through their contents.

"I'll tell you one thing," Bernie said to Libby as she closed the bottom dresser drawer. "Bannon wasn't big on clothes."

There was nothing in the dresser except boxers, socks, T-shirts, jeans, and cargo shorts, while the closet yielded one good suit and a couple of pairs of running sneakers, and the nightstand was full of Kleenex. The bathroom didn't yield much information, either. As she looked at the toothpaste, the toothbrush, the mouthwash, and the razor and shaving cream in the medicine cabinet, it was obvious to Bernie that Bannon hadn't planned on disappearing himself. His essentials were still here.

"So much for Marvin's theory about Bannon playing dead," Bernie said as they closed the door to Bannon's apartment and walked down the porch stairs. "Not that I took it seriously, anyway," she added.

Torn between loyalty to her boyfriend and agreeing with her sister, Libby decided not commenting was best. "So what do you think happened?" she asked her sister instead.

"If Jennie is telling the truth, then I think she interrupted a murder," Bernie responded. She corrected herself. "Or not interrupted, but arrived before the killer had finished the job." She closed her eyes and visualized the scene. "I think Bannon went to work, and then something, maybe a call, made him go outside and get in his car and go somewhere. Then he came back. For some reason, he didn't park in front of Woof Woof. Maybe his killer was already parked at the end of the strip mall and motioned him over."

"Which explains why he was where he was," Libby said.

Bernie nodded. "Exactly. In any case, he or she shot him."

Libby continued the narrative. "Which was when Jennie arrived, something the killer wasn't expecting. So the killer drove around to the back of the strip mall and waited for Jennie to leave. There is that narrow access road in the back that leads to Sparrow Lane, so if worst came to worst, he could have escaped that way. He was probably going to do that, but then Jennie left, and our perp had an idea. A better one. He was going to move Bannon's body out of the driver's seat, jump into Bannon's car, and drive it away."

"Then what happened to the perp's vehicle?" Bernie challenged.

"He came back to get it later," Libby hypothesized.

"Why didn't the police see it, Libby? Tell me that."

"Duh. Because they didn't look."

Bernie conceded that could be the case.

"Of course," Libby continued, "there's another possibility, as well. An obvious one. Maybe whoever killed Bannon was on foot. Maybe he was waiting for him. Maybe he had called Bannon and arranged a meeting."

"Could be," Bernie allowed.

"And maybe," Libby continued, "Bannon knew him."

"Or her," Bernie said.

"At least that's what the bullet wound suggests," Libby said. "From what we saw, whoever killed Bannon had to get pretty close to do it."

Bernie nodded. She was no expert, but it looked as if the shooter had used a .22.

"We should check the back of the strip mall," Libby said as she scanned the street. Everything looked the way it had when they arrived.

"And talk to Denise Alvarez," Bernie added. "See if there's a connection between her and Bannon."

Libby nodded. "Of course, there is a simpler explanation," she said, going back to the topic they'd just been discussing. "Jennie could have arranged a meeting with Bannon, arrived there, and shot him. Then she could have gotten in Bannon's car and driven it and him away and come back. No fuss, no muss."

"That's what the police think," Bernie said as she opened Mathilda's door. The heat rushed out of the van and slapped her in the face.

Libby nodded again. "It is."

"There's just one problem with that scenario," Bernie continued. "If Jennie killed Bannon and had already disposed of the body, why bring him back? Why arrange for the police to find him? Why attract so much attention to yourself when, for all intents and purposes, you've gotten away with murder? Literally."

"It doesn't make much sense," Libby admitted.

"No, it doesn't," Bernie replied, inserting the key into Mathilda's ignition and turning it. The van's engine spluttered. Bernie held her breath and tried again. This time the engine caught and turned over. "If this isn't a frame-up, I don't know what is," she told her sister as she pulled out of the driveway.

Chapter 18

On their way over to Denise's, Bernie and Libby stopped and checked out the back of the strip mall Woof Woof was going to be located in. Just in case. It turned out to be a waste of time, as Bernie had suspected it would be, although she decided as she inspected the landscape that Libby had been correct. Bannon's killer could have hidden Bannon's car and body back here. The vehicle wouldn't have been visible at a casual glance. Especially at that time of day. And Bernie was pretty sure from what she'd seen the evening that Googie had called her to help Jennie out that the cops hadn't bothered to look in back of the strip mall. Hell, they couldn't wait to get out of there.

"Five minutes," Bernie said to Libby as she got out of Mathilda and looked around.

A couple of quick glances told her she wasn't going to find anything here she didn't expect to. The ground was full of weeds, although Bernie spotted a few violets, forget-me-nots, and yarrow hidden among the tall grass. She walked over to a blue tarp lashed to a scrawny linden tree and looked down. An old mildewing blanket lay on the ground, along with two plastic garbage bags, empty beer and soda cans, fast-food wrappers, and a couple of empty bottles of rye.

"Someone's been sleeping rough," Libby noted as Bernie dumped out the garbage bags. They were full of old clothes reeking of weed and sweat.

"For sure. It's looks as if our camper was here for a while," Bernie observed as she bent over and went through the pile on the ground. After a moment, she extracted an ID from the front pocket of a pair of stained khaki cargo shorts, straightened up, and read the name. "Kurt Musso."

"Wasn't that the guy they arrested a couple of months ago for breaking into city hall?" Libby asked.

"Yeah. He died in jail. Heart attack. His widow sued for negligence." Bernie rubbed the small of her back. "So this person definitely isn't our shooter."

Libby grunted in agreement and headed toward the van. Bernie followed.

"It was worth a try," Libby said as she climbed into Mathilda.

The sisters were still discussing the case when Bernie turned onto Winchester on the way to Denise Alvarez's studio. Libby was saying that maybe they should move on from Bannon and concentrate their efforts on Renee and/or her boy toy as she checked Mathilda's rearview mirror again.

"Why do you keep doing that?" Bernie finally asked her.

"Doing what?" Libby asked.

"Checking the rearview mirror," her sister replied. "This is the third time in as many minutes. Well?" Bernie went on when her sister didn't immediately reply.

Libby stuck out her chin. "If you must know, I think we're being followed."

"Think?" Bernie repeated, studying the view in the rearview mirror. They were driving down one of Longely's two main arteries. A six-laner, with three lanes going in one direction and three in the other, 690 was usually bumper to bumper in the morning and evening, but now traffic was light, and when Bernie took a look, all she saw were a handful of vehicles going at a good speed behind them.

"Yes, think," Libby repeated.

"And you're saying this why?" Bernie asked.

Libby stuck her chin out even farther. "I have this feeling. I've had it ever since we were on Bannon's porch."

"Your Spidey-sense kicking in again, is it?"

"As a matter of fact, it is," Libby told her.

Bernie rolled her eyes.

"See," Libby said, "this is why I didn't tell you in the first place."

"Oh, please," Bernie told her, waving her hand in dismissal.

Libby narrowed her eyes. "It's true."

"Which vehicle are we talking about?" Bernie asked as she reached up and readjusted the mirror to give her a better view of the traffic in back of her.

"The gray Civic in the middle lane."

Bernie studied the rearview mirror again. She could see a couple of gray Civics in the mirror. "I see two."

"It's the one in the left-hand lane," Libby stated. "The one with the scratch on the door."

Bernie looked again. "I see the car, but I don't see the scratch."

"Trust me," Libby replied. "It's there."

"Your Spidey-sense again?"

"I saw it earlier," Libby told her as she turned her head and did a quick check. The Civic was still three cars back. "It was parked down the block from Bannon's house," Libby went on.

"So were several other vehicles," Bernie countered.

"This one was in front of the brown ranch with the two gnomes in the front yard. It left right after we pulled out of Bannon's driveway."

"So?" Bernie asked.

"So it's been with us ever since," Libby replied.

"So what?" Bernie exclaimed. "This is a main road, after all. Maybe whoever is in the Civic is going to the mall. Maybe they're going to the post office or the grocery store. Or the gym. Or to the dentist. Have you thought of that?"

"I'll prove it to you," Libby said. By now they were at the intersection of Aspen and Jasper. "Take a right."

Bernie just missed a blue Hyundai as she zoomed across two lanes of traffic.

Libby screamed.

Bernie smiled. "Now what?" she asked. She had to raise her voice to be heard over the other vehicles honking.

"You did that on purpose," Libby accused her sister after she'd caught her breath.

"Do what?" Bernie grinned. "Hey," she added, "I was just following your directions. Now where do you want me to go?"

Libby gestured to the Starbucks on the left. "Pull in here and park."

Bernie followed her sister's orders. "And now what?"

"Now we wait."

Bernie sighed and leaned back against her seat. "You've been watching too many detective shows," Bernie said as she took her cell out of her bag and checked to see if there were any messages from Googie or Amber. There weren't.

A moment later, Libby nudged Bernie in the ribs. "See," she cried as the gray Civic with the scratch on its door made the same right turn they had.

"Yeah, I see," Bernie said as the Civic sailed right by them and turned into Nottingham Plaza. "Told you, Libby," Bernie couldn't help adding. "Can we go now?" Bernie asked when her sister didn't say anything.

Libby sighed. She'd been so positive, too. "I suppose," she conceded.

Fifteen minutes later, they arrived at Denise Alvarez's studio. Bernie parked the van in the driveway and walked up to the studio door. She read the sign tacked on it. It said PLEASE KNOCK, so she did. Denise unlocked the door a minute later.

"It's you," she said when she saw who was standing there.

"You were expecting Matt Damon?" Bernie asked.

"FedEx, if you must know," Denise replied. "What do you want?"

"To talk to you," Bernie told her.

Denise grimaced. "I'm busy, Bernie."

"This will just take a minute," Bernie assured her as she and Libby stepped inside before Denise could close the door in their faces.

Several years ago, in order to house her growing commercial photography business, Denise had taken the large two-car garage attached to her house and converted it into her studio. She'd divided the area into two spaces: a reception area and her studio space.

The room Bernie, Libby, and Denise were crowded into was the reception area. It was small, its dark blue walls were covered with samples of Denise's work, while what space there was, was filled with a small blue settee and a desk overflowing with papers.

"What's this about?" Denise asked, placing her hands on her hips. Her dirty blond hair was up in a bun, and she was wearing an old stretched-out T-shirt, a pair of running shorts, and flip-flops on her feet.

"How do you know Tom Bannon?" Bernie asked her, getting straight to the point.

Denise scrunched up her face, pretending puzzlement. "Who?"

"The dead guy," Libby told her.

"What dead guy?" Denise asked.

"The one that Jennie found."

"Oh," Denise replied. "That dead guy."

"Yeah. Because there are so many around here," Bernie said.

"People die every day," Denise pointed out. "Read the obits."

"True, but they don't disappear and pop up again," Libby pointed out.

"I heard about that," Denise replied. "It was on the news." She shook her head. "Poor Jennie. I guess the wedding is off."

"Not to my knowledge," Bernie said. "Did she tell you that?"

"No, but I just assumed . . . well, that she'd be busy with other things. Legal things."

Libby and Bernie exchanged looks.

"So you're sure you don't know Tom Bannon?" Libby asked Denise.

"I already said that, didn't I?" Denise told Libby.

"Yes, you did," Bernie said, pulling the note she'd taken from Bannon's house out of her pocket and showing it to Denise. "Then how do you explain this?"

Denise shrugged. "What about it?"

"I found it on Tom Bannon's kitchen table."

"Good for you!"

Bernie pointed to the underlining and exclamation points. "It looks like what he wanted to tell you was pretty important."

Denise stifled a yawn. "Well, if it was, he didn't tell me."

Bernie pounced. "So you did know him."

Denise glared at Bernie. "So what if I did?"

"Why did you lie?" Libby asked.

Denise shook her head. "Because I didn't want to get involved. I'm sorry. I know it sounds awful, but there it is. I'm busy, and I don't have anything to contribute that will help you."

"Why don't you let Libby and me be the judge?" Bernie said.

Denise looked at her watch and back at the sisters. "Fine." She waved the fingers of her right hand. "Five minutes. I can give you five minutes."

Libby and Bernie both nodded.

"Go on," Libby said.

Denise did. "All right, I knew Tom. He fenced in my backyard last year, and he was going to come over at some point and rescreen my porch, and that is the limit of my contact with him."

"So you haven't talked with him since?" Libby asked.

After a millisecond pause, Denise shook her head.

"Or texted or emailed?" Bernie said.

"I just told you that, didn't I?" Denise snapped.

"Just closing the loopholes," Bernie responded. Then she added, "And you don't know what he wanted to talk to you about?"

"No, I don't." Denise consulted the watch on her wrist again. "And now, if you don't mind, I have to get ready for a family portrait I'm shooting out at Highland Forest."

"But it isn't five minutes yet," Bernie protested.

"It's close enough," Denise told her. "You can show yourself out." And with that she turned and went into her studio and closed the door.

"What do you think?" Bernie asked her sister as they headed for the van.

"I think Denise knows more than she's telling," Libby replied.

"That's the feeling I got, too," Bernie said as she tapped her fingers on her thigh. "Of course," she added, picturing Bannon's note, "what Bannon wanted to talk to her about could have had nothing to do with his death."

"True. Maybe Bannon was planning on getting married, and he wanted to talk to Denise about his wedding portrait," Libby suggested. "Or maybe he wanted to talk to her about photographing his parents' wedding anniversary."

"Or his trip to Mars," Bernie said.

Libby laughed. "Yeah. I hear reentry is a bitch."

"Me too," Bernie agreed as she got into the van. She was about to start Mathilda when she noticed that the sign indicating one of the doors was open was lit.

She checked her door and asked Libby to do the same. Both were closed. That left only one possibility. Bernie got out and checked the rear van doors. They were ajar. She thought for a moment. The light hadn't been on when they'd left Bannon's house. In fact, the last time she'd opened the back doors was this morning, when she'd picked up eggs from the farmer's market.

She opened the doors and looked inside. *Great*, she thought. Judging from the way things looked, someone had gone through the back of the van when they had been inside Denise Alvarez's studio.

Chapter 19

"I told her," Libby said to her dad as she burst through the door of their flat. "I told her someone was following us."

"That's not necessarily true," Bernie shot back as she flounced down on the couch.

"How can you say I didn't?" Libby demanded, standing over her sister. "I pointed out the car to you!"

"I wasn't talking about that," Bernie clarified.

"Then what were you talking about, Bernie?"

"I was talking about the fact that you don't know that that car was following us, and even if it was, you have no proof that it had anything to do with what happened to the van."

Libby threw up her hands and turned to her dad. "How could the two not be related?" she asked him. "Tell me that. Seriously, I want to know."

Sean sighed, took off his reading glasses, and looked up. So much for the peace and quiet he'd been enjoying. He put the article he'd been reading down on his lap and raised his hands. "Ladies," he told his daughters. "Let's simmer down. And for the record, I have no idea what the hell you two are nattering on about."

It was three in the afternoon, right before the dinner rush, and Libby and Bernie had marched up the stairs to tell their dad what had just happened.

"The thing with the van could be random," Sean pointed out after Bernie and Libby were done talking.

"That's what I said," Bernie told him.

"Someone could have just been passing by," Sean added. He got up and put the article he'd been reading on the escritoire, where it joined his other research for the piece he'd been asked to write. "It's happened before," he said, thinking of the Verizon truck that had been robbed recently. Someone had taken a set of tools and a climbing belt out of the rear of the van. Then he backtracked. "Although the street Denise lives on is residential. It doesn't get a lot of through traffic. What did they take?"

Libby replied, "From Mathilda? Nothing as far as I can tell."

"Are you sure?" her dad asked.

"Pretty sure." Libby turned to Bernie. "Don't you agree?"

Her sister nodded. "And what were they going to take, anyway? There is nothing in there, anyway, except stacks of paper plates, rolls of paper towels, take-out containers, and cleaning products. I mean, what did whoever did this expect to find?"

"Good question," Sean said as he walked over to the window overlooking Main Street. He watched Mrs. Shipley hurry her two-year-old inside. Then he closed the window and sat back down. The wind had picked up and was flapping A Little Taste of Heaven's awning, a harbinger of the rain to come. According to the weather forecast, it was going to be a wet week. "Did any of Denise Alvarez's neighbors see anything?" he asked after he'd sat back down.

Bernie shook her head. She and Libby had gone around and asked. One of the neighbors had been taking a nap;

another one had been in the backyard, mowing the lawn; a third had been taking a walk; and the fourth was due for cataract surgery and couldn't see anything.

Sean clicked his tongue on the roof of his mouth while he thought. After a minute had gone by, he turned to Libby. "So you really think you were followed from Bannon's house?" he asked.

Libby nodded. "I definitely do."

Sean turned to Bernie. "And you don't think that's the case?"

"I think there are a lot of gray Honda Civics out there is what I think."

Libby tucked a strand of hair behind her ear and sat down on the couch. "Maybe. But this one had a scratch on its door."

Bernie snorted. "I'm sure a lot of other gray Hondas do, too. Plus, this one went by us in the parking lot."

"Maybe it was trying to throw us off the scent," Libby objected. "Have you thought of that?"

"Give me a break, Libby. The Civic disappeared into Nottingham Plaza. We couldn't see it."

"But that doesn't mean they couldn't see us," Libby objected.

"And it doesn't mean they could," Bernie answered.

Libby was about to reply when Sean interrupted. "I don't suppose you happened to get the license plate?"

"I got the first two letters," Libby told him.

"At least that's something," Sean said, and then he called Clyde and relayed the information to him. "He'll see what he can do," Sean told Libby after he'd hung up. "Not that he's very optimistic," Sean added. "And in the meantime, while we're waiting for Clyde, let's talk about Bannon's house."

"Works for me," Bernie said.

"What about it?" Libby asked.

Sean leaned back in his chair and began. "So, the door to Bannon's flat was open?"

This time it was Bernie's turn to nod.

"You didn't help it along?" Sean asked his daughter.

Bernie put her hand to her chest and acted shocked. "Dad, would I do something like that?"

"Would you not?" Sean replied, smiling.

"Okay, I would," Bernie admitted, "but I didn't do it this time and I don't think anyone else did either because the lock didn't look forced, and neither did the door." Then she turned to her sister. "Do you agree, Libby?"

Libby looked up. "Yeah," she said. She was still thinking about the gray Honda Civic.

Sean stroked his chin while he thought. "And Bannon's flat wasn't tossed?"

Bernie answered, "Not as far as I could see. I mean, it could have been, but if you mean was the place torn apart, then the answer is no. It wasn't."

Sean turned to Libby. "What do you think?"

"I'm with Bernie on this one," Libby replied, even though it pained her to say it. "Of course, it's hard to tell with something like that."

"True," said Sean, who was thinking it would have made things easier if the lock to Bannon's place had been picked or the flat had been torn apart. Then they would know what they had. There was another moment of silence, and Sean said, "So for the purposes of this discussion, let's assume that if someone did search the flat, they knew what they were looking for, which is why they didn't have to tear the place apart." He looked at his daughters. "I said if because we don't even know that this person or persons were in the house." At that point, the Simmonses' cat, Cindy, came out of Sean's bedroom and jumped on his lap. She cocked her head, and he began to rub her ear gently. The sound of her purring filed the room just as the rain began hitting the windowpane.

Sean watched the rain for a moment. Then he conjured up another scenario. "But for the purposes of this discussion, let's assume that someone had just gone through Bannon's house before you two arrived. You two were lucky," he couldn't help himself from adding. "You could have been shot if the perp was still there when you came in." He bent over and scratched a mosquito bite on his ankle. "Obviously, whoever killed Bannon doesn't play nice with other people."

"I know," Libby and Bernie said at the same time.

"I'm serious," Sean told them. "They could have been armed."

"I know, Dad," Bernie repeated.

"So do I," Libby assured him.

Bernie held up her hand. "I swear."

Satisfied, Sean continued. "Okay, so let's also assume that the someone who looked through the place didn't find what they were searching for. They left and were sitting in their vehicle—talking on their cell, trying to decide what to do next, or maybe trying to decide what to have for dinner—when you came along. At that point, they decided to stick around and see what you guys were going to do." Sean contemplated more scenarios as he watched the sky turn black and the raindrops pound at the window. "Then whomever we're talking about followed you and took the opportunity to go through your van when you were inside talking to Denise because they thought you might have found what they were looking for."

"Hypothetically speaking," Bernie said.

"Of course hypothetically speaking," Sean said. "This is all supposition."

"And the car alarm," Libby said, referring to the one she'd recently had put in. "Why didn't that go off?"

Sean waved his hand in a dismissive gesture. "They're easy enough to disable if you know what you're doing. Obviously, this person or persons did."

"Then why bother having one?" Libby commented.

"Or it could have malfunctioned," Sean told her. Then he leaned forward and said, "All things being equal, Libby, I think you might be right. I think someone might have followed you guys from Bannon's house, and I think that someone might have been the person who searched your van when you were talking to Denise Alvarez. Of course," Sean continued, "this hypothesis is dependent on the Civic following you, and we don't know that it did."

Libby objected. "You just said it did, Dad."

"No," Sean replied. "I inferred it did. That's different."

Libby sighed and looked at the clock on the wall. This was getting them nowhere. Anyway, she and Bernie had to get back to the shop soon. They still had to finish making the mango and cucumber salad. "When do you think Clyde is going to call us back?" she asked her dad as she got up off the couch.

"When he can," Sean told her. Then he went back to petting the cat and watching the raindrops pelt the window, while the sisters went downstairs to work.

Chapter 20

It was five thirty in the afternoon. It was still pouring out, the rain coming down in sheets, flooding the window boxes, and shattering the petals of the flowers on the magnolia trees. Bernie and Libby were getting ready for the dinner rush when Clyde dashed into the store.

"You owe me," he said as he wiped the beads of rain off his face with the sleeve of his windbreaker.

Bernie looked up. "For what?" she asked, doing Little Miss Innocence.

Clyde did his best tough guy imitation. "This." And he extracted the printout from his pocket, smoothed out the damp, crumpled piece of paper, and held it in the air.

Bernie stopped squeezing the lemons for the lemonade she was making and wiped her hands on the dish towel flung over her shoulder. "What is it?" she asked.

"The thing you asked me to get," Clyde replied.

"It looks like it's been through the wash," Bernie observed.

"There's a storm out there, in case you haven't noticed," Clyde responded. "I braved a nor'easter to bring this to you."

"It's hardly that," Bernie said, indicating the street with her chin.

"Hey, you two," Libby said before Clyde could reply, "can we skip the weather debate and get down to business?"

"We're not debating," Bernie told her sister.

"I have to agree with Bernie, Libby." Then Clyde waved the printout in the air. "I didn't find a match, but I did find an interesting possibility."

Bernie reached out her hand. "Okay, then. Let's see what you got."

Clyde brushed Bernie's hand aside. "Not so fast, buster. Not until we discuss payment."

Bernie put her hands on her hips. "Playing hardball, are we?"

"Is there any other kind?" Clyde asked her.

"So you got the information we requested?" Bernie asked him.

"I did, Bernie," Clyde replied. "And at great personal risk, I might add."

Libby and Bernie both laughed.

"Yeah. Looking through a database is a dangerous activity," Bernie told him.

"It could be," Clyde said. "Depending on the database."

"Not in this case," Bernie noted. "We're not talking national security stuff."

"All right, I might be exaggerating a little," Clyde conceded.

"Just a smidge," Bernie commented.

"Anyway," Clyde went on, "I thought I'd deliver it personally so I can pick out my . . . payment."

"I don't remember agreeing on any payment," Bernie replied.

Clyde grinned. "You didn't, but your dad did."

"We didn't authorize him to do that," Libby objected just for the hell of it.

"I can always go home and take my printout with me," Clyde told her.

"No, no," Bernie said quickly. They needed all the information they could get. "Would you take some chicken and a radish salad?" Usually, they negotiated the price for information received beforehand with Clyde.

Clyde laughed. "Get serious. I'm thinking pie."

"What about your wife and your diet?" Libby asked.

"She's in Chicago for the week, visiting her sister," Clyde told her as he patted his gut. "Time to feed the beast."

"Okay. How about a rhubarb and strawberry pie?" Libby suggested. She'd learned to refrain from commenting on her dad's friend's dietary peccadilloes.

Clyde sneezed. "Add in a raspberry one, as well, and you have a deal."

"What about a lemon meringue instead?" Bernie asked. It was a less expensive option.

Clyde shook his head. "Tsk. Tsk. Is this any way to treat a CI, not to mention your dad's best friend? Don't cheap out on me now."

Libby put down the take-out containers that she'd been sorting when Clyde walked in. "How do we know what you have is worth the pies?" she demanded, playing along.

Clyde smirked. "Trust me, it is. Start boxing the pies up and I'll show it to you," he told her.

"Fair enough," Libby replied, and she nodded to Googie as Bernie took the paper out of Clyde's hand and looked at it.

"This lists all the stolen vehicles in this county for the past two years," she said as Googie removed the pies from the display unit and reached underneath the counter for the appropriate size boxes.

Clyde nodded as Bernie scanned it.

"This doesn't tell me anything."

"Sure it does, Bernie," Clyde said, grabbing the printout back and stabbing it with his index finger. "It says right here that a gray Honda Civic was stolen from Denise Alvarez last year."

"We're looking for a gray Honda Civic," Libby observed.

"Exactly," Clyde said.

"I don't get it," Bernie said.

Clyde told her to think about it. Bernie did. She was still puzzled.

"Are you saying that whoever stole Denise Alvarez's car last year is the person who was following us?" Bernie asked him after a minute had gone by.

Clyde nodded. "It's possible. The first two license plate letters are the same."

"Which doesn't mean a lot considering the mathematical possibilities when you think about how many numbers license plates have," Bernie retorted.

Clyde shrugged. "True, but it's not out of the ballpark. Coincidence? Maybe. Maybe not."

Libby rubbed the small of her back. "Could Denise have falsely reported her vehicle stolen?" Clyde nodded.

"But wouldn't she or whoever took the vehicle have changed the license plate?" Bernie observed. "I mean, that would be the first thing I would do."

"Me too," Clyde told her, "but you never know. Like I said before, people do stupid things. And Denise was hanging with some unsavory characters."

Bernie raised an eyebrow. "Like who?"

Clyde explained. "Or rather her friend was involved"—Clyde did air quotes around the word *friend*—"although he was never charged. We don't know the extent of her involvement, but it was pretty clear to Cortez that Denise knew what was going on." Cortez was an investigator with the Longely PD.

"What kind of business are we talking about?" Bernie wanted to know.

"Fencing. Car theft. Burglary," Clyde told her. "Stuff like that."

"I still don't see how what you're saying has anything to do with what happened to Tom Bannon," Libby complained.

Clyde's smile grew broader. "I didn't say it did. I said it could. You should go figure it out."

"You're enjoying this, aren't you?" Libby asked.

"Immensely," Clyde said. "Consider this payback for telling my wife I ate two sticky buns when I came in here the day before Memorial Day."

"It was an accident," Libby wailed. "I explained."

"Not to my wife's satisfaction," Clyde answered, remembering the consequences of Libby's action. He'd been on salad and tofu for a week. He picked up the two boxed pies. "And now, if you don't mind, I'm taking my pies and going home."

Bernie fluttered her eyelashes. "Anything else we should know?"

Clyde laughed. "That worked when you were twelve," Clyde told her.

"Please," Libby begged.

Clyde relented. "Fine. Bannon and Chuck and Denise traveled in the same circles."

"And which circles are those?" Bernie asked.

Clyde did his sinister laugh.

Bernie looked him in the eye. "You have no idea, do you?" she asked.

"As a matter of fact, I might," Clyde cheerfully answered as he headed toward the door.

"Are you planning on telling us?" Bernie asked.

Clyde smiled. "Can't. But what I will say is that if I were you, I would have another chat with Denise Alvarez."

Which was what the sisters decided to do.

Chapter 21

Mathilda shook and shivered as Bernie drove down Westwood Road. The rain had died down to a drizzle, but a windstorm had sprung up in its place seemingly out of nowhere. Five minutes after Bernie and Libby had left the store, the emergency alert on Bernie's phone had buzzed, and the text had told her to expect forty-mile-an-hour gusts.

"If you ask me, I think it feels more like seventy miles an hour," Libby said to her sister when Bernie slowed for a doe bounding across the road, her two fawns following close behind her.

The deer were everywhere this year, Libby reflected. She'd even seen one ambling down Main Street early in the morning last Tuesday. The town board had wanted to bring in sharpshooters, but Libby had argued against that at the monthly meeting. She loved seeing them. She didn't care if they did eat everyone's flowers.

A block later, Bernie slowed for another doe and fawn. Dusk and dawn were the times when they came out to feed, good or bad weather. Then Bernie stopped the van altogether as a half-full trash can rolled across Elderberry

Road and hit a mailbox, spewing garbage in its wake, then continuing on down the street.

Ten minutes later, Libby pitched forward as Bernie slammed on the brakes. A small tree limb from a birch tree had fallen in front of them. "We need to go home," Libby declared. The falling branch concerned her, but the fact that it had missed the overhanging electrical wires by a couple of inches concerned her even more. "We could have been electrocuted."

"Let's not get melodramatic," Bernie told her sister.

"I'm not," Libby replied. She gestured to the road. "It's empty. There's a reason for that."

"Relax. It wasn't even a branch," Bernie argued. "It was a twig."

"It wasn't a twig. It was too large."

"So you're a botanist now?"

"I never said I was. What I am saying is that the next branch that comes down could be bigger," Libby retorted.

"We're not talking tornadoes here," Bernie answered.

"The alert said possible gale force winds."

"Possible, Libby. The key word here is *possible*. Don't worry. It'll be fine," Bernie told her sister as she drove around the branch in the road.

"That's what you always say," Libby replied.

"And it always is," Bernie retorted.

"That depends on your definition of *fine*," Libby pointed out.

"We're alive," Bernie said as she slowed the van to avoid another garbage can rolling across the road.

"That's a fairly low bar," Libby commented.

"I was kidding," Bernie said as she concentrated on driving.

Libby was right, though, Bernie thought. They shouldn't

be on the road now. They should go back home. The van was top heavy, and it could tip over if the wind got much stronger—not that Bernie was going to tell Libby that, because Bernie didn't want to turn around. Now that they were on the road, she wanted to keep going. It would all be fine as long as the wind didn't increase, she told herself.

After Clyde had left, she'd called and texted Denise several times, but Denise hadn't replied. Which made Bernie nervous. She really wanted to know what the hell was going on.

"I don't know why you think something happened to her," Libby continued, referring to an earlier conversation she and Bernie had had. "She's probably out on an assignment somewhere."

"Doing what?" Bernie challenged.

Libby shrugged. "I don't know. Photographing people. Taking pictures of the storm for *National Geographic*. Or getting a pedicure. Having a drink with friends."

"She still could have answered," Bernie replied.

"Maybe her cell is dead," Libby countered. "Maybe she's someplace with lousy reception."

"Possible," Bernie conceded. Libby could be right, she thought, but Bernie still couldn't shake the feeling that something was off. Then Bernie had another idea. "Or she could be leaving town and does not want to let anyone know."

Libby flinched as the wind roared around the van. It sounded like a freight train. "Talk about being totally out of left field. I mean, why would Denise do that, Bernie?"

"Obviously because she's afraid of getting shot," her sister posited.

Libby studied her sister's profile. She was leaning forward, both hands grasping the wheel, concentrating on the road. It was dusk, the time of day when it was difficult to distinguish objects. "Obviously?"

"Yes, obviously."

"Not to me," Libby exclaimed. "Do you know something I don't?" she asked her sister.

"I know lots of things you don't," Bernie answered.

Libby snorted. What could she say? She'd left herself open for that. "No. I mean about Denise being afraid of getting shot."

"Not really," Bernie admitted.

"Because that's quite a stretch. I mean, if that's the case, why didn't Denise take off when it happened?" Libby demanded. "Why wait till now?"

It was a valid question. Bernie thought again of what Clyde had said and the note they'd found in Bannon's apartment, with Denise's name underlined. "Because circumstances might have changed. Because she got spooked by Bannon's death. Remember what Clyde said about Bannon and Denise traveling in the same circles. Something was definitely going on. The question is what."

"Too bad Cortez won't talk to us," Libby said. Not that she'd expected him to.

Bernie had tried speaking to him after she'd tried to get in contact with Denise and failed, but he'd blown her off, telling her to get lost.

"Maybe Clyde's intel is wrong, Bernie," Libby suggested.

"When has Clyde ever been wrong?"

Libby opened, then closed her mouth. She couldn't think of an example.

"Exactly," Bernie said as she struggled to keep the van on the road. She could feel the wind blowing Mathilda into the other lane. She was glad there were no other vehicles around. "Listen," Bernie continued, "maybe you're right. Maybe we shouldn't be out in this weather, but I have a bad feeling that I just can't shake."

Libby snorted. "Ah. The famous gut, huh?"

"You mean it's not famous?" Bernie asked. "I'm hurt."

Libby reflexively checked her seat belt just to make sure it was fastened. "Then tell me this. Why is it that when I have a hunch, you tell me I'm ridiculous, but when you have a hunch, we go out in the middle of a gale?"

"This is hardly a gale, and we didn't go out. We were out."

"That's not the point."

"I'm just highlighting the inaccuracies in your statement."

Libby turned toward her sister. "That's not an answer."

"Okay, then," Bernie replied. "You want me to tell you?"

Libby crossed her arms over her chest. "Yes, I do."

"All right. My hunches are usually correct, and yours are not."

"How can you say that?" Libby protested.

"Simple. I just did."

"Name an incident," Libby challenged.

"Seriously?"

"Yes, seriously. Five bucks says you can't."

"Let's make it more interesting," Bernie said. "Whoever loses has to do the marketing for the week."

"You're on," Libby told her, and she leaned back and waited.

Bernie thought for a moment. Then she said, "Well, there was the time you decided the maintenance man at Adlai Stevenson Junior High School was a serial killer. That's one. And then, and this is my favorite, there was the time you thought that our trashman was a werewolf, and you wanted to sneak out so you could watch him transform from man to beast."

"That was when I was eight years old," Libby protested.

"Hey, you asked me for examples, and I gave you examples," Bernie told Libby as she glanced at the street sign on the corner.

"I was eight!" Libby repeated.

"It's not my fault you didn't specify an age range. You should have been more specific."

"You know what I meant."

Bernie grinned. "Never assume . . ."

"Because it makes an ass out of you and me," Libby said, finishing her father's favorite saying for her sister. "I know."

"Exactly."

"Don't rub it in."

"It'll be hard, but I'll try," Bernie said as she took one of her hands off Mathilda's steering wheel and pointed to the street sign. "We're almost at Denise's," she told her sister, changing the subject. *Quit while you're ahead* was her motto. "Three more blocks."

"I know where Denise's house is," Libby said, still thinking about how she could get Bernie back as she watched the tree branches dancing in the wind. Nothing immediately came to mind.

Then she took a deep breath, told herself she'd figure out something later, and began to think about what they were going to do with tonight's leftover salmon. A Taste of Heaven hadn't had as many dinner customers as they'd planned for that evening, and the people who had come in had wanted the Korean chicken salad, the grilled tuna with green mango slaw, or the lemon pasta with summer herbs instead of the poached salmon. Sometimes that happened. Sometimes you misjudged customers' preferences, which was what made the food business so tricky. So now they had a fair amount of leftover poached salmon to deal with.

The question was, What to do with it? Salmon salad with something pickled? Like gingered beets? That would be pretty. Salmon salad with shaved asparagus? Salmon cakes with homemade tartar sauce on a sweet roll? Corn and salmon chowder? A riff on cold peanut butter noodles with cucumber spears and salmon? Libby wrinkled her nose. No, definitely not that. That sounded terrible. Maybe a salade Niçoise? Libby was deciding that might work—they had everything that they would need on hand—when Bernie interrupted her thoughts.

"As Mom used to say," Bernie said as they turned the corner to Denise's house, "this is definitely inside-out umbrella weather."

Libby smiled. Her mom had had lots of sayings like that.

"I agree with you on one thing, though," Bernie told Libby as they neared Denise's house. "Clyde's hypothesis about the Civic is a little far-fetched."

"Like a pig on a feather bed," Libby said, quoting another of her mother's sayings.

By now they were four houses up from Denise's. Libby pointed to the driveway. Denise's vehicle was parked in it.

Bernie's sense of alarm increased.

"She's probably taking a nap," Libby said as Bernie parked in Denise's driveway, turned off the ignition, and exited the van.

The wind took Bernie's breath away, and she had to

lean into it as she made her way to Denise's house. Libby followed behind. It looked as if no one was home. The same was true with Denise's studio. Bernie rang the bell. The sisters could hear it echoing in the house. When Denise didn't answer, Bernie rang it again. No response. She turned to Libby.

"I don't think she's here."

"Give her a minute."

Bernie leaned on the bell.

"Okay. Maybe she's out with a friend," Libby suggested when Denise didn't come to the door after thirty seconds had gone by. "Maybe she's out with Chuck."

Bernie took her finger off the bell.

"Denise could be asleep," Libby continued, citing another possibility.

"Then she's a pretty sound sleeper," Bernie observed.

"She could be wearing earplugs," Libby posited, "or taking a shower."

"She could be," Bernie agreed. "She could even be sleeping with Chuck."

"That would be convenient," Libby observed.

"Yeah, it would save us the trouble of trying to find him," Bernie agreed. She'd already spoken to Brandon, and Brandon had told her he hadn't seen Chuck—or Chuckles, as he liked to be called—in RJ's for the past year or so. And, no, he didn't know the guy's last name, but he'd try to find out. Bernie was wondering whether Brandon would be able to as she rang Denise's doorbell for the fourth time. Just because. Still no answer.

"I guess we should add Chuck to our list of people to talk to," Libby said as Bernie checked Denise's mailbox. There was nothing in it except a flyer for a landscaping company.

"The ever-growing list." Bernie closed the mailbox flap and nodded her head in agreement. "Not to mention having another chat with Renee and her boyfriend."

"I'm sure they'll be so happy to see us," Libby observed.

Bernie grinned. "I'm counting on it." She was looking forward to the visit.

"Nothing like making pests of ourselves, Bernie," Libby noted.

"It's our stock-in-trade, Libby."

Libby corrected her sister. "No, it's your stock-in-trade."

"I like to think of it as a finely honed craft," Bernie replied.

"That you've been practicing since the age of two," Libby told her.

"It is a skill set."

"I'm glad you think so."

"You mean it's not?"

Libby raised her hands in a gesture of surrender; then she said, "Home, James?" Denise still hadn't come to the door. It was time to go. She and her sister weren't accomplishing anything here.

"Let's check Denise's car, and then we'll go," Bernie said.

Libby nodded her head in agreement. They walked over and tried the door handles. The vehicle was locked.

"So much for that," Libby said.

They turned and were on their way to Mathilda when they heard a crash.

Libby jumped. "What was that?"

"Your guess is as good as mine," Bernie told her. "I think it came from the back of the house," she added.

"I think you're right," Libby agreed.

The sisters looked at each other. Neither one heard anything else. Then they realized that the wind was dying down. It wasn't roaring; it was whistling. Otherwise, they wouldn't have heard the crash.

"It's probably nothing," Libby said.

"You're probably right," Bernie agreed. "But we should check. Make sure."

Libby sighed. "I suppose we should." She sighed again. She had a feeling this wasn't going to be an early night, after all.

Chapter 22

When Bernie and Libby rounded the corner of Denise's house, they saw an outsized round metal-rimmed glass table lying sideways across a fallen Weber grill.

"The wind must have opened the umbrella, and that tipped over the table, and then the table fell on the grill," Libby remarked as she and Bernie picked up the table, closed the umbrella, and righted the Weber, leaving a small mound of black ash on the concrete patio to mark the place the grill had been.

"Sounds like a Rube Goldberg invention or a children's nursery rhyme," Bernie commented as she surveyed the yard. It looked to be average size. Maybe twelve by eighteen feet. The back half was taken up by random clumps of overgrown bushes, which Bernie couldn't identify, and a rusted-out swing set that looked as if it hadn't been used for a decade, while the front half of the yard was home to a garden shed that was listing to the right. From where she was standing, Bernie could see clumps of moss growing on the shed's roof. The only decorative touch in the yard was the fairy lights strung along the back of the house, but they weren't turned on. The backyard was dark. So was the house, except for a light in one of the rooms upstairs.

"It looks as if Denise was going to start a garden," Libby postulated, alluding to the collection of digging tools leaning against the shed.

"Or bury someone," Bernie commented as she walked over to the back door and tried the handle. It looked like that kind of place.

The handle didn't move. The door was locked. As a matter of habit, Bernie studied the windows. She could see that they were old. The frames had grown soft and rotten in places and needed to be replaced. In addition, the white paint on them was peeling off, leaving flecks on the ground. Bernie gently tapped on one of the screens. It wobbled. It had warped, so it no longer fit securely in its track. *Easy to remove*, Bernie thought as she eyed several windows that were half-open to let a breeze in. *No central air. No alarms. Open windows. Why, the house is practically inviting me in*, Bernie decided.

She peered through the screens. The dining room was dark, as was the living room, except for two lit lamps on the tables bookending the sofa. She studied the rooms for another moment. She couldn't detect any movement in either of them or in the kitchen. If this wasn't the perfect opportunity to take a quick peek inside, she didn't know what was, Bernie thought as she took a step back and turned away.

"No, Bernie," Libby said, seeing the speculative expression on her sister's face.

"No, Bernie, what?" her sister asked, all innocence

Libby straightened her shoulders. "You know exactly what I'm talking about."

"No, Libby, I don't," Bernie insisted.

Libby put her hands on her hips. "You most certainly do."

"Don't you want to make sure Denise is all right?" Bernie asked.

"I'm sure she's fine," Libby countered.

"I'm not sure," Bernie replied, suddenly turning serious. The twist in her gut had returned. "Given the weather, the windows should be closed," she observed.

"So she left before it started raining," Libby said. "Big deal. She's one of those people who don't read the weather reports."

"It's been raining since four in the morning," Bernie said.

"Maybe she went out last night and didn't come home," Libby suggested. "Maybe she's having a good time with Chuck."

"Maybe. But I'm still going to check and make sure she's all right," Bernie insisted as she lifted the warped screen out of its frame. "Just to make certain. To put my mind at rest." Then, because she was being honest, she added, "Plus, we need more information. Right now, we're at ground zero in this investigation, and I don't see the elevator going up. We still don't know anything about who killed Bannon and set Jennie up or why they did it." She propped the screen she'd removed against the house. "Maybe we'll luck into something in Denise's house that will point us in the right direction."

"Like what?" Libby asked her.

Bernie shrugged. She had no idea.

Libby put her hands on her hips again. "So this is one of these 'We'll know when we see it' deals?"

Bernie frowned. "All I know is that time is running out for Jennie." She nodded toward Denise's house. "Needs must, as they like to say."

"Who likes to say?"

"People, Libby. People. It's a saying." Then she threw in

the clincher. "After all, we did promise Googie. You want to be the one to tell him we passed up an opportunity to help his girlfriend?"

Damn, Libby thought. Bernie had her. She couldn't come up with an answer to that one. "Okay. You're right," Libby told her sister. She gestured to the window and addressed another concern. "You expect me to get in through that?" She would have to pull herself through and would probably scratch herself in the process.

Bernie grinned. "As a matter of fact, I do."

Libby glared at her. "And you probably expect me to go in first and open the door for you, as well."

"Well, Libby, you are wearing cargo shorts and a T-shirt, and I am wearing my vintage Pucci wraparound."

"You could always take the dress off."

"I could," Bernie agreed. "But it would be easier if you went in. Besides, what would Dad say if I got arrested on an indecent exposure charge?"

"I could get lockjaw."

"The windowsills are wood, and you already got your tetanus shot. Please, Libby." And Bernie walked over and gave Libby a hug.

Libby sighed and pushed her sister away. "I'm a moron," she said as she walked toward the open window.

"No. You're the best big sister ever," Bernie told her as she gave Libby a boost through it.

"Ouch," Libby cried as she scraped her calf on the sill while wiggling in. "I told you, Bernie," she said as she examined her leg when she was standing in the living room.

"You'll live," Bernie replied. "Open the kitchen door."

"I don't know why I listen to you," Libby muttered as she walked to the kitchen. A minute later, Libby unlocked the door and let Bernie in. "Satisfied?" Libby asked her, pointing to the small scratch on her leg.

"For heaven's sake, it isn't even bleeding," Bernie said as she took a quick look around. "Can we dispense with the dramatics and do what we have to do before Denise gets back?"

Libby grunted. Although she didn't like to admit it, her sister was right. She studied the scene in front of her. There were dishes in the sink and a mostly eaten tofu and tomato sandwich on whole grain bread on the kitchen table, along with a half-empty glass of what Libby thought might be iced coffee.

"I guess Denise didn't finish her lunch," Libby observed.

"I know I wouldn't finish it if that were mine," Bernie commented. She pointed to a crumpled-up Hostess Cup-Cake wrapper and a can of Pepsi across the table. "I think Denise had company," Bernie observed, "company with a decidedly different palate."

"Either that or she succumbed to her cravings," Libby noted.

Bernie shook her head. "Then the wrapper and the soda would be next to the sandwich, and they're not. They're across the way. Assuming, of course, that the sandwich is Denise's. It could be the other way around."

"I don't think so," Libby said, pointing to the jar of chia seeds on the far counter. Then she started rummaging through the cabinets. A moment later, Bernie joined her.

Evidently, Denise was into what Libby and Bernie's mother would have called health foods. Her cabinets were stuffed with different kinds of grains and beans, nuts, soy products, and amino acids. She also had a lot of cleaning products and very little fresh food in her fridge. Except for a couple of six-packs of wheat ale, two tomatoes that had seen better days, and half a loaf of bread, the refrigerator was glaringly empty.

"Maybe I was right. Maybe she is about to get out of

Dodge," Bernie hypothesized as she closed the refrigerator door. "After all, if you're eating healthy, you're eating lots of fresh fruit and veggies."

"Either that or she waited till her food ran out to go shopping," Libby suggested.

"I can't imagine doing that, can you?" Bernie asked Libby.

Libby shook her head. "No, but I hear some people do." She thought about their fridge as they walked into Denise's dining room. It was always stuffed to the gills. Just in case. They had backups for their backups. "Because you never know," as her and Bernie's mother would have said. Libby was sure it would be that way even if she and her sister didn't run A Little Taste of Heaven. "I wonder if Denise is one of those people," she mused out loud as she took a look around the dining room.

It was not what she had expected. The room was minimally furnished. There were no pictures on the walls or rugs on the floor. The only pieces of furniture were a mid-century modern teak dining-room table that seated six, the chairs that went with it, and a china cabinet with a pair of candlesticks and seven beer steins etched with the name of a local bar that had closed three years ago.

"She's been in this house for a while," Bernie noted.

"Yes, she has," Libby agreed. "I guess Denise isn't into home decorating," Libby posited as she walked over to the dining-room table. It was piled high with photos. "I wonder where these are from," she said to Bernie as she began to look through them.

"And why they're here," Bernie said as she joined her sister. A moment later, she held up a picture of a rickety-looking tunnel shored up by wooden siding that she'd found off to the side and pointed to the signature scrawled across the bottom left-hand corner. "Denise took this."

Bernie picked up another photo. "And this." Then she put the photos down and began to go through the pile.

The photos were in black and white, color, and sepia. Some were large, and some small. Some were original photos, and some were cutouts from newspapers and magazines. Some had yellow Post-it notes attached to them, while others did not. But all the photos had one thing in common. They were all photos of tunnels of different shapes and sizes and types. It was an eclectic mix.

There were train tunnels. Subway tunnels. Tunnels leading to sewers. Mines. Pictures of tunnels that children had dug. Ice tunnels under mounds of snow in the Artic. Photos of tunnels used as wine cellars, sketches of tunnels used by robbers to access vaults, and renderings of escape tunnels from French and German medieval fortresses. There were photos of the Chunnel, which connected England and France, and of the tunnel El Chapo had escaped through, as well as pictures of the scaffolding holding up the walls of a tunnel that some drug dealers had dug between Mexico and the United States.

Some of the photos went back to the early 1900s and portrayed groups of miners with dirt embedded in their faces and their clothes, carrying lanterns in one hand and shovels in the other. Bernie found a couple of photos of the building of the Holland Tunnel. She even found a photo of a drawing of a tunnel that prisoners had dug while trying to get out of Sing Sing.

"I guess they didn't make it," she said, referring to the photo as she put it down, and then she read aloud the newspaper clipping attached to it. Evidently, the tunnel had collapsed, and the two men in it had died.

"Not the way I'd want to go," Libby said. She was mildly claustrophobic. The idea of being in any tunnel, even the Holland Tunnel, let alone something like a mine, gave her the willies.

Libby gestured to the mass of photos on the table. "I wonder why Denise is collecting these."

"Maybe she's editing some sort of coffee-table book," Bernie guessed. "Picking the photos to go along with the text." It was the best answer she could come up with at the moment.

"Could be," Libby said as she put an old black-and-white picture of a tunnel dug by some prisoners in a penitentiary in North Carolina back on the table and moved on to the living room.

In contrast to the dining room, the living room was stuffed with furniture, most of it far too big to fit the available space. There was a large rust-colored tweed sofa that could easily seat four to five people, two end tables with the lamps made of seashells, which Bernie had seen through the screens, a La-Z-Boy chair that could accommodate two, a large media console with an old-model TV perched on top, plus two empty oak bookshelves that looked as if they'd seen better days. A twelve- by fifteen-foot rug was rolled up along one wall, while several framed pictures leaned up against another wall.

Libby went and turned them around. They were all family portraits. Denise with her parents at the beach when she was little. Denise with her aunts and uncles at what looked like a camp in the Adirondacks. Denise with her cousins at the Grand Canyon. Denise with an elderly-looking German shepherd. As she put the pictures back the way she'd found them, Libby couldn't help but wonder if there was any significance to the fact that they weren't hanging on the walls. That they were stored the way they were. Laziness or something else?

Bernie gestured to the room. "Her parents' living-room

furniture? Or maybe her grandmother's? This doesn't look like stuff Denise would buy."

"No, it doesn't," Libby agreed, studying the room. "It also doesn't look as if she spends any time in here, does it?"

Bernie shook her head. "No, it doesn't."

There were no magazines or books or empty glasses on the coffee table, no dented pillows or throws on the sofa, nothing to indicate Denise hung out here, Bernie was thinking as she went over and opened the doors to the TV console. It contained a VCR and stacks of old VHS tapes.

"Definitely her parents' stuff," Bernie said, straightening up.

"Now what?" Libby asked.

"I guess we take a quick look upstairs and then leave," Bernie told her.

"Works for me," Libby said, heading for the stairs. The sooner they got out of here, the better, as far as she was concerned. They'd spent enough time here already. Denise could be back anytime now. What would they say if she came in the door and caught them? That they'd come by for a cup of coffee and made themselves at home while they waited for her to come back?

Libby was still trying to think of a good explanation as she and Bernie hit the second-floor landing. The walls of the hallway were bare except for a series of ten photos documenting the construction of a building. There were two more photos of the building in the first and the second bedrooms.

"I guess she is into architectural photography," Libby said, pointing at the last photo and thinking of the ones piled on the table downstairs.

"I didn't know that was a thing," Bernie said.

Libby nodded. "I didn't know, either, but it is. One of Marvin's cousins is majoring in it at RIT."

"Kinda like food photography," Bernie noted.

"Yeah," Libby said.

She and her sister were standing in the second bedroom. Neither that bedroom nor the first one had yielded anything of interest. Bernie guessed that like the living room, all the furniture had come from Denise's parents' or grandparents' house. The first and second bedrooms were furnished with matched sets of mahogany furniture. The beds had large quilted headboards, white chenille bedspreads, and tons of throw pillows, while the dressers had crocheted throws with porcelain bowls and ewers on them. There was nothing in the drawers or closets in either room except for extra sets of sheets and towels in the bottom dresser drawers.

"It looks as if Denise doesn't have much company," Libby remarked as she and Bernie arrived at the third bedroom. Denise's bedroom, the sisters assumed. The door was shut.

Bernie paused in front of it. "I wonder why the door is closed. I mean, it's not as if anyone is here." She thought of the Hostess CupCake wrapper on the kitchen table. "Or maybe someone was. Maybe Denise wanted to make sure that whoever was visiting didn't go into her bedroom."

"So it wasn't a friend," Libby observed, making the obvious comment.

"At least not a good one. Maybe a frenemy," Bernie replied, and she opened the door and stepped inside the room.

Denise was sitting up in bed, a surprised expression on her face.

Chapter 23

Bernie screamed and clapped her hand over her mouth. Denise's eyes seemed to be looking straight at her.

Libby ran inside the room. "What's the matter?" Then she stopped in her tracks because she saw what Bernie had seen. "Oh my God!" she cried.

"Somehow, I don't think He is the one who did this," Bernie observed after she'd gotten her breath back.

"Is she?" Libby asked. She couldn't bring herself to say the words, even though she knew that Denise was dead. She couldn't be anything else, given the blood splattered all over her camisole, chest, and sheets.

"Well, let's just say she ain't going dancing anytime soon," Bernie replied, her voice cracking at the end of the sentence.

I'm in shock, she told herself as she studied Denise. Her overriding impression was that it had happened suddenly. Denise had been sitting up in bed, Bernie hypothesized. She'd probably been reading the local paper, which was now lying across her lap, looking at the sales for the week. *Or maybe not*, Bernie thought, noticing the half-packed suitcase on the rug by the dresser. Maybe my gut was right, Bernie told herself. Maybe something had spooked Denise. Maybe she was planning on getting out of town, after all, Bernie decided when Libby intruded on her thoughts.

"We have to call the police," her sister was saying.

Bernie turned and faced Libby. "Agreed."

"Now, Bernie."

"I don't think it'll make a difference if we take ten or fifteen minutes to look around first, Libby. Denise isn't going anywhere," Bernie added. Unnecessarily, in Libby's opinion.

It occurred to Bernie as she resumed studying the scene in front of her that this room was where Denise had lived. This room and her studio. Literally. The rest of the house was nothing but storage space for other people's belongings, but this room, with its handwoven multicolored rug, wicker rocking chair, Shaker furniture, wall-mounted TV, and two series of photos on the walls—one of koi and the second of a doodle named Fred—reflected Denise's personality.

This was where Denise retreated to, Bernie thought, as evidenced by the overflowing pile of newspapers, books, and magazines on the left-hand nightstand and the dirty dishes and empty glasses on the right-hand one. This was where Denise read. This was where she snacked. This was where she streamed her favorite programs.

Bernie was bent over, reading the book titles, when she heard a scritch-scratching sound. Her heart jumped into her throat, but then she saw the squirrel. He was trying to bury something in the window sash. She was breathing a sigh of relief when her sister tugged at her sleeve.

"Yeah, but what about the person that did this?" Libby nodded in Denise's direction. She still couldn't bring herself to say the words.

"What about them, Libby?" Bernie asked.

"They could still be in the house."

"I don't think they are," Bernie told Libby.

"How can you say that?" Her sister's voice rose, grew frantic. "You don't know." The blood on Denise was bright red. This had happened recently. "They could be in the attic." Libby pictured someone crouched down behind a beam, gun drawn, listening to every word they were saying, trying to decide whether to kill them now or let them leave. He could shoot them through the ceiling, for heaven's sake.

Bernie shook her head. "I'm reasonably confident that whoever did this never set foot in the house."

"Reasonably confident," Libby repeated, incredulous.

"Yes. Reasonably confident, Libby." And Bernie walked over to the window directly across from Denise's bed and pointed to the bullet hole in the pane of glass. "See. Whoever did this was outside the house. He or she either parked his car across the street or . . ." Bernie's voice dropped off, another idea having occurred to her.

"Or what?" Libby prompted.

Bernie gestured to the FOR SALE sign planted in the lawn of the house on the other side of the street. "Or the shooter took his or her shot from there. I bet that place is vacant." And Bernie rummaged around in her tote, took out her phone, looked up the address on Zillow, and studied the pictures of the property. Then she passed her phone to Libby. "All the rooms in the house across the way are empty. There's no furniture in any of them, which means the people who lived there have moved out." Then Bernie gestured to the flush mounted light fixture in the middle of Denise's bedroom ceiling. It was on. Bright as hell. She remembered glancing up when she and Libby got out of Mathilda and thinking the room looked like a stage set. "With the light on, it's the perfect arrangement for a sniper."

"It is, isn't it?" Libby agreed as she handed Bernie's phone back to her. "But how did he know . . . ?"

"That Denise was going to be up here reading the paper?" Bernie asked.

Libby nodded. "Exactly."

"Three possibilities that I can think of," Bernie replied as she rewrapped her dress. That was the problem with it. It required too much futzing. "He . . ."

"Or she . . ."

"Or she knew Denise, knew what her habits were." Bernie pointed to the TV. "Maybe Denise came up here every night at the same time to watch her favorite TV show. Or maybe the shooter set up in the house across the street and waited for the right opportunity to present itself. Or maybe he was driving by, saw Denise in the window, and decided to shoot her on a whim."

"Now we're veering into serial killer territory," Libby objected.

Bernie raised her hands in a "You got me" gesture. "You're right. The killer didn't come by on a whim. He or she came by to kill Denise, so they sat in their car and waited for the lights to go on in her bedroom." She paused for a moment, then said, "Although there are people who do carry assault rifles in the trunk of their car and shoot people at random, unfortunately. Too many of them these days."

Libby shuddered. "Scary."

"These are scary times," Bernie said.

Then Libby had another thought. She gestured toward Denise's bedroom door. "What about the closed door?"

"What about it?" Bernie asked.

"Well," Libby replied, "the door was closed, but Denise

lived by herself. There's no one else here, so why was it closed?"

"Maybe she felt more secure that way," Bernie suggested. "Or," she went on, revising the scene she'd pictured in her head, "maybe after the killer shot Denise, he or she came in the house to check and make sure that Denise was dead and then closed the door behind him or her on the way out."

"Why would whoever do that?"

Bernie shrugged. "I don't know. Guilt?"

"Then why shoot Denise in the first place?" Libby protested.

Bernie listed the three possibilities that immediately occurred to her. "She could have been blackmailing someone, or she could have stolen something, or she could have been screwing around with someone's boyfriend."

"Why would the shooter take the chance and come in here?" Libby asked, continuing with her train of thought. "Of course, the shooter could have missed. Denise could have been in the middle of calling nine-one-one."

"Or went in to make sure he'd finished the job," Bernie hypothesized as she walked over to Denise's bed and took a closer look at her.

Denise was wearing pajama shorts and a camisole top. She'd been getting ready to go to sleep. The local paper was on her lap, while the *New York Times* lay off to one side. Her phone was on her nightstand. Bernie picked it up and looked at it. The screen featured a screen saver of Denise and a group of friends at the beach when everyone was younger. *Happier times*, Bernie thought as she tried to open the phone. It was password protected. No big surprise there.

Bernie tried the most obvious passwords, and when

those didn't work, she wiped the phone off with the hem of her dress and put it back where she had found it. Then she used the hem of her dress to open up the drawer in Denise's nightstand. It contained a jumble of Kleenex, hair ties, a couple of tins of hard candy, a bottle of aspirin, and three tubes of hand cream. The usual stuff. She found photographs buried beneath a pile of loose change. Her eyebrows went up when she looked at them. Not the usual stuff. Not the usual stuff at all.

"Now, this is a little more interesting," she said, handing them to Libby. There were four pictures. All of them featured Denise and Tom Bannon. All of them showed the couple in what Bernie and Libby's mother would have called "compromising positions." "I wonder if this is what Denise's killer was looking for. I wonder if this is why the killer came in."

Libby let out a whistle. "Not bad," she said. "Not bad at all."

"Are you referring to the positions they're in or the quality of the photography?" Bernie asked.

Libby laughed. "Both," she said. She studied them for another minute and handed them back. "These were taken in Denise's studio. I recognize the sofa."

Bernie nodded. She had, too.

"I guess Denise and Tom did more than move in the same circles," Libby observed, repeating the comment Clyde had made.

"That's certainly one way of putting it," Bernie said as she put the pictures back where she'd found them. "I wonder if Denise's boyfriend knew about them," she pondered aloud as she and Libby began to go through Denise's dresser and closet.

Libby corrected Bernie. "Putative boyfriend. We don't know that he was, and even if he is, they could have broken up." Libby paused before opening the top drawer of Denise's dresser. "After all, you told me Brandon hasn't seen Chuck for a year. Maybe he left town."

"He could have," Bernie replied, "or he could have just stopped coming to RJ's. He could still be around."

"Brandon said he'd try to find out, right?" Libby asked her sister.

"Right," Bernie answered. "Of course, it would be easier to find out if we knew Chuck's last name." She sighed.

"Yeah," Libby noted. "I wonder if Cortez knows," Libby said, referring to the detective that had blown her sister off.

"If he does, he sure as hell isn't going to tell us."

"Maybe Dad can get it out of him," Libby said.

"Maybe," Bernie said doubtfully. Sean was persona non grata in the Longely Police Department. Clyde was his only working friend there.

Libby continued. "But really, I don't see how those pictures have anything to do with the doggie wedding, or rather with the attempts to derail it."

"Neither do I," Bernie allowed. "So maybe we're dealing with two different things here," she mused. "Maybe Tom Bannon's and Denise Alvarez's deaths have nothing to do with the threatening notes we got, Marcy's keyed vehicle, or Mathilda's flat tires. Maybe their deaths have nothing to do with preventing Jennie from opening up Woof Woof. Maybe those deaths are about something else entirely. Like sex. Jealousy. Betrayal."

Libby laughed. "You mean the good stuff."

"Exactly," Bernie replied.

"But somehow I don't think so," Libby went on. "I think everything is tied together in some way. We're just not seeing it." And she opened Denise's top dresser drawer.

"That's what I think, too," Bernie confessed as she got to work on Denise's closet.

After ten minutes, both sisters abandoned their efforts. If there was anything that would help them figure out who had shot Denise or why they had, the sisters weren't seeing it. There was just the usual stuff. Aside from the half-packed suitcase, that is.

"One thing is clear," Libby noted. "Denise was planning on coming back from her trip. At least for the moment. No packing cartons."

"Maybe she was just getting out of town until things quieted down," Bernie suggested. "Or maybe she was just going to leave all her stuff behind."

"More likely she was just going on vacation," Libby said.

"Possibly," Bernie agreed. Except Denise's bathing suit was still in her top dresser drawer, not that that meant anything. She could have been going to the mountains. "Although the timing is a little too coincidental if you ask me—not that anyone is." Bernie walked over to the bedroom window and looked across the street. Maybe the answer was over there. "Let's take a look at one-ninety-five before we call the police. See if the shooter left anything behind."

"You mean like cigarette butts from a brand that's sold only in one store in the world, like in the movies?" Libby asked.

"No need for sarcasm, Libby," Bernie told her.

"I wasn't being sarcastic."

"Yes, you were."

"Fine. I was."

"I just think that given the fact that someone is setting Jennie up," Bernie said, "it behooves us to take a look. Maybe there's something there that will help us. Point us in the right direction."

"Let's make it fast," Libby agreed begrudgingly after a minute, although she doubted they'd be that lucky.

* * *

According to Zillow, the house across the street was a three-bedroom, two-and-a-half bath Colonial that was built in 1968. It had new kitchen appliances, a new water heater, central air, a new roof, and a finished basement. It also had a lockbox on the front door.

"Damn," Bernie said when she saw it. She should have known there'd be one. She sighed. "Too bad I didn't bring a bolt cutter."

"We should add that to your breaking and entering kit," Libby teased. Then she said, "I guess this means we're not going through the front door."

"Good guess," Bernie replied. Sussing out the combo on a lockbox was definitely beyond her skill set, but at least the house wasn't alarmed, Bernie thought. A small mercy. And she didn't see any cameras.

Libby nodded. She turned and looked up at the second floor of Denise's house. Bernie was right. Denise's bedroom was lit up like a stage set. "So," she said, imagining one of the scenarios Bernie had proposed, "if the shooter was in his car, he'd have been sitting on this side of the street and taken a shot from out of his window and driven away."

"Or taken the shot, gone in the house—he probably got in the same way we did—checked on Denise, and driven away after he closed and locked the door behind him," Bernie added.

"If that's true, the shooter sounds pretty cold blooded," Libby observed.

"This sure wasn't a crime of passion." Bernie frowned. "Which makes it much less likely that the shooter made a mistake and left something behind."

"Maybe a neighbor saw him," Libby said.

"That would be nice, but I wouldn't bet on it," Bernie

countered, thinking that the days of people sitting on their front porch after dinner, talking to their neighbors and watching what was happening on the street, were long gone. "Most of the houses around here have air-conditioning. Everyone was probably in their house, watching TV, or barbecuing in their backyards."

"Maybe they have security cameras," Libby said.

"Ah, yes. The accessory of the moment."

"We should ask."

"Tomorrow," Bernie proposed. "We'll ask around tomorrow."

"Sounds good to me." And Libby turned and pointed to the second floor of 195. "If our shooter was in the house, he'd have to have taken a shot from one of those two rooms up there."

"Most likely," Bernie said. There were really no other options. The two other windows on the second floor faced to the left and right sides respectively. She studied the two front-facing windows for another moment, then turned and followed the driveway into the backyard.

"Where are you going?" Libby called after Bernie.

"To see if there's a lockbox on the back door," Bernie told her.

There was.

"Now what?" Libby asked.

"I'm not sure," Bernie admitted as she looked around. There was a privacy fence on both sides of the yard, as well as neatly clipped privet hedges along the whole length of the fences. The flower beds lining the house were weeded, and a ceramic gnome near the back door held up a sign that said WELCOME.

Bernie studied the windows. Unlike the ones at Denise's house, they were all closed. She went around and tried the lower ones. They were all locked. None of them were broken. None of them showed evidence of being jimmied. Next, Bernie walked around and tried the side door. That had a lockbox on it, as well. The house was sealed up tight. So how had the shooter gotten in? Did he have a key? Or did he shoot Denise from his vehicle, after all?

Bernie guessed that was what he'd probably done. So given that possibility, was it worthwhile breaking a window and trying to get into the house? Probably not. Bernie was debating that question as she was walking back toward Libby when she heard, "Freeze. Hands above your head."

Bernie put on her best smile and slowly turned around. "Funny thing, Officer," she said as she complied. "My sister and I were just about to call you. Not you personally. You in the plural." Evidently, she'd been wrong, Bernie thought. The neighbors had been watching, after all.

Chapter 24

Libby stifled a yawn as she tried to fend off Ernie. And failed. She didn't have the energy to fight with the eighty-pound golden retriever. She was exhausted. She'd gotten three hours sleep in the past twenty-four what with the four hours she and Bernie had spent at the police station, going over what they'd seen and why they'd been in Denise Alvarez's house in the first place.

The only thing that had saved her and her sister from being charged with obstruction of justice at the very least was the fact that Denise had been shot at before, which lent a little more credence to Bernie's protestations that she had been just going in to check on Denise, because she hadn't heard back from her and she wanted to make sure she was all right. Instead, she and Bernie had been let off with a warning to stay out of police business. "A stern warning," Cortez had reiterated. Whatever that meant.

"No," Jennie said as Libby gave up and let Ernie lick her chin, "I didn't know." She had to raise her voice to be heard over the racket the excavator was making. She just hoped the bank would be done remodeling before she opened her place up—if she got to open it up—because the noise would drive the dogs crazy. Thank God the building was in back of them instead of next door, Jennie thought as she scratched Bertha's back.

It was the following day, at three in the afternoon, and Libby and Bernie were standing in the middle of Woof Woof, talking to Jennie. The sisters had been there for the last half an hour, trying to figure out how the murder of Tom Bannon and now Denise Alvarez fit together. Or if they did.

We should be hammering out the final menu details for Bertha and Ernie's nuptials instead of going over what we found out about Denise, Libby thought as she turned her attention to the conversation going on between Jennie and her sister.

"So you didn't know about Bannon and Denise?" Bernie was asking Jennie for the second time.

"That they were a thing?" Jennie's voice rose slightly. "I already told you I didn't. I thought he was seeing Marcy, actually."

Bernie raised an eyebrow. Now, this was interesting, she decided. This group was turning into a regular *Bachelor in Paradise* reality show.

"You're kidding me," Libby said.

Jennie shook her head. "I mean, it wasn't anything serious. Just an occasional . . . you know." And she shrugged her shoulders.

"No, I don't know," Bernie replied. "Tell me so we're on the same page."

"Sure," Jennie replied. She thought for a minute, then said, "The words *nooner* and *quickie* come to mind."

"So Marcy won't be upset if she finds out about Tom and Denise?" Bernie asked her.

Jennie laughed. "No. Not at all. Like I just said, they had a casual thing going. Marcy wouldn't . . ."

"Kill someone over a thing like that," Libby said, finishing Jennie's sentence for her.

"No, never," Jennie exclaimed. "She wouldn't hurt a fly." But Jennie's voice lacked conviction, a fact both Libby and Bernie noted. "On the other hand, she does hunt."

"Hunt?" Libby echoed.

Jennie nodded.

"What does she hunt?" Bernie asked.

Jennie shrugged. "Stuff. Last year she went to Canada to hunt bear—poor thing."

"I take it you mean the bear?" Bernie asked.

Jennie nodded. "She wanted to talk about it, but I didn't want to listen." She made a face. "It's so creepy. I mean, Tom took her to the rifle club. He told me that. Guess she was a pretty good shot."

"Bannon owned a gun?" Libby asked.

"I just assumed, but I don't know for sure. We never talked about it."

"Do you know if Marcy does?" Bernie asked.

"No idea," Jennie responded. Then Jennie said, "Bannon was more of a lover than a fighter. I mean, sex was his thing. Some people golf. Some people play chess. He did this."

Bernie nodded. Something about Jennie's last statement made Bernie wonder if Jennie had been in on the action, as well. "Did you?" Bernie asked her.

Jennie furrowed her brow and brushed away a fly that had been buzzing around her face. "Did I what?" she asked, pretending she didn't understand.

Bernie grinned. "You know. Have a thing with Tom Bannon?"

Jennie tittered.

"I'll take that as a yes," Bernie said when a moment went by and Jennie hadn't replied.

"So what if I did?" Jennie replied belligerently after another moment had passed. "Big deal."

"Well, it does give you a motive for both murders," Libby pointed out. "There is that."

Jennie's face darkened. "How can you say that?" she demanded of Libby as she turned to Bernie. "What about you? Do you think that, too?"

Bernie held up her hands. "Calm down. My sister is just saying what the police will be thinking if they find out, aren't you, Libby?"

Libby nodded.

"That's ridiculous," Jennie scoffed. "My thing with Tom happened years ago, way before I met George."

"George?" Libby repeated, puzzled.

"Googie. You know. Your counterman." Jennie raised her voice again so she could be heard over the construction sounds from the bank.

"Oh yeah." Libby blushed. She couldn't believe she'd forgotten again.

"So is that why you hired Bannon for the job?" Bernie teased Jennie as Bertha licked Bernie's leg.

Jennie drew herself up. "Absolutely not!" she declared. "I hired him because he was good at what he did."

"And other things, as well," Bernie couldn't resist adding.

Jennie sighed. "As a matter of fact, he was," she said, a note of longing in her voice, before she changed the subject. "In any case, I don't see what Tom Bannon's sex life has to do with what's happening."

"Neither do I," Bernie admitted.

"It probably doesn't," Libby agreed.

"On the other hand, you never know what has to do with what," Bernie opined.

"I can assure you that Tom being a player has nothing to do with what's going on here," Jennie told her.

"How can you be so positive?" Bernie asked, glancing around. The place just needed a couple of coats of paint and some trim work, and it would be done.

Jennie hung her head. "I guess I can't. It just doesn't make any sense. None of it does."

"Agreed," Libby said.

"We're almost at Bertha and Ernie's wedding," Jennie noted. She bit her lip. "I'm afraid of what else is going to happen."

"Me too," Libby said, thinking of herself and Bernie. She didn't like the pattern that was developing. "Have you thought of calling the wedding off—at least for the moment?"

Jennie narrowed her eyes. "No. Absolutely not. The invitations are printed, and come what may, the wedding is going on."

"Googie—George—said you were stubborn," Bernie noted.

Jennie smiled. "He's right." Another thought occurred to her. "You two aren't backing out, are you?"

"No," Bernie replied.

Libby seconded Bernie. "Absolutely not." Although, truth be told, she would like to, and she suspected her sister would, as well.

"Good," Jennie said, and she clenched her hands, making them into fists. "Because I'm damned if I'm going to let anyone drive me out of here." Then she swallowed and slumped into herself. "My lawyer says that the DA might bring charges."

"We won't let that happen," Libby assured her as Bernie reflected that Jennie looked exhausted. Denise's death had taken whatever reserves Jennie had had left.

"That's what George keeps saying," Jennie replied. "But I don't know . . . with Denise . . ." She blinked.

"What about Denise?" Libby asked.

Jennie shuddered. "It looks bad."

"Well, it doesn't look good," Bernie agreed.

"I should have taken the photos myself," Jennie said. "I shouldn't have asked Denise. Maybe if I hadn't, she'd be alive today."

Bernie leaned forward. "I'm not sure it would have mattered."

Jennie shook her head. "You really believe that?" she asked Bernie. "You really believe she was shot because of the wedding?"

"Honestly, I don't know," Bernie responded.

Jennie swallowed. "Why is this happening?" she wailed. "Maybe my brother was right. Maybe I have bad feng shui."

"That's ridiculous," Libby said. "Your brother doesn't know what he's talking about. People don't have bad feng shui. Maybe bad luck, but that's a whole different thing."

"I know," Jennie replied. "My brother is a moron." She bit her lip. "I haven't spoken to him in years."

"That must be hard," Libby said, thinking of her own family.

"Not really," Jennie answered. "Actually, it was a relief. He joined some cult in Oregon, and we haven't heard from him since." Then Jennie changed the subject. "I just feel so bad about Tom and Denise. Truly terrible."

"I'm sure you do," Libby told her while she wondered if Jennie's regrets were real. She wasn't sure. Maybe her dad's cynicism was contagious, or maybe, to paraphrase Shakespeare, Jennie seemed to be protesting too much.

"Well, I do," Jennie insisted, even though neither of the sisters had disputed her claim. "But honestly, I feel even worse for myself. I'm being blamed for Tom Bannon's death. Probably Denise's, too. I know I sound like a horrible person, but they're dead. It's over for them, God rest their souls, but I'm here!" She rubbed her hands together.

"I could go to jail! I could lose everything I own. Some detective came by this morning and wanted to know where I was when Denise was shot! They wanted to know if I had a gun!"

"Do you?" Bernie inquired.

"Of course not," Jennie exclaimed. "I hate guns!" She looked from Libby to Bernie and back again suspiciously. "Why are you asking?"

Bernie soothed, "We're just trying to stay ahead of any unpleasant surprises."

"Okay," Jennie said, mollified. "I just don't understand. Who is doing this?"

"I wish we knew," Libby said.

"Who hates you?" Bernie asked.

"No one," Jennie replied, and then she pulled Bertha off Libby and told the golden to sit. "At least no one that I know of."

Chapter 25

Jennie opened the door to let the dogs out. Bernie and Libby watched Bertha wag her tail and rush off to the backyard. Ernie followed.

"No, no," Jennie yelled after the dogs when they started digging in the left-hand corner of the backyard. "There must be a woodchuck or something down there," Jennie explained to the sisters as she ran after the goldens. "They keep on going there. At this rate they're going to dig under the fence. I'm going to have to call someone and put in those Fence Defenders, or whatever they're called." She shook her head. "More money."

Bernie was just about to follow Jennie when Renee walked through the door. She stopped when she saw Bernie and Libby. "What are you doing here?" she demanded.

"I could ask the same of you, Renee," Bernie said, noting that today Renee was wearing a pale pink and white Missoni sundress and white Prada sandals.

"I was going to offer my condolences to Jennifer," Renee said.

"For what?" Bernie asked.

"For Denise, of course." Renee brandished the copy of

the local paper she was carrying. The headline read SEC-
OND MYSTERIOUS DEATH. POLICE MUM.

"What about Denise?" Jennie asked Renee as she
stepped back inside, muddy-pawed goldens in tow.

"Poor thing. In her own bedroom, too. The world has
become a dangerous place." Renee gave a little laugh.
"Well, I don't mean to blather on. I just came by to say
how sorry I am. First, Tom and now Alvarez."

Jennie nodded her thanks.

"I know it's hard," Renee continued, "but you've done
the right thing by giving this place up."

"Who said I'm giving this place up?" Jennie asked. "I'm
most definitely staying. Who did you hear that from?"

Renee shrugged her shoulders. "I just assumed. What
with the story in the paper." She leaned forward. "Do you
think anyone will leave their dog here, considering what's
going on? I know I wouldn't."

"Well, hopefully, we'll have everything cleared up by
the time it opens," Bernie suggested.

Renee smiled. "That would be lovely, Bernie. I certainly hope that's the case." She turned to Jennie. "But
it's always good to be prepared for any eventuality, don't
you think, my dear? I mean, it would be hard to run a
place like this from jail, not that I'm saying that will happen," she quickly stated. "I can't imagine the strain you
must be under." Renee made fake sympathetic noises.
"Perhaps you should call Ruffo and work out a deal with
him to sublet the place. Take some of the stress off your
shoulders. I think that would be the smart thing to do,
don't you?"

Jennie narrowed her eyes. "No, I don't. Anyway, he
wouldn't agree."

"I think he will. At least he said he would."

"You talked to him?" Jennie demanded.

"Just a little chat."

"You had no right to do that," Jennie cried.

"We were just having a hypothetical conversation," Renee explained.

"You still had no right," Jennie told her.

Renee put her hand to her mouth. "Oh dear. Sorry. I didn't mean to offend. I was just trying to be helpful to you in your time of need."

"Well, you're not," Jennie told her.

Renee slapped an expression more of sorrow than of anger on her face. "If I were you, Jennifer, I'd take all the help I can get. What do they say about beggars can't be choosy?"

Jennie took a couple of quick steps toward Renee. In the process she let go of Bertha and Ernie. They headed toward Renee.

"No, you don't," Bernie said as she and Libby got the goldens by their collars before they could pounce on Renee. Then they watched as Jennie walked over and grabbed Renee by her shoulders.

"I don't need your help," Jennie told Renee through clenched teeth. "Do you understand?"

"Let go of me," Renee cried, trying to free herself. "You're hurting me."

Jennie tightened her grip. "You're enjoying this, aren't you? You've come here to gloat."

"Do something," Renee cried to Bernie and Libby. "She's going to kill me."

"Coming from you, that's pretty funny," Jennie continued. "You killed Tom Bannon and Denise and set me up. You've hated my being here from the beginning. You'll do anything to make me leave."

"You're crazy," Renee said, still struggling to get free.

"Am I?" Jennie shouted.

Bernie and Libby exchanged glances. This was not going to end well. They let go of the dogs' collars and ran over to the two struggling women, but Bertha and Ernie beat Libby and Bernie to it. They got between the two women, jumped up, and began to lick their faces. Jennie loosened her grip, and Renee took a step back.

"Oh, my God," Renee said, rubbing her shoulders. Bernie could see Jennie's fingerprints on Renee's skin. "You really are nuts," she told Jennie as she pushed Bertha off her. "Get down." Then she noticed the muddy paw prints on her dress. "Look what you've done," she screamed at Bertha, who put her tail between her legs, ran over to her mistress, and cowered between her legs.

"Don't yell at my dog like that," Jennie snarled as she stroked Bertha's head.

"Don't yell?" Renee said, amazement in her voice. She pointed at her dress. "This is the second piece of apparel your animals have ruined."

"Good," Jennie said.

"Good?" Renee repeated incredulously.

"Yes, good. I'd ruin them all if I could. It would serve you right." Jennie turned to Bernie and Libby. "She's behind this whole thing. She's the one the police should be arresting."

Renee shook a finger at Jennie. "I'm going to sue you for libel."

Bernie tried intervening again. "Let's all calm down and take a breath, shall we?"

"Calm down?" Renee screeched. She pointed to herself. "Me calm down? I'm the one who was attacked."

"I didn't attack you," Jennie countered. "If I had attacked you, you'd be in the hospital."

Renee rubbed her shoulders. "Then what would you call what you did?" she demanded of Jennie. "You could have crippled me."

"Don't be ridiculous," Jennie scoffed. "I was trying to get you to tell me why you did it," Jennie told Renee.

"Did what?"

"What I just said, Renee. Take your pick. Kill Bannon and Denise. Key Marcy's car. Write threatening notes." And Jennie took a step toward her.

"You are crazy," Renee cried as she took a step back. "Stay away from me," she yelled as she ran for the door, the goldens in hot pursuit. "I'm calling the police."

"Maybe I went a little too far," Jennie allowed as the shop door slammed.

"Ya think?" Bernie asked.

Jennie laughed nervously. "Could you maybe go talk to Renee? Smooth things over?"

"I can try," Bernie agreed, "but I wouldn't hold my breath if I were you."

As it turned out, Renee had something else in mind.

"I've been thinking," she told Bernie and Libby when they stepped inside her store.

Bernie snorted.

Renee ignored her and continued. "I have a little problem."

"That's one way of putting it," Bernie muttered under her breath.

"Do you want to hear what I have to say or not?" Renee snapped, glaring at Bernie.

"We want to hear it," Libby quickly answered.

Bernie lifted her hands up in a gesture of surrender. "Sorry. I was out of line. Go ahead."

"Okay then." Renee fingered one of her diamond earrings. "Anyway, as I was saying," she continued, "I have a small problem, and it occurred to me that you two might be able to solve it for me."

"And why would we want to do that?" Bernie asked.

Renee answered, "This is why. Because I won't call the cops on Jennie if you'll help me out."

"What kind of problem are we talking about here?" Libby asked.

"I'll tell you what it is after you tell me whether or not you're going to do what I need done," Renee replied.

"That's messed up," Bernie observed.

Renee shrugged. "Take it or leave it. Those are my terms."

"Is what you want us to do legal?" Bernie asked.

"Yes, it is," Renee said. She smiled. "Not that that should matter to you." Renee held up her hand before Bernie could speak. "And don't get all self-righteous on me. I've heard about your antics. So, what's it going to be? A yes or a no?"

Bernie and Libby looked at each other. The last thing Jennie needed was another visit to the police station, Bernie decided.

"We did promised Googie," she said to Libby.

"I know, Bernie."

"So, Libby, what do you think? Are you in or out?"

"In," Libby replied promptly.

"Ditto," Bernie agreed.

"Good," Renee said, and she explained what she had in mind.

Chapter 26

After Bernie and Libby's conversation with Jennie, talking to Marcy went from a low to a high priority. The sisters were curious to see if what Jennie had said about Marcy and Bannon was true, but they were especially curious to find out if Marcy knew her way around a rifle, and if she did, what her reaction would be when they asked her.

It was almost eight in the evening, and Marcy was just about to close when Libby and Bernie parked in front of Flowers by Design. The strains of Beethoven's Fifth and the smells of greenery greeted the sisters as they walked into the postage stamp–sized shop.

"Nice background music," Libby said.

"It helps keep me calm when I'm doing this," Marcy replied, gesturing to the papers on the counter.

"Paperwork, the scourge of the small businessperson," Bernie commented when she saw the familiar forms spread out.

"Tell me about it." Marcy put down her pen. It had a violet on top of its cap, which matched the bunch of violets on the front of her T-shirt and the painting of violets on the far wall. Obviously, Marcy had a theme going on, Bernie thought.

"Good day?" Libby asked, noticing that there weren't many flowers in the cooler, just ten or so bouquets of daisies, a bucket full of gerberas, and some roses that were about to open.

"No. Not really. Summer is my slowest season," Marcy explained, "so I try to keep my stock on the low side. Otherwise, I'd have to throw everything out." She made a face. "Like those roses. I don't know why I bought them. They're a winter flower—saleswise." She corrected herself. "Winter and fall."

"Summer is our slow season, too," Bernie said. "Everyone is outside barbecuing."

"And gardening," Marcy added. "Why buy flowers when you can pick your own or get them from a neighbor? I tried selling seedlings last year, but I can't compete with the big-box stores." She pushed the papers she'd been working on back into their folder, closed the folder, and shoved it aside. "So what brings you two here this time of night?" she asked, folding her hands in front of her.

"A few questions," Libby said.

"We need some advice," Bernie said.

Marcy cocked her head. "About what?" she asked.

Bernie told her the story she and Libby had concocted on their way over. "Our boyfriends have offered to take us hunting in the fall, and we decided we need to practice before that."

"Hunting what?" Marcy asked.

"Deer," Bernie said.

"Really?" Marcy said.

Bernie and Libby nodded.

"Odd, because neither of you strike me as the type," Marcy observed.

"We decided to try something new," Libby said.

"Why come and ask me about it?" Marcy inquired.

"Well, because Jennie said you shoot deer and stuff," Libby answered.

"I do," Marcy replied. "My dad taught me."

The sisters nodded again.

"So my sister and I figured you could show us how to do it," Libby told her.

"Do you have a license?" Marcy asked.

"Do we need one?" Libby inquired.

"Definitely. Funny, but I thought you came to talk about this." And Marcy pointed to the front page of the morning paper which lay on the counter.

"That too," Bernie said.

Marcy frowned and pulled a dead leaf from one of the African violets on the right side of the counter. "Horrible. Just horrible. I can't believe she's gone. I called a couple of times later in the day, but Denise never called back. I thought she was busy. I was really annoyed."

Libby and Bernie both nodded.

Marcy shivered. "I had just spoken to her that morning, too. I keep thinking about that. About how you just never know when your time is up."

"What did you two talk about?" Bernie asked.

"The wedding. We talked about Bertha and Ernie's wedding." Marcy sighed. "I guess it's off now. I was just going to order the dogwood branches, too. Lucky thing I haven't. There isn't a big market for them this time of the year."

Bernie leaned on the counter with her forearms. "The wedding is still on," she informed Marcy. "At least that's what Jennie is saying."

Marcy cocked her head. "Really? You're kidding me. Given everything that happened?"

Bernie pushed a strand of hair off her forehead. "No,

I'm not kidding at all. Well, at any rate, that's what Jennie said this morning, when we talked to her."

"Wow." Marcy straightened up. "I just assumed . . . she's got more . . ." Marcy searched for the word she was looking for and couldn't find it. "More . . . I don't know. I don't think I'd go ahead with it if I were her." She stopped for a minute, then confided, "Frankly, I don't know if I want to go ahead with the job now considering what happened to Denise."

"And Tom Bannon," Bernie said.

"Not to mention your keyed van and Mathilda's flat tires," Libby added.

Marcy bit her lip. "Are you still catering the thing?"

"The wedding? Yes, we are," Bernie replied.

"I don't know." Marcy shook her head. "Given everything that's going on . . ." She stopped talking, her voice drifting off.

"I'm sure we'll have this sorted out by then," Bernie reassured her.

"You think so?" Marcy asked.

"Definitely," Bernie said. "Right, Libby?"

"Absolutely," Libby lied.

"Boy, I hope so," Marcy said to the sisters.

"So do I," Libby echoed.

Marcy brushed a rose petal off the counter and into the trash basket under the counter. "You don't think Jennie had anything to do with what's been happening, do you?" she asked anxiously.

"Definitely not," Bernie replied. "I think she was set up."

"The police don't think so," Marcy observed. "The article I read in the paper said she was a person of interest."

"Which is why we're helping Jennie out," Bernie explained.

"Aren't you scared?" Marcy asked.

"Should we be?" Libby inquired.

"I am," Marcy replied. She shuddered.

"Why?" Bernie asked. "You have a gun in the house to protect yourself, and you're a good shot."

Marcy corrected her. "I have a rifle, and being a good shot doesn't help in this kind of situation. The article said someone shot Denise through her window. Can't defend against that."

"I suppose not," Bernie allowed.

"Getting back to Denise," Libby said. "When you talked to her, did she say anything about going away?"

Marcy shook her head again. "No. Nothing. Where was she going?"

"I have no idea," Bernie said. "We were hoping you would know."

"Was she going on vacation?" Libby asked Marcy.

"Well, if she was," Marcy replied, "she didn't mention it to me."

"Maybe on an assignment," Bernie suggested.

"She never mentioned anything about leaving," Marcy told Bernie. "And I can't imagine what assignment she'd be going on. It's not as if she was doing freelance stuff for magazines or working for a paper. She did portraits. Family stuff, like graduations, weddings, anniversaries," Marcy informed the sisters. "In fact, we made a date to have a late dinner at Chase's tomorrow night." Chase's was a diner over by the Eastgate Mall, whose claim to fame was their raspberry pie.

"So you guys were friends?" Libby asked.

Marcy thought for a moment, then said, "Yeah. I guess you could say that. Not BFFs or anything like that, but we'd hang out once in a while."

"Surprising," Bernie observed.

"How so?" Marcy asked.

"Well, with Tom Bannon and all."

Marcy dusted the leaf of another of the African violets with the tip of her ring finger. There were five plants in a row. "What about him? I don't understand."

Bernie turned to her sister. "If Marvin was sleeping with one of your friends, wouldn't you be upset?"

Libby nodded. "Definitely. I definitely wouldn't be having dinner or lunch with her, that's for sure."

"I wasn't sleeping with Tom Bannon," Marcy protested.

"That's not what Jennie said," Bernie informed her.

"Well, she's wrong, Bernie," Marcy declared.

"Is she, Marcy?" Bernie raised an eyebrow. "Is she wrong about Tom Bannon sleeping with Denise, too?"

"Not to mention Jennie," Libby said. "Don't leave her out."

Marcy's eyes widened. "He slept with Jennie!" she exclaimed.

"It happened a long time ago," Bernie told her. "At least that's what Jennie says, but I'm not so sure." She pretended to think for a moment. "Yeah, otherwise you guys would have a regular ménage à quatre instead of a ménage à trois going on. Bad joke, huh?" Bernie said as Marcy glowered at her. "Jennie says you were cool with it, Marcy. Were you?"

"Jennie has a big mouth," Marcy observed.

"She said you didn't care that Tom was screwing around. Is that true?" Libby asked, chiming in.

Marcy clenched her jaw. "Tommy could do whatever he wanted."

Bernie's raised eyebrow went higher. "Tommy?"

"Fine, we hooked up from time to time," Marcy admitted. "Big deal. What the hell do you care, anyway?" she demanded. "My private life is my private life."

"It is until two of the participants in your—" Bernie

stopped. "Group . . . are killed. Then it becomes something a little more interesting."

Marcy took a deep breath, held it, and let it out. "Like what?"

"Like a motive for murder," Bernie informed her.

"Is Jennie saying—"

Libby cut Marcy off. "No, she said you wouldn't hurt a fly." She pointed to Bernie. "My sister is saying it."

"That's absurd," Marcy scoffed. "I wouldn't kill one person, let alone two, for something like that. No one would."

"You'd be surprised what people will do," Bernie answered.

"And you have a gun," Libby said.

"A rifle," Marcy corrected her. "And so do a lot of other people."

"I hear you're a pretty good shot," Bernie told her.

"So what if I am?" Marcy replied. "And your point is?"

"Did you shoot Denise?" Bernie said.

"And Tom?" Libby added.

"I can't believe you're asking me that," Marcy cried.

"We understand if you did," Bernie continued, her voice quietly soothing. "It would be hard to care about someone and then find out you were sharing him. The way I figure it is you must have been overcome with jealousy when you found out that Tom was sleeping with Denise as well as with you, so you shot Tom first and then Denise." Bernie shook her head in sorrow. "I can't imagine what it must have been like to feel that much hate. Is that why you tried to frame Jennie? Because you found out about her, too?" Bernie sighed sympathetically. "The guilt you must be feeling."

Marcy laughed. It was not the reaction Bernie was expecting.

"Are you listening to yourself, Bernie?" Marcy asked. "If what you said is true, why would I kill Tom and then wait to kill Denise? Why wouldn't I do them both together? What you're saying makes no sense."

"She has a point, Bernie," Libby said.

Bernie put her hands on her hips. "Maybe she didn't know about Denise then, Libby."

"Then why would I shoot Tom?" Marcy demanded. "Answer me that."

Libby turned to Bernie. "Yes, why would she, Bernie?"

"Whose side are you on, anyway, Libby?"

"The side of truth, justice, and the American way, of course," Libby responded.

Marcy did a double take, and Bernie laughed. "It's a catchphrase from the Superman comics," she explained to her.

"It's been a long day," Libby said.

"For me, too," Marcy answered, her voice softening. Libby's comment had broken the tension. Marcy moved the third African violet in the row on the counter a fraction of an inch to make it align perfectly with the other four plants. "It's true Tom and I were fooling around," she allowed, "but that's all it was. He was fun . . . but that's it. Nothing to take seriously. And as for Denise." Marcy took a deep breath and let it out. "Poor thing. She was free to do what she wanted."

"One more question," Bernie said.

"I think we're done here," Marcy told her.

"Please, Marcy."

"Why should I answer, Bernie?"

Bernie grinned. "Because then we'll stop coming around and making pests of ourselves," she answered.

"Which my sister is really good at," Libby noted.

This time it was Marcy's turn to laugh. "Yes, she is,"

Marcy agreed. She turned to Bernie. "Okay," she said to her. "Ask away."

"Where were you when Bannon was killed?"

"I don't know when that was," Marcy replied.

Libby told her.

Marcy chuckled.

"What's so funny?" Bernie asked.

"Guess I'm off the list. The police were over at my place around then, taking a statement. My house was robbed. Whoever did it took my laptop, my Apple Watch, and my rifle." She sighed. "Actually, I'm really lucky. Good thing I was having a drink with Liam, otherwise I would have been home when the robber broke in."

"You know Liam?" Bernie asked.

"Tom recommended him. He was giving me an estimate for a small fence I want to put up in the backyard."

"Nice of Tom to recommend someone," Libby observed.

"Tom had more work than he could handle, and he and Liam were friends," Marcy replied. "They grew up together in Cali. He was just trying to do him a solid."

"Does the name Chuck mean anything to you?" Libby asked suddenly.

"You mean Denise's ex?" Marcy asked.

Libby nodded.

"Oh, he's out of the picture. I heard he's up in Canada."

"What's he doing up there?"

"I heard he's hiding out."

"From what?" Bernie asked.

Marcy shrugged. "A drug deal gone bad. I hear the Feds have a couple of warrants out on him, but I could be wrong. Boy, was I glad when Denise stopped seeing him, I can tell you that. The guy was nothing but trouble." She looked at her watch. Then she pointed to the outside. "I fulfilled my part of the bargain, and now it's time for you to fulfill yours."

"Fair enough," Bernie answered.

She and Libby were halfway out the door when Marcy called them back and handed them a small clay pot filled with a four-leaf clover plant.

"For luck," she told them. "I have a feeling you're going to need it."

Chapter 27

Bernie indicated the potted plant Libby was holding in her hand with a nod of her head. "I have a feeling Marcy is right about our needing some luck."

"To solve this case. I think so, too," Libby said as she got into Mathilda. Libby cradled the plant Marcy had given her and Bernie in the palms of her hands and leaned back in her seat. "So where do we go from here?"

"First off, we call Clyde and ask him to pull Marcy's robbery report," Bernie said as she took out her cell and dialed. "Make sure it happened."

"Of course, my queen. I exist but to do your bidding," Clyde told her when Bernie made her request.

"I'll take that as a yes," Bernie replied.

"You're just like your old man," Clyde told her. "Can't take a hint."

"A little grumpy this evening, aren't we?" Bernie observed. "Tofu and kale for dinner?"

Clyde's silence told Bernie her assumption was correct. "I have a strawberry shortcake in the cooler downstairs with your name on it," she said.

"The biscuit kind?" Clyde asked.

"No, the cake kind," Bernie said.

"Deal," he told her. "See you in twenty."

As it turned out, Clyde beat Libby and Bernie to their flat by a good ten minutes. When they arrived, Clyde was upstairs, sitting on the sofa, eating a piece of the strawberry shortcake Sean had brought upstairs and apportioned out. Both men looked up when Bernie and Libby walked through the door. Libby sighed with pleasure as she sniffed the smells of butter, cream, and strawberries that filled the room.

"This is exceptionally good," Clyde said, indicating with his fork the piece of cake he was working on.

"It is," Sean said, nodding his agreement. "Even better than usual." Then he said, "Clyde was just telling me the weapon stolen from Marcy's house was a custom-made long-range three hundred Remington Ultra Mag."

"That sounds like a serious weapon," Libby observed as she went over to the coffee table, cut herself a slice of cake, and sat down next to Clyde on the sofa. Bernie followed suit, sitting on Clyde's other side.

"Expensive too," Clyde said after he'd swallowed.

"Good for killing deer or people," Sean added before he downed one of the whole strawberries decorating the top of his slice of the cake.

"I talked to Dick," Clyde went on, taking a sip of the iced coffee Sean had made a second trip down to the kitchen for.

"Dick?" Bernie asked after she licked a dab of whipped cream off her finger. The ratio of cream to vanilla to powdered sugar was perfect. "Do I know him?"

"No. He's a friend of mine," Clyde replied. "A major gun guy. Belongs to the gun club over on Bleeker. He knows Marcy. Says she an excellent shot."

"Figured she had to be owning a weapon like that,"

Bernie commented as she balanced her plate on her lap. Then she told Clyde and her dad what they'd found out while talking to Marcy.

"So Marcy has a motive, not to mention the ability, to kill Denise," Sean observed.

"Not according to what she said," Bernie pointed out.

"Of course she'd say that," Sean opined.

"And you believe her version?" Clyde asked Bernie. "You believe everyone was fine with what was going on?"

"I'm not sure," Bernie said after a moment's thought. "I wouldn't be if it was happening to me, that's for sure."

Sean turned to his oldest daughter. "And you?" he asked. "What do you think?"

"I think she's lying," Libby said. "Maybe not about the sex thing, but about something."

"Why?" Clyde asked her. "Why do you feel that way?"

Libby shook her head. "She was too nice. Too forthcoming. But I could be wrong."

"Not helpful," Sean said as he ate another piece of cake. He especially liked the fact that his daughters had moistened the cake with a mixture of Grand Marnier and orange juice this time.

"I was hoping Marcy was lying about the police report," Bernie said. "It would have made things simpler."

"Unfortunately, she wasn't. She did report a robbery. Of course, she could have staged it herself to get rid of the weapon," Clyde replied. "Don't look at me that way," he told Bernie and Libby. "It's happened before."

"The Richards case," Sean said.

Clyde nodded. Tim Richards had shot his wife two days after he'd filed a stolen weapon report.

"You could get a search warrant to see if it's still in her house or place of business," Sean suggested after he'd eaten another whole strawberry.

Clyde shook his head. "It wouldn't be granted. No reason for it to be. And, anyway, it's not my case. I can't apply for one."

"True," Sean said. He sighed as everyone sat there, eating strawberry shortcake and listening to one of the neighbors' dogs barking outside.

"I'll tell you what gets me," Bernie said after a few minutes had passed. "The timing between the two deaths doesn't make any sense. Why the interval? Why not kill one vic right after the other?"

"It could be because Denise wasn't a threat and then she became one," Clyde replied. "Or it's possible the deaths aren't related, after all. Preliminary evidence suggests Bannon and Alvarez were shot with different weapons."

"Do you believe that means the crimes aren't related?" Sean asked.

"No," Clyde said. He shifted his position. "Not at all. Not with everything that's been going on." He finished the last bite of his piece of cake, leaned over, and cut himself another slice. "By the way," Clyde told everyone, "the DA still likes Jennie for Bannon."

"I wouldn't expect anything less," Sean commented. Once McKenzie made up his mind, he rarely deviated. "And Denise? Does he like Jennie for Denise, as well?" Sean asked.

Clyde shrugged. "Not sure. Cortez is still investigating."

"Maybe we need to look at this from another angle," Sean suggested as Sean's cat, Cindy, jumped on his lap and began to eat the whipped cream left on his plate. "Take it in a different direction."

"Do you have anything specific in mind?" Clyde asked.

"A glimmering of an idea," Sean told him.

"Want to share?" Bernie asked.

Sean shook his head. "Not yet. Maybe in a couple of days."

"I wait with bated breath," Clyde said. He stayed for another twenty minutes, had a third slice of cake, then went downstairs. Libby and Bernie walked him out. They still had dough to make, scones to bake, and chicken to brine.

Chapter 28

Bernie had just fallen asleep when Renee called. "Come now," she whispered. Her voice was so low that Bernie had trouble hearing it.

Bernie opened one eye and looked at the clock on her nightstand. It read two o'clock. "Are you crazy? Do you know what time it is?" she croaked.

"I don't care. Ivan's getting ready to leave the house," Renee told her. "I can hear him getting dressed in the bathroom. If you don't come now, you're going to miss him."

Bernie didn't say anything. She was too sleep fogged.

"A deal is a deal," Renee snapped.

"Fine." Bernie clicked off. She lay in bed for a minute, watching the ceiling fan go around and willing herself to get up. Her eyes were crusted with sleep, and she had a slightly sick feeling in the pit of her stomach. *Screw this*, she thought. Then she thought about her promise to Googie and sat up. This whole "keeping your word" thing really sucked. It took another moment for Bernie to stand up. She pulled on a pair of shorts she had lying on the chair next to her bed, threw on a tank top, slipped into a pair of flip-flops, and went to wake her sister.

"You're kidding," Libby said when Bernie shook her awake and handed her some clothes. "We went to bed at one."

"I know, and I wish I was kidding, but I'm not," Bernie said.

"This is what comes of taking up with younger men," Libby muttered, wiping away a drop of sweat from her face.

"Brandon is younger," Bernie said, giving Libby the T-shirt she'd spotted on the floor.

"By a year, not by twenty," Libby replied.

"You think it's that much?" Bernie asked her.

"I have no idea," Libby replied. "All I know is that I need coffee." She moaned as she slipped the shirt Bernie had given her over her head and put on a pair of Bermuda shorts. "I need coffee bad."

"Ditto," Bernie said, rubbing her eyes.

Fortunately, there was some left over from last night out in the living room. Bernie and Libby gulped the dregs down. While they did, Bernie considered taking her dad's car, then decided against it. It wasn't worth the repercussions, she thought as she hurried downstairs. Besides, if her dad woke up and saw the car was gone, he'd assume it was stolen and call the police. *Definitely not worth it*, Bernie thought. She and Libby would just have to make do with Mathilda, Bernie concluded as she opened the door, stepped outside, and breathed in the air laden with moisture.

Their street was empty at this hour of the night. Two moths fluttered around the streetlamp in front of A Taste of Heaven. Except for the porch light on at Mrs. Sullivan's house, the surrounding houses and shops were dark. Even the flowers were asleep in their window boxes, their petals closed for the night. A slight breeze ruffled the leaves on the trees as Bernie drove toward Renee's house. Except for an occasional truck speeding along, no one else was out.

"No moon," Libby said, commenting on the sky. It was dark aside from Venus twinkling off in the distance.

"Thank God for small favors," Bernie noted. It would make following a car a little easier, but not much, since Mathilda was white, and she'd be one of the only things on the road. When they arrived at Renee's street, Bernie parked down the block, behind a large oak tree where she had a reasonable view of Renee's house. It was the best she could do coverwise.

"They say nothing good happens after midnight," Libby observed as Bernie turned Mathilda's motor off and killed her lights.

Bernie grunted, her eyes peeled on Renee's house. "It's more like nothing good happens after two in the morning," she noted, an observation she'd found to be true.

"Whatever," Libby replied. "How do we know Ivan hasn't left yet?" she asked, changing the subject, as she rubbed the last grains of sleep out of the corners of her eyes with the edges of her hands.

"I'm assuming Renee would have called if he had," Bernie said. She yawned. "I just hope I can stay awake."

"I hope you can stay awake, too," Libby said. "Maybe you should let me drive."

Bernie was just about to say something about how she drove better half-awake than her sister did fully awake when she heard a groan. She startled. So did her sister. They both looked. Renee's garage door started going up.

"The door needs oil," Bernie observed.

"It needs something," Libby agreed as they watched Ivan's car, a red Porsche, back out of Renee's driveway.

Bernie whistled. "Nice ride."

"It looks new," Libby said. "Do you think Renee bought it for him?"

"Well, I don't think he bought it for himself," Bernie replied. "I don't think he could afford a ten-year-old rust bucket let alone something like that." She nodded in the Porsche's direction. "One thing is for sure, though. He'll definitely be able to outrun us."

Libby snorted. "Anything could outrun us." She rubbed the back of her neck. It was stiff. She must have slept on it the wrong way. "That being the case, why do you think Renee asked us to do this? Why not hire a private detective? This is like mission impossible. She knows what we drive."

"Interesting observation," Bernie said after a moment's thought. That hadn't occurred to her. "Maybe she doesn't have the money."

"Yeah, because she's paying off the Porsche. What does Ivan do for a living, anyway?" Libby replied

"According to Brandon, not much," Bernie responded. "He advertises himself as a personal trainer, but surprise, surprise, Renee is his only client." Bernie corrected herself. "Was his only client." She put air quotes around the word *client*. "It looks as if he may be taking on another one."

"Renee didn't say that," Libby pointed out.

"She didn't have to. Why else would she have hired us?" And Bernie started whistling the tune to "Just a Gigolo."

"I wonder if he's worth it," Libby mused.

"I'd wager Renee is asking herself that very question right about now," Bernie said as she waited till Ivan was at the corner before she pulled out.

Libby rubbed her eyes again. God, she'd kill for an iced coffee right about now. "I wonder where he's going."

"That's what we're supposed to find out." Then Bernie stopped talking and concentrated on her driving.

She wasn't about to turn Mathilda's lights on—that would be tantamount to saying, "Here we are." The lack of a moon and no streetlights in Renee's neighborhood made it easier to follow Ivan, but it also made it difficult to stay on the road, and the last thing Bernie wanted to do was pop a tire on a curb.

She was thinking about what Libby had said when Ivan got to the next corner. He turned left, and Bernie sped up a little. She didn't want to lose him. For the next fifteen minutes, they followed Ivan as he zigged and zagged his way through the warren of streets that made up Renee's neighborhood.

"Do you think he's trying to lose us?" Libby asked as Ivan made yet another turn.

"No. Not at all. He certainly could do that if he wanted to," Bernie pointed out. "All he has to do is step on the gas and he'd leave us in the dust."

"Then what the hell is he doing?" Libby demanded as Ivan made a left onto Meadowbrook and stopped at Nice N Easy.

"Playing cat and mouse? Having fun at Renee's expense? I mean, if you were Ivan and wanted to sneak out, wouldn't you park your vehicle in the driveway?" Bernie said, the thought having just occurred to her, as she watched Ivan go inside the shop and come out with a cup in his hand five minutes later. "Or getting coffee."

"Boy, I wish I had one of those right now," Libby said wistfully.

"Me too," Bernie agreed as Ivan got into the Porsche and roared away. "Even if it is gas station joe."

"Do you think he's going to RJ's?" Libby wondered aloud as Ivan hung a left onto Clarke Street. RJ's was a third of a mile away.

Bernie shook her head. "At least not if he's meeting someone of the female persuasion. Too public. Renee would hear about it by tomorrow morning, if not sooner."

"Maybe that's the idea," Libby hypothesized.

"How do you mean?" Bernie asked as she slowed down, looked both ways at the intersection of Geneese and Grand, checking for oncoming vehicles, and then sailed through the red light when there weren't any.

"Maybe he's negotiating with Renee for better working conditions."

Bernie chuckled. "Interesting thought. Or he could be taking a ride because he can't sleep. Panning for gold. Meeting his long-lost sister. Hunting for Sasquatch."

"So you have no idea," Libby said.

"None, but I think we can rule out RJ's," Bernie mused a moment later, when Ivan took a right onto Bradford Avenue. "Maybe he's going to Renee's store," she observed. "At least he's headed in that direction."

Libby stifled a yawn. "What would he want there?"

"Again, I don't have a clue," Bernie replied. She was about to say something else when Ivan sped up and took a left on Hurlbert. Bernie cursed under her breath and sped up, as well, but by the time she got around the corner, Ivan was nowhere in sight. She hit the steering wheel with the flat of her hand. "Game over. We lose."

"If it is a game," Libby said as Bernie scanned the area for the Porsche.

They were in front of Longely High School. The large brick building's marquee read TWO MONTHS TILL WE OPEN. Bernie remembered they'd had those words on the marquee when she had gone there. It seemed like a different lifetime. She'd wanted to work in the movies then. Had sworn she'd never work in her mom's store and moved to LA to pursue her dream. Funny how things worked out,

Bernie was reflecting as she slammed on Mathilda's brakes. Libby jerked forward.

"It is a game," Bernie said after she apologized to her sister. "Everything is a game."

"I wouldn't go that far," Libby replied as she sat back in her seat and rubbed her neck again. Bernie's maneuver hadn't helped it.

"I would. At least in this case. Do you have another explanation?"

"But why do this now?" Libby persisted.

Bernie cocked her head. "What do you mean?"

Libby explained. "Why lead us all over the place and then decide to lose us? You said it yourself, Ivan could have gotten rid of us anytime he wanted. So why did he choose this time?"

Why indeed? Bernie thought. "Valid point," she told her sister. "Maybe he was just having fun and got tired of leading us around and decided to go home," Bernie suggested as she surveyed the streets in front of her. They were in the hilly part of town, which meant that Bernie and Libby couldn't see over the crest of the hill on Hurlbert. Ivan could be on the other side, but the only way to find out would be to drive over there.

"Or maybe," Libby countered, "we're near the place Ivan wanted to go, and he didn't want us to find out where it was."

"Meaning he led us on a wild-goose chase just for the hell of it and then took off. I'm beginning to like this guy less and less," Bernie noted as she remembered they had a few chocolate chip cookies in the glove compartment. They wouldn't be in the greatest shape, but what the hell. *Beggars can't be choosers*, Bernie recalled her mom saying as she asked Libby to open the glove compartment and hand her a cookie.

"These aren't bad," Libby said after she ate one.

"Better than I expected," Bernie replied after she licked a smear of chocolate off her fingers. Actually, they were quite good, even if they had turned into a gooey mess.

"So what do you want to do?" Libby asked Bernie as she downed her second cookie, leaving the last one for her sister.

Bernie frowned. "As far as I can see, the only thing left to do is drive around for a little while longer and see if we can locate Ivan's vehicle and then, if we can't, call Renee and give her the bad news."

Libby brushed cookie crumbs off her lap. "That should be fun." Then she said, "You can do it."

"Thanks."

Libby nodded. "My pleasure."

"Maybe we'll get lucky and spot the Porsche in someone's driveway," Bernie opined.

"Maybe," Libby said, but she wasn't counting on it, and truth be told, neither was Bernie.

The sisters spent the next fifteen minutes driving up and down the streets in the area they'd lost Ivan in. The neighborhood around the high school was composed of private houses with neatly mowed lawns, edged flower beds, basketball hoops in the driveways, and two-car garages. Bernie was hoping that Ivan's vehicle would be in one of those driveways, but it wasn't.

"I give up," she said as they drove up and down their last hill.

Libby was going to say, "Good," but then she heard the words "Let's check out Renee's shop" come out of her mouth instead.

Bernie slammed on the brakes again. Libby fell forward.

"What is the matter with you?" she demanded.

"Nothing. I'm in shock," Bernie said as she pressed the accelerator.

"*You're* in shock? What about me! I can't believe those words came out of my mouth! I guess I just don't want to have to do this again," Libby told Bernie. "Especially at this time of night. Make that at any time," Libby clarified.

The sisters drove in silence for the ten minutes it took them to get down to the strip mall Renee's shop was located in. They had just gone over the bridge and were turning onto Chestnut Street when Bernie thought she saw a flash of red rounding the back of the strip mall.

"Did you see that?" Bernie asked Libby.

"See what?" Libby inquired of her sister. She didn't see anything. From her vantage point, the strip mall was deserted, as were the shops across the way.

"I thought I saw the Porsche going around the back of the strip mall," Bernie explained.

Libby took another look. "I don't."

"It was a flash of red."

"That could be anything," Libby protested.

"Let's find out," Bernie said and she turned into the strip mall and followed the access road to the back. It looked the same way it had the last time they'd been back there. If anything, Bernie thought, there was even a little more garbage lying on the ground. "I must have been seeing things," she commented while she listened to the frogs croaking. "I suppose he could have followed the creek," Bernie said as a ginger cat ran through the weeds and disappeared behind one of the dumpsters. A moment later, she heard an anguished squeak. She was about to say, "One less mouse in the world," when Libby started to speak.

"With that car?" Libby said to her sister. "Ivan would rip the Porsche's undercarriage right out."

"Maybe, maybe not," Bernie countered.

"All right, I concede there's a slim, very slim possibility

that Ivan could have managed to drive the Porsche through here." Libby waved her hand in the creek's direction. It was shallow, and the rocks lining the creek bed were on the smaller side.

"But a possibility nonetheless," Bernie insisted. "We need to check."

"I guess," Libby agreed unenthusiastically, thinking of the bugs down there.

So she and Bernie got out of Mathilda and followed the creek for a little way. But there was no car, no tire tracks in the mud, indicating a vehicle had passed that way, although Libby and Bernie did spot some watercress growing along the creek bank.

"We should come back and pick that," Libby said, referring to the cress as she swatted at the mosquitoes buzzing around her head.

"We will," Bernie replied as they made their way back to Mathilda. "In the daytime, after we spray ourselves with insect repellent."

Next, they got back in Mathilda and drove up and down the streets flanking the strip mall. There were no Porsches, red or otherwise, in any of the driveways.

"I think we are out of options," Libby observed after another ten minutes of fruitless activity.

"There's one last possibility," Bernie said, making a U-turn. She'd just remembered the culvert. It was a long shot, but what the hell. They were already here. Well, almost here.

The culvert Bernie was thinking about was located in back of the strip mall, not too far from the bank that was being renovated. Visible in the winter, the area was hidden in the summer by several large willow trees. Normally, it was accessible from a skinny dirt road that ran off Route 21, but now that access was blocked by several pieces of the construction equipment that was being used to renovate the bank.

"I don't think Ivan went anywhere near here," Libby said as she studied the diggers and the trucks parked there from her vantage point in Mathilda. "There's no reason he should have."

"I can't think of a reason, either," Bernie agreed. She was out of ideas. "I don't suppose you'd like to call Renee, Libby?"

Libby snorted. "Yeah, right. Nope. I already told you this one is all yours."

"I just thought I'd give you another crack at increasing your social skills, but if you don't want to . . ."

"I don't . . ."

"It's okay with me," Bernie said as she made a U-turn. She was thinking about what she was going to say to Renee when she saw bright lights approaching. She slowed down even more. For a moment, she thought about backing up but decided against it. She was afraid she'd get Mathilda stuck in the mud or pop a tire on a rock. No, they were cut off. Heart beating, Bernie killed the engine and waited.

"Who do you think that is?" Libby asked as she shielded her eyes with her hands. The lights were blindingly bright, illuminating everything.

"Security, if we're lucky," Bernie's said, wishing she had a weapon.

"And if we're not?" Libby asked, thinking about what had happened to Denise.

"We will be," Bernie replied with more confidence than she felt. She smiled when she saw the squad car come around the bend and stop in front of them. For once, she was glad to see the police.

"You," the officer said when he got out of his car and started walking toward the van.

"Oh, Officer, thank God you're here," Bernie trilled, doing her best maiden-in-distress impersonation. "We need help."

"Can't stay out of trouble, can you?" the officer replied.

"We're trying," Bernie answered. *Damn*, she thought. *Talk about bad luck.* It was the cop who had arrested them the last time.

"And not doing a very good job," the officer observed as a second squad car pulled up behind him.

Bernie sighed. It was going to be another long night.

Chapter 29

"Nice to see you home," Sean said to Bernie and Libby as they tiptoed into their living room.

The sisters jumped. The lights were off, and their dad was sitting in his chair, fingers tapping, waiting for them.

"What are you doing up, Dad?" Bernie asked in her best fake cheery voice, not that she didn't have a pretty good idea what Sean's answer was going to be.

"Listening to the birds sing," he growled.

"It's five in the morning," Bernie observed.

"I know what time it is," Sean snapped. "More to the point, what are you doing up at this hour of the morning?" he countered.

"Now, that's a funny story," Bernie said.

Sean crossed his arms over his chest and leaned back in his chair. "Is it now? I can hardly wait to hear it," he told Bernie at the same that Libby asked her dad if he wanted some coffee.

Bernie put on a big smile. "Good idea, Libby. We could all use some, don't you think, Dad? I know I can."

Sean didn't answer.

"Well, I want a cup," Bernie continued. "And a corn

muffin. A corn muffin would be nice. See if there are any corn muffins downstairs, too, won't you, Libby?" Then Bernie took a look at the expression on her dad's face and decided helping Libby in the kitchen would be a good idea. "As a matter of fact, I'll give you a hand bringing things up," Bernie told her sister.

Sean drummed his fingers on the arm of his chair. "I'll be waiting."

"I'm sure you will," Bernie said.

"You're not helping your cause," Sean called after her as she scurried down the stairs.

Bernie and Libby came back up fifteen minutes later, Libby carrying a tray with three cappuccinos, three-day-old split and toasted corn muffins, a pot of clover honey, and a dish of cultured butter from the Dobys' farm.

"This isn't going to put me in a better mood," Sean said, indicating the tray Libby was holding with a nod of his head.

"Have a cappuccino, anyway," Libby coaxed. "I sprinkled cocoa and cinnamon on just the way you like it."

Sean grumbled something about bribery not working but accepted the drink and a toasted corn muffin. Then he watched Libby place the tray on the coffee table and she and Bernie sit down next to each other on the sofa and help themselves.

"Just be glad I still have friends on the force," Sean said after he'd taken a sip of his cappuccino and wiped a bit of foam off his upper lip. He really did love this stuff. "Who would have opened the store if you had been arrested?" he continued after another sip. "Have you thought of that?"

"Amber and Googie," Bernie promptly responded as she bit into the corn muffin. Heaven. The slight crust outside contrasted with the crumbly inside. "They're perfectly capable. Anyway, we just got an appearance ticket for trespassing." She put a little more butter and a dab of honey on the muffin and took another bite. "Who knew we were trespassing? There wasn't even a sign posted anywhere. Did you see one, Libby?"

Libby shook her head, broke off a piece of the muffin, and ate it. She hadn't realized how hungry she was.

"Anyway, it's not a big deal," Bernie went on.

"It could have been," Sean shot back. "You could have been slapped with an intent to commit a criminal act."

"What criminal act?" Bernie demanded. "We didn't do anything."

"Destruction of property. along with whatever other stuff the arresting officer could find to throw at you and your sister," Sean clarified. "And then there's the DA."

"That's ridiculous," Bernie spluttered.

"That may be," Sean told his daughter, "but that's what I was told Lucy was considering."

"The judge would dismiss it," Bernie countered.

"Maybe he would," Sean said. "Okay. He probably would. But meanwhile we'd have to hire a lawyer."

"Harlen's son would represent us for free," Bernie told him.

"That's not the point," Sean told her as he watched a squirrel scurry up the drainpipe of the house across the way, scamper across the roof, and disappear down the other side.

Bernie took a sip of coffee. Then she took another one as she considered what her dad had said. "They're harassing us," she observed after she'd taken a third swallow. "I should file a complaint."

Her dad corrected her. "No, you shouldn't. They're being nice."

"Nice?" Bernie squeaked. "How can you say that?"

"Yes, nice," Sean said firmly. "Lucy already told you

and Bernie to keep away from the case," Sean told Bernie. "This is your second warning. He will probably run you in the next time he catches you and will find something to hold you on." Then he turned to Libby. "And what do you have to say for yourself?"

"Me?" Libby stopped sipping her coffee.

"Yes, you," Sean said.

"Nothing." She pointed at Bernie. "It's her fault."

Bernie turned toward her sister. "What's my fault?"

"This whole mess."

"Excuse me, Libby. Where do you get that from?"

"The culvert was your suggestion."

"And going to check out the strip mall was yours," Bernie told her sister.

Sean held up his hands. "Both of you stop. Why were you two there in the first place?"

"We were following Ivan," Libby answered.

"Trying to follow Ivan," Bernie corrected.

Sean looked from one of his daughters to the other. "Who is Ivan, and what does he have to do with Jennie?"

"He doesn't have anything to do with Jennie," Libby replied.

"Well, in a way he does," Bernie contradicted.

"A very loose way," Libby said. "If that."

"No. It's a little more than that," Bernie countered.

Sean tapped his fingers on the arm of his chair. "Well, which is it?" he demanded.

Libby and Bernie took turns explaining.

"We didn't think we had a choice," Bernie ended with.

"You always have a choice," Sean noted as he got to work on his muffin, carefully spreading the butter and then the honey on first one side and then the other. "Jennie seems to have quite the temper," he observed after he was done and had taken a bite of his handiwork.

"It sounds worse than it was," Bernie assured him.

"It was bad enough that Renee could threaten to file assault charges," Sean pointed out.

"It's not like Jennie punched her out," Bernie told her dad. "She just grabbed Renee by the shoulders and shook her a little. The problem is Jennie is a lot bigger than Renee."

Sean wiped his fingers on a napkin and watched the sun come up. They were heading toward the summer solstice, the longest day of the year. Soon they'd be going in the opposite direction. Sean sighed. It was a depressing thought. "Size is not relevant in this case. Actually, not in most cases of this," he informed Bernie.

Bernie tried to think of an appropriate answer, but nothing came to mind. She was too tired to make the effort. Instead, she finished her coffee and muffin and ran through the coming day in her mind. Fortunately, they didn't have any events to cater on the calendar, just a meeting with their insurance agent at two. Then she leaned back, snuggled into the sofa, and closed her eyes. Five minutes, she promised herself. She'd just take a five-minute nap, and then she'd call Renee, tell her what had happened, and start prepping for the morning rush. She was drifting off when an idea occurred to her.

"How did they know?" she asked, opening her eyes and sitting up.

Sean turned from watching the light break on the street and thinking about all the years he and Rose had gotten up at this time of day and how his wife had loved watching the sun come up over the horizon.

"Know what, Bernie?" Sean asked. "Who are you talking about?"

"I'm talking about the cops," she replied. "How did they know that we were there?"

"I don't understand the question," Sean told her.

"Well, we had our lights off, and you can't see anything from the road, because of the willow trees, and no one lives around there—it's vacant land—so how did the cops know we were there?" Bernie asked. "Someone must have called it in. But who? We didn't see anyone."

"I don't know," Sean said. "Unless, of course, it was Ivan."

"Assuming that he knew we were following him."

"It sounds to me as if he did."

"Can you see if you can find out who made the call?" Bernie asked her dad.

Sean nodded. "I'll see what I can dig up."

"Appreciate it," Bernie said, and she closed her eyes for her five-minute nap.

Chapter 30

"The call was anonymous," Sean announced when he came downstairs three hours later, at nine o'clock. "At least that's what Clyde told me. He also said that the cops might have spotted you, anyway. Evidently, they're getting complaints about activity going on around there from the construction company doing the bank build-out, so they've upped the patrols in that area."

"What kind of activity?" Bernie asked.

"I don't know. I didn't ask," Sean replied. He grabbed a couple of cinnamon rolls from the display case, wrapped them in a napkin, poured himself a cup of coffee, and headed back out the door.

"Where are you going?" Libby called after him.

Sean paused at the door. "For a drive," he said.

"Really? Where?" Bernie asked, thinking her dad could pick up some eggs for them if he was heading in the direction of Sunshine Farms.

Sean indicated the street with the hand holding the coffee. "Just taking care of some business."

"What kind of business?" Libby asked.

"See you for lunch," Sean answered, pretending he hadn't

heard Libby's question. Then he pushed against the door and opened it. It shut behind him, making the bells on it tinkle.

"Notice he didn't answer your question," Bernie said to her sister.

Libby nodded as she watched her dad heading for his vehicle. "I wonder what he's up to," she said as she went back to wiping off the two-tops. She was getting them ready for the yoga class regulars who dropped by A Little Taste of Heaven after their nine o'clock session for coffee and homemade cheese Danish.

"To meet someone, I'll wager," Bernie observed. "He took two cinnamon rolls." She was just about to add that her dad was wearing one of his newer polo shirts when Renee walked into the shop.

"Since I haven't heard from you, I thought I'd drop by before I opened my store," Renee told the sisters. Today she was wearing a vivid pink Dior dress and matching strappy sandals.

She looks perfect, Bernie thought. *The vision of summer.*

"Sorry about that," Libby said.

She started to explain, but Renee cut her off with a wave of her hand. "Don't bother. I know what happened with you and the police," she said. "Ivan saw it."

"Did he now?" Bernie commented as she thought about what a mess she looked like in contrast to Renee. She'd put her hair up in a topknot and slipped on a white tank top, a light blue cotton cardigan, and the voile dark blue peasant skirt that she'd bought at Les Puces when she'd been in Paris.

Renee nodded.

"Odd, because we didn't see him," Bernie noted as she tidied up her hair.

"Well, he was there," Renee assured Bernie. "He feels terrible about what happened to you two. So do I."

"I bet you guys do," Libby said.

"We do," Renee assured her. "Ivan told me all about it when he got home. He said there was nothing he could have done to help."

"What time did he get home?" Bernie asked as she spotted a small spot on her cardigan.

Renee gave a little laugh. "Honestly, I wasn't keeping track. I was just so happy to see Ivan walking through the door."

Right, Bernie thought.

"Nice of you to let us know that he was home, Renee," Libby commented before Bernie could say anything.

Renee smiled. "Given what Ivan told me, I figured you were busy with other things," she replied. "That you wouldn't be answering. Excuse me. Wouldn't be able to answer your phone, being in handcuffs and all." Renee put her hand to her mouth. "Sorry. I shouldn't have said that so loudly." She lowered her voice and took a step toward them. "So, are you two going to have a record?"

Bernie ignored the dig. "So where was Ivan?" Bernie asked. "Where did he disappear to?"

Renee laughed again. "He didn't disappear."

"You could have fooled me," Bernie said, moving over to let a customer go by.

"Then where did he go?" Libby asked.

"To visit a place he and his mom used to go to when he was little."

"I thought he lived in Cali," Bernie noted.

"He did, but he and his mom had an aunt out here that they used to come out and visit once or twice a year until she died."

"Specifically what area?" Bernie asked.

Renee shrugged. "I don't know. You'll have to ask him."

"And before that, I suppose Ivan was just driving around, testing out the Porsche," Libby said.

Renee brightened. "That's exactly what he was doing. It turns out Ivan wanted to see how fast the Porsche would go and how well it cornered when no one was on the road." She lowered her voice. "I just got it for him two days ago," she said.

"Nice present," Libby replied.

"It is, isn't it? Ivan works so hard, poor baby. I figured he deserved it."

Living with you, absolutely, Bernie thought but didn't say as she watched Renee finger the diamond pendant she was wearing and remembered what Ruffo had said about Renee being behind in her rent. Well, if she was, Bernie had a good idea why.

"I came to apologize for all the drama," Renee went on. She gave an embarrassed little laugh. "It turns out this was all a silly misunderstanding. Ivan just didn't want to wake me up."

"Very considerate of him," Libby observed.

Renee smiled. "He's a very considerate person. He told me that I looked so beautiful sleeping, he couldn't bear to wake me up."

"That's very . . ."

"Sweet," Renee said, finishing Bernie's sentence for her. "It is, isn't it? I can't believe how lucky I am. Sometimes, I just get worried that Ivan and I aren't real, that he's just pretending to have feelings for me," Renee leaned over and confided to Libby and Bernie. "But that's just silly. He is the kindest, the most honest person I've ever met," she gushed. She was about to say something else when she caught sight of the clock on the wall. "Oh my God," she cried. "It's almost ten. I have to open the shop." And she ran out the door.

"Do you think she believes what she just said?" Libby

asked Bernie as she watched Renee get into her Infiniti and pull out into the street.

"No. But I think she's trying real hard to convince herself that it's true," Bernie replied. "I'll tell you one thing, though. If she does believe what she's throwing down, I know someone who is going to be very unhappy in the future."

Libby balled up the paper towels she'd just been wiping the two-tops down with and tossed them into the nearby trash can. "And that story Ivan told her?"

Bernie snorted. "Good luck with that. Talk about being gullible. We need to speak to him."

"Speak to whom about what?" Googie asked. He had been in the prep room, doing dishes, and had just come out and caught the tail end of Bernie and Libby's conversation.

Bernie brought him up to speed.

Googie dried his hands on the towel slung over his shoulder. "What does that have to do with Jennie and Woof Woof?" he asked when Bernie was done talking.

"Probably nothing," Bernie allowed. "But it's a loose end, and we need to tie it up."

"You do know the DA is thinking of charging her with Denise's death, as well?" Googie said.

Bernie and Libby both nodded.

"She told us," Bernie said.

"And that she has every last cent invested in Woof Woof?" Googie continued. He swallowed, his Adam's apple bobbing up and down. "I don't know what to do."

Libby gave him a quick hug. "Don't worry. We'll figure it out."

Googie ducked his head and studied a spot on the floor. "There isn't much time left," he noted.

"It'll be fine," Bernie reassured him.

"No, it won't be, because even if Jennie isn't arrested," Googie said, continuing on with his train of thought, "people are going to be scared to leave their dogs with her." He looked up and pointed at himself. "I mean, I wouldn't want to leave Ernie and Bertha with a murderer! Would you?"

"Don't worry. We'll find out who is behind this," Bernie reassured Googie. She raised her hand. "I swear."

"I do, too," Libby said, hoping as she said it that she and her sister could fulfill their promise.

Chapter 31

Bernie and Libby knocked on Renee's door at three thirty that afternoon. By then, thanks to the Internet and Brandon, they'd found out a little bit more about Ivan. Fifty dollars to an outfit called Find Out showed that Ivan Esposito was twenty-nine years old and had been born in Los Angeles. He and his mom had moved around a lot for a while, but then his mom had settled down. Ivan had graduated from the Pismo Beach high school and gone to a local community college for a year before dropping out. He also had an arrest record: two DWIs, one drunk and disorderly, one public intoxication, and a shoplifting charge. He'd done a couple of court-mandated stints in rehab and six months of community service for each offense.

As for work, he'd had a number of jobs. He'd been a cook at Wendy's and Burger King, worked for two landscape companies and a pool maintenance outfit, been a janitor at Greene's Gym, and put in a couple of years with a roofing company. According to Brandon, Ivan had told him he met Renee when he was working as a bottle boy at a bar in Santa Monica called the Rodeo.

"So was it love at first sight?" Bernie had asked Brandon as she made him his two grilled salmon, avocado, and tomato sandwiches on fennel-raisin bread to go. Lately, he'd been coming in for a bite to eat and a chat before heading off to work.

Brandon had sniggered. "Well, that's what Ivan said."

"And what do you say?" Bernie had asked.

"I say he's a smart guy, and he saw a good meal ticket and took it."

"I wonder what he'll say," Libby had mused as she'd poured Brandon a cup of coffee and added cream and two sugars.

"Just be sure he's sober when you ask him," Brandon warned. "He's a bad drunk. He got himself banned from RJ's."

Bernie raised an eyebrow. "Impressive," she said as she spread a thin layer of store-made horseradish mayonnaise on the bread and laid a layer of sliced tomato over it. "And I thought you let anyone in."

Brandon grinned as he grabbed a peach from the pile on the counter and bit into it. "We do," he told Bernie as he wiped away the trickle of juice running down his chin with the back of his hand. "That's . . . why . . ."

Bernie lifted up her index finger and wagged it at Brandon. "Don't say it."

"I can't help it. You left yourself wide open."

"What did he do?" Bernie asked, changing the subject, as she sliced half an avocado and put it on top of the tomato.

"Ivan? Two fights. Three broken chairs and a collapsed table. One guy in the hospital with a concussion. The boss finally said enough was enough." Brandon shook his head. "Personally, I would have kicked Ivan out long before then, but it wasn't my call."

"There are never fights in there," Bernie noted. She carefully placed the two pieces of grilled salmon on top of the avocado, added a couple of shredded basil leaves and the second slices of bread, pressed down lightly with the flat of her hand, then wrapped everything up in wax paper.

"Exactly my point," Brandon replied as he finished his peach and reached for his sandwiches.

Bernie was remembering what Brandon had told her as she rang Renee's doorbell. While she listened to the five-note chime, she watched a sparrow fly into the soffit above the door. A moment later, she heard cheeps and looked up. There were strands of grass and sticks sticking out of the soffit. *Has to be a nest in there*, Bernie thought as she rang Renee's doorbell again. No one answered. A moment later, she watched another sparrow fly in and the first one fly out. The cheeping got louder. Dinnertime. Bernie wondered if Renee knew about the nest as she leaned on the bell one last time.

"There's no answer," Bernie told Libby as Libby walked over to the garage and peeked in. The Porsche was there.

"Maybe Renee came back, picked Ivan up, and took him to the shop," Libby hypothesized.

"Maybe," Bernie said as she tried the doorknob. It was locked.

"Or he could have gone for a walk," Libby suggested as she and Bernie went around to the back. Ivan wasn't there, either. Not that they had expected him to be. The sisters studied the backyard for a moment. The grass needed to be mowed, the hedges needed to be trimmed, and the flower beds needed to be weeded.

"So much for Ivan's landscaping expertise," Bernie observed as she tried the back door. It was locked, too.

"I guess we're going to have to pay him a visit some other time," Libby observed, stepping around a thistle that had sprouted between the pavers.

The sisters had almost rounded the side of the house when a black Cadillac Escalade stopped in front of Renee's. As Bernie and Libby watched, they saw Ivan lean over and kiss the blond, middle-aged, heavyset woman who was driving. When he got out, she blew him a kiss. Ivan blew a kiss back, then started wending his way up the path to Renee's house, staggering a little as he went.

"I think we just got lucky," Bernie said to Libby as she took in Ivan's appearance. It looked as if he'd just gotten out of bed. Literally. His hair was tangled, his polo shirt was buttoned incorrectly, and his belt buckle wasn't buckled.

"Must be Marcy's four-leaf clover is working," Libby agreed. "The timing is certainly fortuitous."

"For us, not Ivan," Bernie said, thinking it was too bad they hadn't gotten the Escalade's license plate number, let alone a picture of the woman. "How old would you say she was?" Bernie asked Libby as they increased their pace. She didn't want to give Ivan a chance to get inside the house before they could talk to him. She had a feeling he wouldn't come back out when she rang the bell.

"I'd say she was Renee's age," Libby replied. "Maybe a little older."

"That's what I think, too," Bernie said before she called out Ivan's name.

He froze when he heard it.

"Just the person we want to speak to," Bernie said as she and Libby caught up with him a moment later.

"What do you want?" Ivan asked.

"Now, is that any way to greet your girlfriend's friends?" Bernie asked.

"She's not my girlfriend, and you're not her friends," Ivan growled. Bernie noted that he was slurring his words.

"Be nice," Bernie admonished.

"Why should I be?" Ivan demanded, his bicep muscles tensing as he brought his arms up.

"Because I'll hurt you if you aren't," Bernie told him.

Ivan started to laugh and ended up snorting. "Seriously?"

"Yes, seriously," Bernie answered. She'd always wanted to say that.

"You and who else?" Ivan asked.

Bernie stuck out her chin. "Try me and find out." Another line she'd always wanted to say.

Libby intervened. "We have some questions about last night," Libby told Ivan before Bernie could say anything else.

"Good for you." Ivan belched. Bernie waved away the fumes with her hand.

"I guess rehab didn't work that well," Bernie observed, taking a step back. "Maybe the fourth time's the charm. Or is it the sixth or the seventh time?"

Ivan's eyes narrowed. "How do you know about rehab?" he demanded through clenched teeth. "Did Bannon tell you?"

"As a matter of fact, he did," Bernie lied, seeing an opening and taking it. "He told us everything."

"That son of a bitch," Ivan spit out. "He always did have a big mouth."

"Did you kill him?" Libby asked.

Ivan blinked his eyes. They looked bloodshot. "Kill him?"

"Yes," Libby said.

For a moment, Ivan looked genuinely puzzled. "Why would I do that? He was my friend."

"That's not what it sounds like," Libby noted.

"Well, he was," Ivan said.

Interesting, Bernie thought as she listened to Libby asking Ivan whom he had been fighting with at RJ's.

"Some a-holes from the city. Now bug off," Ivan snarled, reverting to his original attitude.

"I'll tell you what," Bernie said to him. "You answer our questions, and I won't tell Renee about that lady I just saw you with."

"She's my aunt," Ivan told her as he started to sway back and forth. Bernie and Libby rushed to grab him. "Don't touch me," he cried, making "pushing away" motions with his hands. "Leave me alone."

Bernie raised her hands and took a step back. "You really don't want the neighbors to see you this way, do you?" she asked.

"I don't care," Ivan told them.

"Renee will care," Bernie pointed out. She held out her hand palm up. She'd felt a couple of drops. "Besides, it's starting to rain."

"So what?" Ivan shook his head from side to side. He opened and closed his eyes. "I need to sit down," he declared abruptly.

"You can sit down inside," Bernie suggested, and with that she moved to Ivan's right side while Libby moved to his left, and they both guided Ivan up the path to Renee's house. Then Bernie took Ivan's key, opened the lock, and escorted him inside. Once there they led him to the living room.

"I should never have had those margaritas," Ivan muttered as he plunked himself down on the dove-gray sofa over by the far wall.

Bernie took a seat on the wooden coffee table in front of him, while Libby remained standing.

"We have some questions we need you to answer," Bernie repeated.

Ivan belched again. His eyes narrowed. "You can't make me," he declared. "You're not the police."

"You're right. We're not the police. We can't make you talk," Libby told him. "On the other hand, what we can do is tell Renee what we just saw."

"My aunt," Ivan insisted. "You saw me with my aunt."

"You two have a pretty close relationship," Bernie observed.

Ivan smiled slyly. "We do."

Bernie turned toward her sister. "I don't know. I don't usually kiss my aunt on the mouth, do you, Libby?"

"Nope," Libby said. "That's a little weird. Maybe a little too much family closeness going on. But I have blown her kisses."

Ivan struggled to get up, then sank back down.

Bernie turned back to Ivan. "All I'm sayin' is that I don't think Renee's going to like that very much. She strikes me as the jealous type."

"Really jealous," Libby emphasized. "Look at what happened last night."

"And poof." Bernie snapped her fingers. "There goes the Porsche."

"And your nice lifestyle," Libby added.

"But that doesn't have to happen," Bernie continued.

"Indeed, it doesn't," Libby said.

"Just answer a few questions and we'll forget everything we saw."

"It was my aunt," Ivan insisted.

"All right," Bernie said. "We'll forget we saw you kissing your aunt."

"That's blackmail," Ivan said indignantly.

Bernie smiled benignly. "Indeed, it is."

Ivan clenched his fists. "You can't do that."

"But we are," Libby said.

"I'll report you to the police," Ivan cried, trying to get up again and failing. "I'm calling right now."

"Be my guest," Bernie said as Ivan belched again. The fumes rolled out, slapping Bernie in the face. She flinched. What had he been drinking?

Ivan laughed, his anger forgotten. "Pretty good," he said. "I should patent that. Bet I could make a lot of money."

He's just a kid, Bernie thought, moving away from the smell.

"A lot of money," he repeated, momentarily entranced by the idea. "Then I could buy a house in Venice Beach. Or Santa Monica."

That would be nice, Bernie thought as she urged Ivan to tell them what he was doing last night. She could see that they didn't have long before he passed out.

He grinned, showing off a set of perfect white teeth. "Ask Honey Bear. She knows."

"Honey Bear?" Libby repeated. "Who is Honey Bear, Ivan?"

"That's for me to know and you to find out," he sang.

"Renee," Libby guessed.

Ivan pouted. "You're no fun."

"That's what they tell me," Libby replied. "Why do you call her that?"

"Guess."

"I can't, Ivan," Libby replied.

"'Cause she's my sugar mama." This time Ivan's words came out slower. He had to work to form each one.

Bernie moved closer to Ivan again. "Were you trying to lose us last night?"

Ivan shook his head. He closed his eyes, then opened them. "Fun. Just having a . . . little . . . fun with you. Trying to see if you could keep up." He giggled. "You couldn't."

"Where were you going?" Bernie asked.

"Anywhere. Nowhere. I don't know. The beach. Riding the curl."

Bernie waited for Ivan to say something else. When he didn't say anything else, she threw out another question. "Were you meeting someone?"

Ivan closed his eyes.

"What were you doing near the culvert?" Bernie asked.

Ivan's head drooped. Bernie clapped her hands. Ivan startled. His eyes flew open.

"Ivan," Bernie said. "Pay attention. Focus." Ordinarily, she would have shaken him, but she didn't want to get that close to him in the state he was in.

Ivan nodded, and Bernie repeated her question.

"The culvert?" he mumbled. "What's a culvert?"

"The big pipe," Libby explained.

"Oh, that," Ivan said.

"Yeah, that," Libby repeated.

Ivan half rose and fell back down again. He patted the sofa. "I need to sleep."

"You can sleep after you answer our questions," Bernie told him.

"Now," Ivan said. "Sleep now."

He was closing his eyes when Bernie took a pillow off one of the club chairs and threw it at him, hitting him in the chest.

Ivan's eyes flew open. "Hey," he cried. "Don't do that!"

"Then answer me," Libby said, wondering as she did how much alcohol Ivan had consumed to get in the state he was in.

Ivan thought for a moment before replying. Finally, he mumbled, "I was . . . I was checking it out."

"Why?" Libby demanded.

"Ask Honey Bear. She knows." Then Ivan closed his eyes. He was fast asleep. A minute later he started to snore.

Chapter 32

Bernie studied Ivan for a moment. He was sprawled out on the sofa, a line of drool snaking its way down his chin. "He's definitely down for the count," she noted as she checked her phone. It was 3:50 p.m. She figured that gave them a half hour for a quick look-see before they had to pick up some flour and baking powder at the mill and head back to the shop for the evening dinner rush. "Shall we take a peek?" she asked Libby, indicating the house with a wave of her hand. "Seeing as we're already here and all."

"And if Renee comes back?" Libby asked as she bent to take the pebble she'd picked up in Renee's backyard out of her Croc.

"She won't," Bernie assured her. "Her shop doesn't close till seven tonight."

"But what if she does?" Libby insisted. "What if, let's say, she doesn't feel well and comes home early?"

Bernie shrugged. "Then we're just two good citizens who found Ivan outside and helped him into the house."

Libby nodded, walked over, and began studying the pictures on the living-room walls. Four of them were original watercolors of the ocean and the beach, while three of them were photographs of Renee's wedding.

"I bet this was their honeymoon," Libby said, referring to the photo of Renee and her husband standing in front of the mouth of a cave. The caption read BELIZE. "They seem happy, don't they?"

Bernie stopped going through the contents of Renee's media center and came over and took a look. "Yes, they do," she agreed.

"He was a good-looking guy."

"Yeah. Too bad he died so young," Bernie said.

Libby was quiet for a moment. Then she said, "I've been thinking . . ."

"An unusual occurrence," Bernie couldn't help herself from saying.

"No, seriously. Do you think Renee sent Ivan out and then called us to chase him around?"

"You're thinking that because of what he said, aren't you?" The thought had crossed Bernie's mind, as well.

Libby nodded. "Do you think Renee set us up, Bernie?"

"For what?"

"I don't know," Libby admitted. "But then why would Ivan say what he did?"

Bernie shrugged. "Maybe he thought he was being funny. I guess we'll just have to ask Honey Bear and see what she says."

"That should be amusing," Libby noted.

Bernie grinned. Actually, she was looking forward to it. "I think so."

"I was being sarcastic," Libby told her.

"I know, but I wasn't," Bernie replied as she and her sister started climbing the stairs to the second floor

They started with the first bedroom, then moved on down the hall to the second and third ones. The first one was clearly a guest room. It was small and neat. The bed was covered with a floral-print duvet and matching pillows, which Bernie recognized from one of the catalogs they got in the mail. An area rug color coordinated with the window blinds and an oil painting on the wall of a vase with wildflowers carried through the color scheme. Libby characterized the room as tasteful and anonymous as she peeked in the closet and Bernie did the same with the dresser drawers. The only thing in either of them was surplus sheets and towels.

The second bedroom proved more surprising. It was clearly Ivan's. His clothes were scattered on the bed and the floor, and there were two large posters of surfers riding the waves on the walls. A framed photo of a smiling Ivan carrying a surfboard sat on top of the dresser, along with a blue ribbon with the inscription *First Place, Huntington Beach Surf's Up Competition*. There was another first place ribbon next to it from a similar contest at Pismo Beach. Next to that was a large polished conch shell and a pint glass jar full of sand. Bernie picked up the jar and studied it for a moment before putting it back down.

"I guess Ivan really loves the beach," Bernie observed as she began going through Ivan's dresser drawers. They were stuffed with high-end briefs, socks, workout gear, sweaters, and T-shirts, half of which bore the names of California surfing meccas. "And his booze," Bernie added, holding up a bottle of Jack she'd found buried under a stack of T-shirts. Somehow, she wasn't surprised.

"He's not trying very hard to hide his bottle," Libby noted as she tackled Ivan's closet. It was filled with designer jeans, hoodies, shirts, ties, and suits, as well as both a long and a short wet suit, not to mention a rack of expensive sneakers, the kind that cost five hundred dollars a pop.

"Maybe his drinking is one of those non-secret secrets," Bernie hypothesized. "As long as he performs . . ."

"And she did get him that Porsche," Libby noted as she closed the closet door. "On the other hand"—she nodded toward the room—"he is sleeping in here."

"I'm guessing that was probably Renee's choice," Bernie replied as she and her sister headed to Renee's bedroom. "She's smarter than I gave her credit for."

Libby stopped at the doorway. "Why do you say that?"

"I say that because Ivan probably looks better in the morning than she does," Bernie answered.

"Do you think that matters?" Libby asked.

"It obviously does to Renee," Bernie observed as she surveyed Renee's bedroom. "Probably to Ivan, too."

In contrast to Ivan's room, the bed here was made, and everything was put away. The room smelled of Chanel. The word *romantic* popped into Bernie's mind. So did the word *boudoir*. The walls were a soft pink; the bedcover and the dust ruffle, white eyelet. The dresser looked to be an old marble-topped piece, while the mirror on the wall above it was an oval Louis XVI. A vase of perfect yellow roses stood off to one side.

"Nice," Libby said, looking around, before she got to work on the dresser drawers, while Bernie took the closet and the nightstands.

Five minutes later they stopped. To Bernie's surprise, there wasn't a lot in the closet. Five bags from low-level Italian designers, a bunch of jeans from Target, some sweater dresses, five pencil skirts, plus four designer dresses and twenty pairs of inexpensive shoes, except for the Manolos. On a whim, Bernie opened a black leather Hermès clutch and read the label.

"Oh my God," she cried. "This is a rental."

Libby stopped what she was doing. "Rental?"

Bernie showed Libby the tag inside the bag. "Renee is renting this." And she explained about companies that lent you items of clothing for short periods of time.

"Kind of like a car rental," Libby said.

"In a way."

Libby scratched behind her ear. "But why would you do something like that?"

"Most women do it because they're going to a special event and they want a really nice dress, but they don't want to spend the money on something they'll wear only once," Bernie explained as she checked the labels in the other designer items in Renee's closet. Except for a Missoni dress, these items were rentals, as well. "In Renee's case, it makes her seem better off than she is. No wonder she was so upset when her clothes got dirty," Bernie observed, remembering the incidents with Renee and the goldens. "Those must have been rentals, too. If they got damaged, she'd have to buy them."

"I wonder if the Porsche is leased," Libby said as she finished up what she was doing.

"I'm guessing not," Bernie replied. "I'm guessing Renee would want to give it to Ivan as a present. More impressive that way."

"She could lie and not tell him it's leased," Libby pointed out.

"I suppose she could," Bernie replied.

The sisters were still talking about the implications of what they'd found as they walked into Renee's en suite bathroom. It contained a large soaking tub, candles, and enough grooming and beauty products to stock a small store. In contrast, the hall bathroom, which Ivan was using, had a small shower, a pedestal sink, and a medicine cabinet full of supplements.

"I wonder if Renee sold off her Birkins to help cover her

expenses," Bernie mused as she and Libby went down the stairs. She knew that Renee had owned two: an alligator and a crocodile one. They were her pride and joy. Bernie had expected to find them in Renee's closet, but they weren't there. If she remembered correctly, bags like that had sold at auction recently for one hundred thousand each. And then there was Renee's jewelry. They hadn't found any of the good stuff. Was it in a safety-deposit box in the bank? Or had she sold it?

Bernie was betting on the latter as she looked at her phone. They'd spent fifteen minutes upstairs. That left fifteen minutes for the rest of the house. Before they started, though, Bernie and Libby walked into the living room and checked on Ivan to make sure he was still sound asleep. He was. The sound of his snoring filled the room.

Chapter 33

The saying *A place for everything and everything in its place* popped into Bernie's head as she studied the dining room. There were more watercolors of the beach and the ocean hanging on the light blue walls. Bernie walked over and took a closer look at them. Studying them, Bernie realized the watercolors were of the same locale at different times of the day and during different seasons of the year.

So obviously, the place meant a lot to Renee. Bernie wondered where the beach was. It reminded Bernie of some of the places she had hung out in, in Southern Cal when she was younger. She smiled at the thought, remembering the smell of suntan lotion and salt.

Then Bernie wondered if Renee's late husband had painted them—the scrawled signature on the bottom was difficult to read. If she squinted, she could make out a capital *L*, a space, and then a capital *P*, or was that a capital *R*? She wasn't sure. A moment later she gave up trying to decode the artist's signature and turned and studied the room. It was eclectic, though mid-century modern dominated. The Tiffany-style lamp above the teak table glowed in the sunlight, while the rush-bottomed chairs added a note of comfort and informality, which saved the yellow and blue Chinese rug on the floor from being overly formal. The china cabinet on the right displayed a collection of blue-and-white Chinese pottery, while the drawers underneath turned out to hold table linens and place mats.

"I don't think Renee used this room a lot," Libby guessed as she closed the last cabinet drawer. Then she and Bernie headed for the kitchen.

"I'm guessing Renee and Ivan ate most of their meals in here," Bernie said, stepping inside the kitchen and looking around. The place was definitely well equipped and, she guessed, had been renovated recently. It had a Viking oven with a dark blue enamel hood over it, a white porcelain farm sink, and a midrange double-door stainless-steel refrigerator, all of which looked relatively new. The granite countertops had a Vitamix, a sous vide machine, and a high-end coffee maker resting on them.

The custom-made light blue Formica table in the corner held the remains of this morning's breakfast—whole wheat toast, scrambled eggs, and a French press half full of coffee—along with a yellow legal pad and a pencil, which lay near a jar of strawberry jam. Bernie thumbed through the pad, while Libby checked out the kitchen cabinets.

"Who is Gangemi?" Bernie asked, reading off a name sandwiched in between the words *insurance* and *orders*.

Libby turned from opening the middle kitchen cabinet door. "Who?"

"Gangemi," Bernie repeated. "His name sounds familiar, but I can't remember where I heard it."

"Maybe from Dad," Libby said as she eyed the cans of protein powder and supplements populating the first shelf. Someone was into smoothies big-time. "Why?"

"Because Renee has his name underlined, and she's written, *Is it worth it*? next to it."

"Hmm. I wonder what that's about," Libby said as she went back to the kitchen cabinets. A minute later she held up a white bag and said, "Cricket flour. What is cricket flour?"

"Flour made from crickets, of course."

"Of course," Libby said, mimicking her sister. "Who doesn't know that?"

"Obviously, you don't."

Libby lifted the bag up higher. "This is a joke, right?"

"Nope," Bernie replied. "It's the latest thing."

"With who?" Libby demanded.

"Our eco-friendly brethren." Bernie laid the yellow legal pad back down next to the jar of strawberry jam. "You know, saving the planet. Cutting our carbon footprint. Not eating beef. Evidently, cricket flour has a very high protein content, among other things."

Libby made a face. "I don't care what it has."

"It is also really expensive," Bernie continued. "Like somewhere between fifteen and twenty dollars for a twelve-ounce bag. I think someone even makes a chocolate chip cookie mix made with cricket flour. The writer of the review I read said it wasn't bad, that she couldn't taste the difference between chocolate chip cookies made with regular or cricket flour. Interested in trying it?"

Libby made a face. "I think I'll pass," she replied as she put the bag back where she'd found it.

Bernie smiled. She had an idea. "Maybe we could make cricket chocolate chip cookies for April Fools' Day as a gag gift. Take orders in advance."

"Possibly," Libby allowed. She had to admit it was a fun idea. Good marketing.

Five minutes later, the sisters were done with the kitchen.

"Shall we move on?" Bernie said, taking a last look to make sure everything was the same way they'd found it.

Libby held out her hand. "After you."

Renee's office was a little ways down the hall and off to the left. Libby figured the room was an add-on as she stepped inside it. Small and cluttered, it was noticeably hotter than the rest of the house. Someone had started to paint the walls and stopped, so that one wall was light green, while the other three had only primer on them. There were no pictures on them. A desk piled high with papers was situated to the left, and a duct-taped office chair sat next to it. Two bookcases, a file cabinet, three racks full of clothes, and several cardboard packing cartons stacked on top of each other completed the decor.

"It's a little crowded in here," Bernie observed as she and Libby edged their way past the unsealed cartons.

"And messy," Libby noted as her sister stopped and peeked inside a couple of the boxes. The top one was full of sweaters, while the second one contained expensive Italian woolen scarves, scarves Bernie recognized as stock from last fall. As Bernie maneuvered her way toward the desk, Libby studied the bookcases. They were filled with engineering texts of one kind or another and stacks of fashion magazines.

"I'll wager the engineering books were Renee's husband's," Libby observed as she studied them before joining Bernie at the desk. "There's no computer," she noted.

"She keeps her laptop at the shop," Bernie told her sister as she opened the file cabinet's upper drawer.

Meanwhile, Libby picked up the top piece of paper on the pile. It was a tax statement from New York State. She read it and let out a whistle.

Bernie turned in her sister's direction. "What's going on?" she asked.

Libby waved the piece of paper she was holding in the air. "It says here that Renee owes thirty thousand dollars in back sales tax."

Now it was Bernie's turn to whistle. That was a lot. Especially since the penalties built up really quickly. "So she's in trouble," Bernie observed.

"Well, she's sure not doing great," Libby noted, remembering the days after their mother had died and she'd been running A Little Taste of Heaven by herself. She'd lain awake at night, trying to figure out how to keep going, which vendor to pay 15 percent of the bill to. It had been awful. She'd gotten an ulcer.

Bernie nodded toward the rest of the pile. "I wonder what else is in there."

It turned out to be mostly unpaid bills. Evidently, Renee owed on her fixed expenses as well as to her vendors.

"Robbing Peter to pay Paul," Libby commented.

"Which she's been doing for a while," Bernie noted as she put a file marked WORKMEN'S COMPENSATION back in the file cabinet. She was just closing the drawer when she and her sister heard a loud crash coming from the direction of the living room.

They looked at each other and ran in. Ivan had rolled off the sofa and was lying on the floor next to the coffee table.

"Are you okay?" Bernie asked him.

Ivan blinked, then blinked again, and rubbed the back of his head. "What are you doing here?" he croaked.

"You were about to pass out, so we brought you in the house," Libby lied.

Ivan stared at her.

"Don't you remember?" Bernie asked, hoping that he didn't recall what had happened, but she could tell from the expression on his face that he did.

Ivan sat up. "You tried to blackmail me," he cried as he pulled himself up using the coffee table as leverage.

"That's putting it a bit strongly," Libby told him.

Ivan scowled. "That was my aunt."

"If you say so," Bernie replied, watching as Ivan swayed back and forth. "Maybe you should sit down," she suggested.

"Don't tell me what to do," Ivan snarled. He took a step toward her, fists up.

Bernie took a step back. "Hey, buddy, calm down."

Ivan took another step forward. "Don't tell me to calm down," he said, taking a third step. "You think you're something special, don't you?"

"That's what they tell me," Bernie told him as she retreated.

She scanned the area, looking for something she could hit Ivan with if it came down to that. Something heavy. Something that would lay him out, but she didn't see anything that would fill the bill. Ivan was a foot away when he swung. And connected. The blow didn't have a lot of force behind it, but it had enough so that Bernie felt a shock go through her when Ivan's fist connected with the left side of her jaw. She wobbled. A flash of light exploded in front of her eyes. The world spun. For a moment, Bernie thought she was going to fall, but she managed to grab on to one of the club chairs and steady herself.

Ivan was drawing his fist back for another punch when Bernie spied a small metal sculpture sitting on one of the side tables. She was reaching for it when she saw Libby running up behind Ivan. She was holding one of the wooden rush-bottomed dining-room chairs above her head when

Ivan, sensing someone was behind him, turned. He lunged at Libby and stumbled on the pillow that Bernie had thrown at him earlier. Then he straightened up.

"You," he said, making a grab for the chair. His hand closed on it. He was wrenching it out of Libby's hands as Bernie picked up the metal sculpture. She was just about to bring it down on the back of Ivan's head when he stopped and let go of the chair. The color drained from his face. As Bernie and Libby watched, he turned and ran for the bathroom. A moment later, the sound of retching filled the air.

"Well, I guess that takes care of that," Bernie said as she pointed to the chair Libby was holding. "You can put it down now," she told her sister as she replaced the sculpture of a woman releasing a bird back on the table.

Libby laughed and put the chair on the floor. "It was the only thing I could find," she told Bernie.

"It would have done the job," Bernie commented. "More than done the job, actually."

Libby indicated the bronze with a nod of her head. "That would have done worse."

"Probably," Bernie allowed.

"I thought we didn't believe in physical violence," Libby said.

"We don't," Bernie replied. "Unless someone else believes in it first." Bernie rubbed the left side of her jaw with the palm of her hand. It had started to ache. "I'm going to have a bruise, aren't I?"

"A nice fat yellow and purple one," Libby told her.

"Not my best colors." Bernie rubbed her jaw again. She needed to put ice on it to keep the swelling down. "I hope I still have some concealer left," she said, sighing as she thought about what her dad was going to say. And Brandon. She could hear Brandon now.

"I think it's time to go," Libby suddenly announced. She'd just realized that she didn't hear Ivan retching anymore.

"I think you may be correct," Bernie agreed. She might not know much, but she did know that she didn't want to be around when Ivan emerged from the bathroom.

Chapter 34

"What happened?" Sean asked when Bernie and Libby walked through the door of their flat fifteen minutes later.

Bernie forced a laugh and edged toward the bathroom, being careful to keep her right side to her father. "Why would anything have happened?" she inquired as Libby headed for her bedroom.

"That's what I just asked you," Sean said, shifting his weight to accommodate his cat, who was lying on his lap. "Bernie, face me."

Bernie increased her pace. If she could just put some of her concealer on the bruise, it wouldn't be so bad, she told herself. The stuff she had worked really well. It was Hollywood grade.

"Bernie, stop right now," her father commanded.

Bernie groaned silently, reflecting as she did that she'd made a strategic error. She should have stayed downstairs and sent Libby up to get the concealer for her while she slapped some ice on the swelling. Then, at least by the time she saw her dad, it would have gone down a little.

"You should have seen the other guy," she joked as she turned around.

Her dad wasn't laughing. "I repeat. Tell me what happened."

"It wasn't our fault," Libby said as she emerged from her room. "He started it."

Sean drummed his fingers on the arm of his chair and looked from one of his daughters to the other. "Really? That's the best you can do?" He waited for an answer, and when there was none forthcoming, he went on. "You said that when you were two. It didn't work then, and it's not working now. So first of all, who is he?"

Libby answered. "Renee's boyfriend, Ivan."

Sean frowned. "The live-in?"

Bernie nodded. "I suppose you want an explanation," she told her dad after a minute had passed and Sean hadn't said anything else.

"That would be nice," Sean replied. "A detailed explanation, if you don't mind."

Libby and Bernie began at the beginning with Ivan's putative aunt.

Sean's eyebrows shot up when he heard that. "Ivan seems like a busy boy."

"He does indeed," Bernie said.

Sean stroked the cat. "And you're sure it's not his aunt?"

"Did you kiss Aunt Roberta on the mouth?" Bernie asked.

Sean grimaced at the thought.

"Exactly," Bernie said, and she went on with the story.

"You two got lucky," Sean commented when his daughters were done talking.

"You always said timing is everything," Bernie quipped.

"I did," her dad replied. "And given the way your jaw looks, you need to work on yours."

Bernie touched it. "Yeah. I suppose I do."

Sean cupped his right hand behind his right ear and leaned forward. "Say again."

Bernie threw up her hands. "I get it, Dad. We should have left after Ivan passed out . . ."

"Because," Sean prompted.

"We could have been seriously hurt."

Sean clapped. "Very good, Bernie."

Libby jumped into the conversation. "But then we wouldn't have any new information."

"Information that can't be used, because it was illegally obtained," Sean observed.

"Clyde can't use it to get a warrant, but at least it points us in the right direction," Bernie noted.

Sean rubbed the tips of the cat's ears with both hands. Cindy began to purr. "And which direction is that?"

"We have a working theory," Libby said.

"A fairly weak one," Sean pointed out when Libby was through.

"A poor thing but our own," Bernie said.

Sean leaned forward. "On the other hand, what you say about Renee fits in with what Ruffo told me," he conceded. "Money is a great motivator, but then," he mused, "so is sex and revenge. People sleeping with other people's love interests can make their partners do stupid things."

Bernie swallowed and tried not to think about her aching jaw. "I still like the money angle. It's more compelling. Given what we didn't find in Renee's house, I think there's a pretty good chance that Renee sold her jewelry and some of her more valuable possessions to cover her expenses. If she goes under, she'll probably lose everything—her house, her business and, most important, Ivan."

"And now she's down to the wire," Libby said. "This is crunch time for her."

"And it's not going to get any better," Bernie added. "Not unless she wins the lottery."

Now it was Libby's turn to conjecture. "I'll wager that Renee owes a lot of money to a lot of different vendors. And then not paying your sales tax . . ." Libby's voice trailed off.

"Or your liability insurance," Bernie added. She shook her head. "It's usually the beginning of the end, business-wise at least."

"That what your mom always said," Sean replied, remembering what Rose had told him.

"The fines are really high. The amount owed just snow-balls," Bernie observed.

"And Renee's expenses are high, as well," Libby added. "For one thing, Ruffo is charging her four thousand in rent for a nine-hundred-square-foot space. Plus, Renee has beaucoup bucks invested in her inventory. I mean, it's not as if you can return the stuff if it doesn't sell," Libby said, thinking of the racks of clothes in Renee's home office.

"And Libby hasn't even mentioned the most expensive item of all," Bernie said. "The item that's probably responsible for Renee's current situation."

"I take it you mean Ivan?" Sean asked.

"Exactly," Bernie said. "He's got expensive tastes. We found lots of designer clothes and sneakers in his room. Not to mention the Porsche. He's not cheap to keep."

"Is the Porsche bought or leased?" Sean asked.

"Bought," Bernie said. She'd found the paperwork in one of the folders in the file cabinet. "According to what I saw, Renee is two months behind on her payments."

"Unlike Renee's clothes," Libby chimed in. "She's paid up on that."

Sean gave Libby a blank look. "What are you talking about?"

"Her clothes are leased."

"Leased, Bernie?"

"Yes, Dad. Leased." And Bernie told her dad what she'd told her sister.

Sean shook his head. "Amazing. What will people think of next? And this is a business? People make money doing this?"

"They most certainly do," Bernie said, and she got her laptop out of her bedroom and showed her dad the website for Stepping Out.

"Unbelievable," Sean was saying when Libby remembered what she'd wanted to ask her father.

"Dad, who is Gangemi?"

Sean frowned and began tapping the fingers of his left hand on the arm of his chair. Then Cindy gave him a dirty look, and he stopped. "Why does that name sound so familiar?" he mused. "I know I know it from somewhere."

"Renee wrote, *Is it worth it*? next to that name on a yellow pad, if that helps," Libby informed him.

Sean held up his hand. "Give me a few minutes," he said. "It'll come to me. It always does." Ten years ago, he wouldn't have needed to think about it, he reflected. He would have remembered the name instantly. Even five years ago that would have been the case. He was losing it, sitting around. It was a depressing thought. On the other hand, at least now that he was in remission, he could walk around. He was thinking he really shouldn't complain when it came to himself. *Of course.* How could he have forgotten?

"Gangemi," Sean said. "He used to run a loan-sharking operation out of the No Name Bar on Sifton Avenue. He was involved in a shooting outside of Todd's Steak House about five years ago. Left him paralyzed." Sean rubbed his chin. "I thought he was out of the business, but maybe not."

"You think Renee was going to ask him for money?" Libby asked.

Cindy butted Sean's hand with her head, and he went back to petting her. "That's what the note you found sounds like to me, and it certainly fits in with Renee leasing her clothes."

For a moment everyone was quiet as they listened to the sound of the Metro North heading down the track to Manhattan.

"So we're back to money as a motive," Libby remarked.

"We never left it," Sean told her. "But this is all speculation. All the information you and Bernie collected is suggestive, but I still don't see any way to connect the dots between Renee and the two homicides."

"What about connecting the dots between Ivan, Renee, and the two homicides?" Bernie asked her dad. "How does that work for you?"

"That's a little more plausible, but . . ." And Sean was just about to tell Bernie about the theory he'd been turning over in his mind when the downstairs door opened and closed.

"Hello. Who's there?" Bernie called out as she heard the *clomp*, *clomp* of feet on the steps.

A moment later, Jennie appeared at the door. She was panting and out of breath. Her topknot was falling apart, and she had a smear of dirt on her white T-shirt.

"He's leaving," she said. "He's leaving today. You have to talk to him before he goes. You have to get him to confess. Make him admit what he's done."

"Who's leaving?" Sean asked her.

"Liam," Jennie said. "Liam is getting out of town. I keep telling everyone he's the killer, the one that set me up, but no one believes me."

"And your proof is?" Sean asked.

Jennie turned and faced him. "I just know." She tapped her chest with her fist. "In here."

"In here." Sean mimicked her gesture. "Well, in that case, I'll call my friend Clyde in the Longely police force and have him pick this Liam up right now. I'll just tell him Jennie told me to."

"Please," Jennie begged. And she burst into tears.

Bernie and Libby got up and hugged her.

"Really, Dad," Bernie admonished.

"I'm sorry," Jennie cried before Sean could say anything. "I'm so sorry. I don't know what to do. My lawyer told me I should be prepared to surrender. You guys are my last hope."

Sean sighed. He should have kept his mouth shut.

Chapter 35

Bernie held the ice pack away from her jaw for a moment, then put it back on and instructed Libby to take a right at the next corner. They were almost at Liam's house. They'd called him when Jennie was still at the flat and set up a meeting at A Little Taste of Heaven at seven, after the shop closed.

"Nice going," Bernie had said to her dad after Jennie had left.

"Everyone is so sensitive these days," Sean had complained. "Well, maybe I was a bit harsh," Sean had conceded when both of his daughters had given him the fisheye.

"Maybe?" Libby had said. "A little harsh?"

Sean frowned. "Okay, I was a lot harsh. But I apologized. And Jennie was fine when she left. Just pointing that out." Then Sean suggested Bernie get some ice on her bruise. Bernie came up a few minutes later with a plastic bag filled with ice, a pot of sweet mint tea, a bowl of strawberries, and a small dish of sugar cookies.

"To pass the time while we wait for Liam," Bernie explained.

But Liam didn't come. He didn't show up, he didn't call, and he didn't answer his cell.

"So what do you think?" Bernie asked her dad after they'd waited a half an hour.

"I think you gave your word to Jennie," Sean replied after he'd bitten into his second cookie and swallowed. "Which means you're obligated to go find him and see what he has to say." Then he added, "Who knows? The fact that he didn't show up lends a small amount of validity to Jennie's accusations. Although I would be surprised if she is right."

"And what are you going to do?" Libby asked. She'd assumed her dad would want to come with them.

Sean finished the cookie and reached for a strawberry. "I just need to take care of some business."

"Like what?"

"Maybe have a chat with Gangemi for old times' sake," Sean replied.

"You know him?" Libby asked.

"We have a passing acquaintance," Sean answered.

Five minutes later, the sisters were out the door.

"You think Liam is guilty?" Libby asked as she stopped to avoid a biker whizzing past them.

"Jennie thinks so," Bernie said.

"I didn't ask about Jennie. I asked about you, Bernie."

"I think . . . probably not, but I think he knows something." Bernie indicated the next street over with a nod of her head. "Make another right on Maxwell, then a left onto Antler Drive. According to Jennie, Liam is renting the bottom flat of the light green house in the middle of the block, the one with the two pink flamingos stuck in the front yard."

"Got it," Libby said as she looked around. It had been a

while since she'd driven through Elwood Pines. "Looks like things are changing."

"I'd say," Bernie agreed.

Ten years ago Elwood Pines had been a solid working-class neighborhood, the last of its kind in Longely. The houses had been built in the thirties and forties for the people working in the factories around Albany. Most of the homes were small wooden Colonials with postage-stamp lawns, tiny backyards, driveways but no garages, and overgrown laurel hedges. Their big attraction was their price: inexpensive. But in the past five years a growing number of the houses had been bought by people moving out of New York City, who had rehabbed them or even knocked them down and rebuilt. The new builds weren't McMansions, but they weren't working class, either.

"Look, Bernie." Libby took one hand off Mathilda's steering wheel and pointed as she turned onto Antler Drive. "Do you see what I see?"

Bernie did. She leaned forward to get a better look. "Do you mean Ivan or the red Porsche at the end of Liam's driveway or both?" she asked as she watched Ivan walk down the driveway. She could see he was carrying a small wooden box in his right hand. Then he turned, waved at the house, got into his Porsche, and backed out of the driveway.

"Both," Libby said as she slowed down.

"Interesting that those two know each other," Bernie observed.

"It is, isn't it?" Libby agreed as Bernie wiped off the drops of water running down the side of her cheek onto her arm with the hem of her blue-and-white-checked gingham skirt.

Evidently, the ice in the ziplock plastic bag had started to melt. Bernie opened the bag up and dumped the contents out the window. "I wonder why Ivan was here. I wonder what they were talking about."

"Good question," Libby commented as the Porsche's taillights turned the corner and vanished into the summer evening.

"Isn't it, though?" Bernie said as Libby pulled in behind the Jeep in Liam's driveway and parked, thereby effectively blocking the Jeep's exit.

As they got out of Mathilda, Bernie and Libby noted that the back of the Jeep was filled with suitcases and cartons. They were taking a closer look when Liam walked out of the house. The door slammed behind him, the sound echoing down the street. He was carrying a large cardboard carton and was wearing a Hawaiian shirt, khaki shorts, and flip-flops. When he saw the sisters, he froze.

"That's quite the fashion statement," Bernie told him. "I haven't seen one of those shirts for a while."

"Wow. A visit from the fashion police. How lucky can I get? What the hell are you doing here, anyway?" Liam demanded.

"Well," Libby explained, "when you didn't show up at the shop, we decided to come around and make sure you were okay. Can't be too careful, with everything happening these days."

"Yeah," Bernie chimed in. "We wouldn't want the same thing that happened to Tom Bannon and Denise Alvarez to happen to you."

"I'm touched that you care," Liam said.

"We're caring people," Bernie told him.

"Well, I'm sorry you came all the way out here," Liam told Bernie. "I'm fine. My phone died." And he started walking toward the Jeep.

"How convenient," Libby observed.

Liam came to a stop and shifted the weight of the box from his right to his left side before replying. Bernie and Libby could tell it was heavy from the way Liam was standing. "It's an old phone," he told Libby. "They do that."

Bernie pointed to the flamingos. "Are you taking those with you, too?"

Liam laughed. "Hardly. They belong to the house's owners."

"So where are you going?" she asked.

Liam tried for a nonchalant shrug and failed. "To my mom's lakehouse for a couple of days."

"That's an awful lot of stuff for a couple of days," Libby observed.

Liam laughed a little louder this time. "Just stuff I'm storing at her place."

"Why not leave it here?" Bernie asked. "You are coming back, right?"

"Of course I'm coming back. It's my old high school stuff," Liam explained. "We're having a family reunion, and my mom thought it would be fun to go through it." He nodded with his chin toward the carton he was carrying. "This is my last carton, so if you don't mind moving your van, I'll be on my way. I don't want to be late."

"In a minute," Bernie said. "We need to chat first."

"Do we?" Liam asked.

"Yeah, we do," Libby replied.

Liam looked Bernie up and down. "What happened to your face?"

"Didn't your friend tell you?" Bernie asked.

"My friend?" Liam repeated, looking confused.

"Ivan," Bernie said. "You know, the guy that just left your house."

"Oh. That Ivan," Liam said.

"You know others?" Libby asked.

Liam shrugged. "It's a fairly common name." He indicated Bernie's jaw with a nod of his head. "He do that to you?"

Bernie nodded.

Liam tsk-tsked. "I bet he was drunk."

"Yes, he was," Libby said.

Liam shook his head. "He's okay when he's sober, but not so okay when he's soused."

"So I was told," Bernie said. "I should have listened." Then she said, "I'm surprised he didn't tell you."

"Why would he?" Liam asked.

"Friends tell each other things."

"We're not friends."

"Then why was Ivan here?"

Liam shrugged again. "He was collecting for the Leukemia Society."

"Or maybe he came to pick something up," Bernie said, thinking of the box Ivan had been carrying.

"Like a contribution to the Leukemia Society," Liam retorted. "But more to the point, why are you here?"

Bernie answered, "We already told you. We were concerned when you didn't show up."

"Yeah. Right. Sure you were." And Liam started walking toward his Jeep again.

"Aren't you going to ask why we called you in the first place?" Libby asked him.

Liam stopped, put the carton down, opened one of the Jeep's doors, and shoved the carton inside. "I don't have to ask. I can guess. Jennie came whining and weeping to you, begging you to make me confess."

"That's fairly accurate," Libby allowed.

Liam smiled unpleasantly. "She's good. She puts on quite

the performance. I'll give her that. But then most pathological liars do." He slammed the Jeep door shut. The sound reverberated down the street. "You know what they say," Liam told Libby. "If you can't take the heat, stay out of the kitchen."

"Are you saying that Jennie killed Bannon and Alvarez?" Bernie asked.

"Well, I know I didn't," Liam said.

"That's not what Jennie thinks," Libby informed him.

Liam frowned. "So I've been told. And that's supposed to concern me, how? I don't care what Jennie thinks. She is nuts. No, I take that back. She's a vindictive bitch. I've already talked to the police. Twice, thanks to Jennie. I don't have to talk to you."

"You're right, Liam, you don't," Bernie was telling him when her sister tapped her on her shoulder. Bernie turned and Libby pointed to the wet suit lying across the back seat of Liam's vehicle.

"Bernie, didn't Ivan have one of those in his closet?" Libby asked.

Liam cocked his head and lifted an eyebrow. "Is that why he punched you?" he asked Bernie. "Because he found you poking through his stuff?"

"Something like that," Bernie allowed. "Do you two surf?" she asked him, taking a wild guess.

Liam glanced at his phone. "As a matter of fact, we do," Liam replied, not looking up.

Bernie switched tactics. "Is that how you met?"

Liam grunted as he texted something.

"You must miss Cali," Bernie said.

Liam snorted.

"What's that supposed to mean?" Bernie demanded.

"It means that I know what you're doing—trying to get

all cozy with me—and it's not going to work," Liam told her as he kept texting.

Bernie continued talking, anyway. "Ivan told me he won a lot of surfing awards."

Liam looked up from his phone. "Two, to be exact."

Bernie smiled her most winning smile. "I bet you won more."

"As a matter of fact, I have." Then Liam laughed. "You're doing it again. Now, are you going to move your van, or am I going to do it for you?"

"And how are you going to do that?" Bernie asked.

"Two possibilities," Liam said. He corrected himself. "Actually three." His smile vanished. His eyes narrowed. The genial surfer-boy dude mask was gone, and in its place was something else, something cold and hard. "You can move, I can push you out of the way with my Jeep, or I can call the police."

"Or you can shoot us and be done with it," Bernie quipped, curious to see what Liam's reaction to her statement would be.

Liam smiled again. This time Bernie was reminded of a shark.

"That also is a possibility," he said, a speculative tone in his voice.

"We'll move," Libby informed Liam before Bernie could say anything else. She figured they'd had enough aggravation for one day.

Liam turned to Libby. "In case you were wondering, I was kidding," he told her, but Libby wasn't sure he was.

"Are you a good shot?" Bernie asked Liam.

"Good enough," Liam said.

"So is Marcy," Bernie noted.

"And I'm supposed to care, why?" Liam replied.

"Do you know her?" Bernie asked instead of answering his question.

"You want advice?" Liam said to her as he got into his Jeep. "Let it go."

"So you do know her," Bernie said.

"Yeah. I know her. She's a friend of Jennie's. You got questions, go ask my ex about her. But if I were you, I'd go back to baking blueberry muffins, or whatever the hell it is that you do."

"And if I don't?" Bernie said.

Liam shrugged and started the Jeep up. "Do what you want. I don't care."

"The line is, 'Frankly, my dear, I don't give a damn,'" Bernie replied.

Liam gave her a blank look.

Bernie enlightened him. "You know, the last line from the movie *Gone with the Wind*."

"I don't know about the movie, but the line works for me," Liam told her. "Now, are you moving or not?"

"Moving," Libby said, and she and her sister got into the van.

"God, I could use a drink," Bernie said after they'd pulled out of Liam's driveway. "Make that two."

"Ditto," Libby agreed. "RJ's it is."

"I wonder if Liam is going to his mom's," Bernie mused as she watched him make a right at the corner without pausing for the stop sign.

"I don't know, but he sure is in a hurry."

Bernie rolled down her window. "I bet Ivan would know."

"Probably," Libby said as she headed toward the bar. She needed a shandy. And maybe a few chicken wings. Make that a dozen.

"We should ask him," Bernie said as she rested her feet on the dashboard. She touched her jaw. It still hurt. She had a feeling it was going to be sore for a while.

"You can ask him," Libby told her sister, "but as for me, I second what Rhett Butler said. At least for this evening."

"Me too," Bernie agreed, stifling a yawn. There was something else she needed to check out.

Chapter 36

Sean hummed as he drove along. He was happy. He was happy that he had a car again. He was happy he was out of the house. He was happy the shots he was taking for his MS were working. He was happy that it was a beautiful summer night, but most of all, he was happy that he'd remembered who Gangemi was. Happy he wasn't losing it, at least not yet. He couldn't believe he'd forgotten the guy, but as Clyde had pointed out, Sean had been out of the game for a long time, and so had Gangemi, for that matter. . . . Or at least he'd been out of the public eye.

It had taken a couple of phone calls, but Sean had managed to arrange a meeting with Fred. He smiled and thought about the last time he'd seen him. That had been when he'd arrested him for menacing. He sighed. It seemed like another lifetime when he'd been on patrol.

His arrest, to Sean's knowledge, was the only time Gangemi had been taken into custody. After that, he'd hired out the strong-arm stuff and concentrated on building up his loan-sharking and bookmaking business. Things had been going great for him. He'd just taken over

Fatty Stein's business when he'd gotten shot by a person or persons unknown while coming back from the track. Two bullets had lodged in his spine, paralyzing him from the waist down. Now, according to Clyde, Gangemi's son, Fred Junior, ran the business, but Fred Senior was still the brains of the operation.

"I never understood this whole junior business," Sean had told Clyde. "It argues a lack of imagination."

"And a massive ego," Clyde had added. "Why do you want to speak to him, anyway?" he had asked Sean. "Does it have to do with that article you're trying to write?"

Sean corrected him. "Have written. I finished it, and in case you're interested, it's appearing in the *Gazette* in two weeks. And no, I'm just helping the girls out. That's what good parents do."

"If you say so."

"What's that supposed to mean?" Sean demanded.

"Exactly what I said," Clyde replied. "And by the way," he added, "you owe me four of those mocha cupcakes, you know, the ones with the coffee icing."

"You're kidding," Sean squawked.

"Not in the least. Whadda you think? I work for free?" Clyde said. "That I exist for the sole purpose of answering your questions?" Then he hung up before Sean had a chance to ask Clyde if his wife had him on another diet. He could always tell from Clyde's mood. Especially if Clyde's wife was back to serving him coffeeless coffee, which was coffee made out of sunflower-seed hulls, watermelon seeds, and God knows what else.

Sean was thinking that this would certainly put him in an unspeakably bad mood as he pulled up in front of Fred Gangemi Junior's residence. The guy hadn't done bad for himself, Sean decided as he got out of his vehicle. Fred Junior's house was located in one of the ritzier sections of

Longely, and if it wasn't a McMansion, it was pretty damned close.

Sean wondered as he walked up to the door whether Fred Junior's neighbors knew what he did or whether they believed he really did import lawn furniture from China and Vietnam instead of loaning out money at 20 percent interest. He rang the bell, and Fred Junior answered the door immediately. He must have been watching for him, Sean thought as he took in the man standing in front of him. He looked like the CEO of a tech company, Sean reflected, instead of the head of a successful criminal enterprise. But then again, some people would argue they were the same thing.

"He's waiting for you," Fred Junior said, pointing to the staircase. It curved up and looked as if it belonged in a thirties movie. "Second bedroom to the right. He doesn't get too many visitors these days."

"I'll be quick," Sean assured him.

Fred Junior waved his hand, indicating that wasn't necessary. Sean noticed that he was wearing a Patek Philippe on his wrist. "No. Stay as long as you like. He can use the company."

Sean nodded his thanks. "That's quite the staircase," he noted.

Fred Junior smiled. His veneers were bright enough to reflect the light from the chandelier. "My wife got it sent over from some country house in England. Cost a fortune. Put in an elevator, too, speaking of costing a fortune, so my dad could come downstairs if he wanted to, but he prefers to stay in his room." Fred Junior frowned. "Just between you and me, I think he's depressed. I think he misses the old neighborhood. I offered to take him there to visit, but he refused. I don't think he likes anyone seeing him in his wheelchair. At his age, you'd think it wouldn't matter."

"But it does," Sean replied, thinking about the time when he couldn't walk very well or very far without the aid of a cane. There had been lots of times he hadn't wanted to go out of the house, because he'd been embarrassed to be seen by his neighbors. Which was ridiculous. He knew that. But it hadn't mattered. He'd still felt that way. Certainly, he couldn't have climbed these stairs back then, he thought as he started up them, his feet sinking into the carpet as he went. He climbed slowly, running his hand over the banister. It was chestnut, and the wood was smooth under his hand and emitted a pleasing glow.

When he got to the landing, he started down the hallway. It was long, with a high arched ceiling, thick carpeting on the floor, and oil paintings hung on the walls at regular intervals. The paintings looked as if they'd come from the same place the staircase had, and Sean decided that the place reminded him of a museum as he reached Fred Senior's room. He could hear the TV going through the door. He knocked, and a thin, wavering voice told him to come in.

Sean carefully opened the door and entered. Fred Gangemi Senior was lying in a hospital bed, facing floor-to-ceiling windows that looked out on a carefully landscaped backyard that contained an in-ground pool, a vine-covered gazebo, and a perennial garden. The TV that Sean had heard in the hall was mounted on the opposite wall.

"Long time no see," Fred Senior told Sean.

"Yes, it is," Sean replied as he reflected that Fred Senior looked old and frail. Sean wouldn't have recognized him if he'd seen him on the street. What hair he had had turned white, his cheeks had sunk in, and there were deep circles under his eyes and liver spots on his hands.

"You look good," Sean lied as he wondered what people whom he hadn't seen for thirty years would say if they saw him now. How would he look to them? Not good, he suspected.

"Right," Gangemi rasped. "So do you."

"At least we're still both here." Sean indicated the scene out the window. "Pretty view," he observed.

"My son did it, so I'd have something to look at. I like watching the deer in the morning."

"Nice of him," Sean observed.

"Yeah, it is," Fred Senior said. "He's a good kid." He pointed to the chair next to his bed. "Sit."

Sean sat.

"So?" Fred Senior said. "What do you want? I presume you didn't come here to talk about the landscaping."

"I have a question," Sean said.

"I'm not going anywhere," Fred Senior noted when Sean didn't ask it immediately.

"It's for my girls," Sean explained.

Fred Senior nodded and waited. Sean noticed his chest was going in and out and he was having trouble catching his breath.

"It's about Renee," Sean explained.

Fred Senior started to cough. "Who?" he asked after he'd dabbed his mouth with the handkerchief lying on his lap.

"Renee Hickenloop. She owns a fancy dress store in a strip mall."

"The strip mall owned by Ruffo?"

Sean nodded. "Yeah, that's the one."

"What about her?"

"Did she borrow money from you?"

Fred Senior studied the view out the window. "Why ask me?"

"Because that's what you and your son do."

"We got out of that business a while ago."

"That's not what I heard."

"Well, you heard wrong."

"That's your story, and you're sticking to it," Sean said.

"Exactly," Fred Senior replied.

"You know," Sean said after a minute had passed, "it occurs to me that you and I aren't so different, after all."

Fred Senior raised an eyebrow. "How do you get that?"

"Well," Sean said, "we're both old, we both live with our children, and until recently I wouldn't have been able to get up the stairs without a cane."

"Anything else?" Fred Senior asked.

"Yes," Sean replied. "We both worked in the same type of enterprise—crime—on different sides."

Fred Senior chuckled. "That's good. I like that."

Sean continued. "And our kids have gone into the family businesses, so to speak, yours full-time and mine part-time. And we're both retired—supposedly."

Fred Senior looked at him. "Okay. I get it. But what's your point?"

Sean leaned forward in his chair. "My point is this. I'm no longer in law enforcement, and my daughters never have been. The piece of information I'm asking for is for background purposes only, but it may save an innocent person from going to jail."

"You're talking about the whole Bannon and Alvarez thing, aren't you?" Fred Senior guessed.

Sean nodded.

"I thought that was a slam dunk," Fred Senior said,

wheezing between the words. "I thought you guys like Jennie for it."

Sean corrected him. "That's what the DA thinks. My daughters think otherwise," Sean explained.

"And why does their opinion matter?"

"Because Jennie hired them to figure out what happened. I'm just tying up loose ends for my daughters. You know, dotting the i's and crossing the t's."

Fred Senior resettled himself on the bed. "I see. So how does the fact that someone owes us money, hypothetically speaking, factor into this equation?" he asked Sean.

"Money always factors into everything," Sean replied.

Fred Senior let out a half snort. "Now, on that we can agree. Is there another reason you're here?"

"Like missing your handsome face?"

Fred Senior smiled. "The ladies always have found me irresistible. No. Besides that."

"Like I already said," Sean told him. "Just doing a favor for my kids."

Fred Senior sighed. "It's nice to be needed," he reflected.

"Yes, it is," Sean agreed.

"I don't get consulted much these days," Fred Senior revealed.

"Me neither," Sean said.

For the next five minutes, the two men were silent as they watched the clouds move in and the wind rustle the leaves in the trees.

Fred Senior broke the silence first. "Renee owes a lot," he confided to Sean. "I told Fred Junior not to do the deal, but he didn't listen. Now she's in really deep. Too deep. You never want to let it get to that point if you can help it. It makes people feel hopeless, and that's when things get dangerous." Here Fred Senior paused for a minute. "But Freddy thinks he knows everything."

"So do my daughters," Sean said.

Fred Senior laughed. "I bet that's what my dad said about me."

"I'm sure mine said the same, too," Sean replied as he watched the wind pushing the clouds across the sky. He stayed for another hour, sitting in companionable silence with Fred Senior and reflecting on the ironies of life.

Chapter 37

The dream woke up Bernie at three in the morning. She sat up, heart pounding. In the dream she'd solved the case. The answer had been obvious. She remembered there had been wooden planks and nails. She'd been talking to someone when he'd drawn his gun and shot her. That was when she'd woken up.

But try as she might, she couldn't remember who the guilty person had been, who had killed her. And now she was wide awake. Her mind was racing. She couldn't go back to sleep. She kept on thinking about the case and about the last call she'd fielded from Jennie, the one in which Jennie had told Bernie that she wanted the wedding to go on whether she got arrested or not, the one where she had begged Bernie to track down the shooter.

Like she and Libby hadn't been trying to do that all along, Bernie had thought glumly after she'd hung up. She felt as if she was trying to put together one of those thousand-piece jigsaw puzzles, the kind that are all the same color, only some of the pieces were missing. Finally, after an hour of tossing and turning in her bed, Bernie decided to hell with it.

She'd get up, get dressed, and drive down to Woof Woof and check the place out one last time. Maybe there was something there that she'd missed. She didn't think there was, but at least if she looked, she could tell herself she'd done the necessary work. Bernie had collected her lock-picks, bag, and gloves and was looking for the keys to the van when she heard Libby's bedroom door open.

"Where are you going?" Libby whispered, taking a step into the living room. Her voice was hoarse with sleep, and she was rubbing her eyes.

"I'm going to Woof Woof to check things out," Bernie explained, taking care to keep her voice low. The last thing she wanted to do was wake her dad up.

Libby stifled a yawn. "I thought we already did that."

"We did," Bernie told her sister.

"So why are you doing it again?" Libby asked.

"Because I just can't get it out of my head that there's something in that place that we're not seeing. Something that will explain what the hell is going on."

"Like what?" Libby asked.

"Like if I knew, I wouldn't be going out there again," Bernie snapped. Then she apologized. She never did very well when she didn't get enough sleep, and tonight she'd gotten about an hour and a half's worth. "Go back to bed."

Libby stifled another yawn. "If you wait a couple of minutes, I'll get dressed and go with you," she told her sister.

"Are you sure?" Bernie asked as she spotted the keys. They'd been half hidden under her dad's newspaper. "You don't have to."

"I know I don't have to," Libby said, remembering how Jennie had sobbed in this room, "but I want to. Besides, I'm up. I might as well, because I'll never get back to sleep now."

Ten minutes later, Bernie had left a note for their dad,

and she and Libby were out the door. Seven minutes after that, they were at the strip mall. Usually, the drive over would have taken fifteen minutes, but tonight there was literally no one on the road except for a tabby cat darting across the street at Fifth Street and Crescent Drive and a red fox sitting in the Kirbys' garden, next to a garden gnome. When they got to the strip mall, Bernie drove around to the back of the mall and parked there to avoid attracting the attention of any patrol cars that might be cruising by. Then they got out of Mathilda.

"No security cameras in the back," Bernie noted as they walked around to the front. The last thing either of them needed was yet another confrontation with the police.

Libby nodded and pointed to the cameras across the street. "But there are two in the front." Fortunately, Bernie noted, they weren't pointed in the direction of Jennie's place. Nevertheless, they were both careful to keep their heads down and out of view. A moment later, Bernie popped the lock on Woof Woof's door. The sisters stepped inside, and Bernie shut the door after them. That way, a random check wouldn't arouse suspicions.

"It's nice," Libby said, looking around at the place. "Jennie did a good design job."

"Yes, she did," Bernie agreed.

The place looked bright and cheerful. Gone was the dark-colored wood paneling, the dim lighting, the uncomfortable long wooden benches along the walls, the small round tables, the beer signs, and the bar. The place seemed more spacious, airier. After opening the door, you walked into the reception area. A sign on the desk told everyone to please wait for the staff to help with drop-offs or pick-ups. Next came a waist-high white picket fence decorated with a picture of a small black-and-white terrier lifting his leg. The sign on it read PLEASE DO NOT ENTER. STAFF ONLY.

Then, after you walked through the gate, you passed through two separate areas, one for big dogs and one for small. The areas were painted different shades of yellow, while the door leading to the outdoor fenced-in area was painted a bright orange. There was a large mural on the right wall, showing a pack of dogs at play, while the left wall featured cartoons of different breeds of dogs. The gates that were going to separate the areas hadn't gone up yet, because Jennie planned to set up the tables for the reception inside Woof Woof, while Bertha and Ernie's wedding ceremony was going to be in the backyard.

Libby idly ran a finger over one of the folding tables leaning against the wall. "Where do you want to start looking?"

"I guess you take the right side and I'll take the left," Bernie said.

"Not that there's much to look through," Libby noted.

It was true. Except for the tables, a few chairs, the fences, a couple of boxes of dog toys, a carton of treats, and a toolbox, there wasn't much there.

For the next twenty minutes Bernie and her sister went through the place. They sifted through the business cards on the reception desk and studied the appointment book and the list of emergency numbers to call. They moved the tables and chairs away from the walls and then put them back the way they had been. They tapped on the molding and the walls and got the ladder that was lying on the floor and examined the lights and the ceiling tiles. They didn't find anything they hadn't expected to see.

Libby stretched and rubbed the back of her neck. A wave of exhaustion hit her. "Let's go home." Maybe if she was lucky, she could get a couple of hours in before she had to start her workday.

Bernie held up her hand. "In a minute. We haven't checked the storeroom yet."

"Why is that going to be any different?"

"It probably won't be, but as long as we're here . . ." Bernie's voice trailed off as she walked toward it.

"I know," Libby said, quoting another of her dad's favorite sayings. "If you're going to do a job, do it right."

"Exactly," Bernie said. She was determined to finish the job, even though every bone in her body was aching with fatigue.

The storeroom was at the rear of Woof Woof. Previously, the space had been used to store cases and kegs of beer, but now, according to Jennie, it was going to be used to keep cleaning supplies, doggie beds, dog food, water bowls, and other doggie paraphernalia.

Bernie opened the door and went inside the storeroom. Libby followed. The door swung closed behind them. "Must need a doorstop," Bernie observed as she wrinkled her nose.

The place smelled of stale beer. Unlike the rest of the space, this room hadn't been touched. The walls were still paneled in wood, and stained linoleum squares covered the floor. The only things in the room were a water bowl, a small bag of Pro Plan puppy food for large dogs, and a couple of metal tie-out stakes.

"So that's that," Libby said as she looked around. "I think we're done here."

"I guess we are," Bernie admitted, even though she didn't want to be. Then she heard something. *A squeak*, she thought. "Did you hear that?" she asked Libby.

Libby shook her head. But a minute later, she heard the noise, too. Something was squeaking.

Bernie pointed. Libby followed her sister's finger. It was

a mouse. No. Two mice. As the sisters watched, the mice scurried away and seemed to disappear into the space between two of the linoleum squares

"Where did they go?" Libby asked.

"Good question," Bernie said as she went over to where they had been, and squatted down.

"There's nothing there," Libby protested after she'd joined her.

"Exactly," Bernie said, pointing to a hairline space between two of the black-and-white linoleum squares. "See. The glue is gone."

Libby studied the tiny line Bernie was indicating. "Nothing could get in there."

"I'm not so sure," Bernie told her. "Remember how the mice were getting into the prep room a couple of years ago?" There'd been an infinitesimal crack in the wall between the molding and the floor. That was when Bernie had learned that, like bats, mice could get into the smallest of crevices.

"Yeah, I remember," Libby said. "How could I forget?" They'd tried everything, and then Cindy the cat had come into their lives and the problem had solved itself.

Libby scowled at the memory as Bernie reached out a finger and ran it down the line. She felt something. She just wasn't sure what. She pressed the middle of the linoleum square. It gave slightly. She pressed the next one over. That one did, too, but the next one in line didn't.

"What are you thinking?" Libby asked her sister as Bernie got up, went over to her bag, and got her tweezers out.

"I'll show you, Libby," Bernie told her. Suddenly she wasn't tired anymore.

"Seriously, what are you doing?" Libby asked as Bernie returned to the spot and squatted back down.

"Following a hunch," Bernie replied.

Chapter 38

Bernie took a deep breath, placed the tweezers in the hairline space, worked her way under a tile with them, grabbed the end of the linoleum square, and lifted. She felt a slight movement. She did it again, and the tile came away, revealing a piece of plywood with a small hole in it. Bernie tried a second and then a third and a fourth linoleum tile, with the same result.

"Am I good or am I good?" Bernie crowed while she studied the plywood square in front of her. She could see where it had been cut out of the floor.

Libby snorted. "I'd say overly optimistic. It's probably some old repair."

Bernie pointed to the small hole. "Or an entrance to a tunnel," she replied, thinking of the article her dad had written.

Libby raised an eyebrow. "That's quite the leap," she said.

Bernie tried to put one of her fingers in the hole to lift the plywood up, but her finger was too big. The tweezers didn't work, either. She needed something longer and stronger. She stood up, walked over, and got one of the tie-outs. Then she stuck it in the hole, angled it toward her, and pulled. The plywood square moved. Bernie pushed it aside.

"And you were saying?" Bernie said to Libby as she shone her cell's flashlight into the opening.

The sisters could see a ladder. It looked old and wobbly. Libby counted the steps. There were four in all. Then when Bernie leaned in and lowered the light a little farther down, she saw that there were wood slats holding up the walls, and a dirt floor.

"Okay, I was wrong," Libby allowed.

Bernie cupped a hand under her ear and cocked her head. "Say again."

"I was wrong. Happy?"

"Yes." Bernie pointed. "Because that is definitely a tunnel."

"I'm not saying it isn't," Libby said.

"But you did."

Libby threw up her hands. "Enough. I'm too tired to do this." She brushed a lock of hair off her forehead and changed the subject. "So where do you think it leads to?"

Bernie sat back on her heels. "I'm not sure, but I can guess. You know the article Dad's been working on?"

"You mean the one about the robbery?" Libby asked. "The one where they robbed the bank vault and the robbers made off with bearer bonds and gold and cash and jewelry? It was the biggest crime in Longely's history."

Bernie nodded. "Yeah. That one."

"They never found the crew that did it."

"No, they didn't. Whoever did it tunneled into the vault and left the same way. No one knew anything was wrong until the bank manager opened the vault on Monday." Bernie gestured toward the opening in the floor. "I'm thinking that that's part of the tunnel they used to get to the bank vault."

"I thought the police destroyed it," Libby replied. "At least that's what the TV show I watched said."

Bernie shook her head. "Evidently not. According to Dad, the police were going to fill it in, but before they could, the tunnel caved in on its own. At least part of it did. It happened when the bank repaired the hole in the vault. All that vibration."

Libby thought of the pictures of the tunnels on Denise's dining-room table and of Renee's husband's textbooks. "Renee's husband was a mining engineer, wasn't he?"

"Structural," Bernie said. "I know where you're going with this, and no, he didn't have anything to do with the robbery. He died before it happened. Dad checked."

"And Renee?"

"What do you think? I can't exactly see her down here with a miner's light and a shovel in her Prada heels," Bernie replied. "Can you?"

Libby laughed. "Hardly, but she could be directing the operation. And then there's Ivan."

"Although," she reflected after a moment's pause, "I can't see him getting his hands dirty." She scratched a mosquito bite on her arm. "Or his sneakers, for that matter."

"Yeah. I have a feeling physical labor isn't exactly his thing," Bernie said. She was wondering whether they should wake her dad up and tell him what they'd found when she heard a car driving by. Then that noise stopped, and Bernie and Libby heard car doors slamming shut and people talking.

"Someone's here," Libby hissed.

"No kidding."

"What do you want to do?"

"Sit tight. It's probably security checking the place out," Bernie told Libby.

"Or the police," Libby said as the voices outside got louder.

"They'll leave in a minute," Bernie predicted.

But they didn't. Woof Woof's door creaked open. Bernie put her hand to her mouth. She should have locked the door. Then a muffled male voice said something about checking something out, although neither Bernie nor Libby could make out what that something was.

"Maybe it's Jennie and Googie," Libby suggested.

"Are you nuts? It's four thirty in the morning."

"Maybe they couldn't sleep, either."

"Seriously, Libby," Bernie whispered, "does that sound like Googie's voice to you?"

"No," Libby admitted.

"Good, because it doesn't sound like Googie's voice to me, either. How's this for a thought? What if these are the people that killed Bannon and Alvarez? Because if they are, something tells me they're not going to be happy finding us here."

"They might not open the storeroom door," Libby said.

"It's true, they might not, but are you willing to take that chance? It's not like there's any place to hide in here. They'll see us the moment they open the door." Bernie nodded toward the tunnel. "We need to go down there. We need to go down there now."

Libby's heart started beating faster. Just the thought of climbing down there took her breath away and not in the good romance kind of way. She pointed to the linoleum and the plywood. "They'll know someone has been here. Those are not exactly invisible."

"True," Bernie said. "But at least we'll have a head start."

Libby didn't say anything.

"We have to go," Bernie repeated, her voice growing more urgent.

"You go. I'll stay and hold them off," Libby said.

Bernie laughed. "With what? Your flip-flops? Don't be ridiculous. That's not happening. You're coming with me."

Libby swallowed. Her throat felt very dry.

"Hey, this isn't a refrigerator," Bernie said.

Libby put her hands on her hips. "It was very traumatic," she said indignantly.

"I'm sure it was, but going down there is better than the alternative," Bernie said.

"You mean possibly getting dead?"

"Exactly."

"Well, when you put it that way," Libby told her sister. The voices were getting louder, and as much as she didn't want to believe that what Bernie said was true, she knew that it was.

"I'll go first," Bernie said.

"I'm certainly not," Libby replied.

She opened and closed her eyes and took a deep breath. How bad could it be? she told herself, trying to fight the panic rolling around in her stomach. She hated tight spaces, but she wasn't five anymore, and Bernie was right: the tunnel wasn't a refrigerator someone had left on the street with its door attached. It was time she got over her fear. She hadn't even been in there that long, though it had felt like forever.

"You ready?" Bernie asked, picking up her bag.

Libby nodded.

"Then let's do this," Bernie said, and she turned the flashlight function of her cell back on. The first step was a ways down, and she had to fish around with her foot to find it. The second and third steps were easier, although she wished she wasn't wearing flip-flops. They were great for the beach, but not for this. "Made it," she announced when she reached the ground. She started to stand up and hit her head on the ceiling. She was going to have to crouch over. "I'll tell you one thing," she said to Libby. "Whoever dug this thing had to be pretty small." Then she moved into the tunnel to make room for her sister.

"Well?" Bernie said after a moment had passed and Libby hadn't moved. "I'm waiting. Don't make me come up and drag you down."

"You said it. I didn't."

"Ha. Ha. Very funny. Are you coming or not?"

"Coming," Libby replied. She said a silent prayer and began climbing down. When she got to the second step, she reached over and pulled the plywood square halfway over the opening When she reached the third step, she pulled the cover completely across.

"Don't freak out," Bernie told Libby.

"I'm not going to," Libby lied.

"I'm glad I left a note for Dad," Bernie reflected as she started out. "At least he'll know where to start looking for us if anything happens."

"You're not helping matters, Bernie."

"Sorry." And Bernie stopped talking and concentrated on what she was doing. After a few feet of crouching, she got down on her hands and knees and crawled. It was easier on her back but harder on her legs, because there were bits of gravel in the dirt.

"What's with the gravel?" Libby asked as she brushed it off her knees. Actually, she was glad it was there. The pain was providing a distraction.

"Don't have a clue," Bernie said. She heard more squeaks and felt something brush past her hands. "I hope that was a mouse," she said, "and not a rat."

Libby shuddered. "I hope so, too." Actually, she thought

mice were rather cute as long as they weren't running around the shop's silverware drawer. But rats, on the other hand . . . "Don't tell me if you see one," Libby said. "I don't want to know."

"Roger that," Bernie replied. She crawled another couple of feet, and her hand landed on a piece of paper. It was a wrapper from a bag of M&M's Fudge Brownie candies. They'd come out in 2020. Bernie knew this because she'd eaten way too many of them. Her guess had been right, after all. She stopped and passed the wrapper back to Libby. "It looks as if someone was down here not too long ago. I think my hypothesis is correct."

"Tom Bannon?" Libby mused after she noticed a Gatorade bottle lying next to a wooden slat that was holding up the wall. There had been Gatorade bottles and wooden boards on Bannon's dining-room table.

She'd thought he was building bookshelves for his house, but then she and Bernie had agreed that made no sense, because he was moving to Hollywood. What if he had been working on the tunnel? What if that was what had gotten him killed? It was possible, Libby thought as she soldiered on. No, it was more than possible. It was likely.

"How long have we been down here, anyway?" Libby asked a moment later, as she stopped to blink the sweat out of her eyes. She didn't want to use her forearm or her shirt, because they were both coated with dirt.

Bernie checked her phone. "Maybe five minutes, if that."

"It feels like twenty," Libby observed.

"What do they say about time flying when you're having fun?" Bernie cracked. Then she started crawling again. A little later she heard a creak and then another one. It was the kind of sound that old houses made at night,

Bernie thought. She swept the beam of light over the tunnel in front of her, but she didn't see anything. Then she directed the light toward the ceiling. A trickle of dirt was coming through the slats on the top.

"What was that?" Libby asked.

"Another mouse," Bernie lied, picking up her pace. She wasn't going to tell her sister what she'd just seen. She'd totally freak.

"That doesn't sound like a mouse," Libby observed.

"Trust me, it was," Bernie said.

"What was it really?"

"Actually, you don't want to know," Bernie told her. "Ignorance is golden."

Libby corrected her. "You mean ignorance is bliss and silence is golden."

"I like my way better," Bernie told her.

A minute later, Libby stopped. "I just thought of something," she said. "You know what we haven't heard?"

"What?" Bernie asked.

"We haven't heard any footsteps above us or voices in the tunnel."

"So?" Bernie said.

"So I'll tell you what it means, Bernie. It means this whole thing was unnecessary. We could have stayed where we were."

"You don't know that."

"Yeah, I do."

"Are you saying you want to go back?"

It took Libby two seconds to decide. "No. We've come this far. Let's finish it."

"Good," Bernie said. "Saves me the trouble of dragging you along."

Five minutes later, Bernie thought she saw a light at the end of the tunnel. Well, a glimmer of light, really. More like less dark. She turned off the flashlight to check, but it was hard to tell, because she kept on seeing explosions of yellow and red in front of her eyes. Who knew an absence of light could do that?

"Come on, Libby," she said as she turned the light back on. "We're almost there."

"Where is there?" Libby asked her sister.

"I don't know," Bernie admitted, "but wherever it is, it's better than being in here." She looked again, and the glimmer of light ahead was gone. Had she imagined it? God, she hoped not.

"Agreed," Libby said. She took a deep breath and continued crawling.

And then Bernie's phone died, and the light went out.

"Oh no," Libby cried.

"It'll be fine," Bernie told her. "We must be near the end of this thing. There has to be an exit here somewhere." Which was when they heard a low, faint rumbling.

Libby gasped as the rumbling got louder and the floor of the tunnel shook. Libby and Bernie stopped and held their breath. Then there was another rumble, a smaller one, after which there was nothing.

"I bet we're going under Route Thirty-Two," Bernie posited.

"So?"

"It's a truck route. Hence the vibrations."

"At least there are no earthquakes around here."

"No. There are, Libby," Bernie told her. "Smaller ones."

"Not what I need to hear now," Libby responded.

"Sorry."

A moment later, Libby began to sing, "You Make Me Feel Like a Natural Woman."

"Please stop," Bernie begged.

"You don't like the song, Bernie?"

"No. I love the song, Libby. That's the problem."

"Are you saying you don't like my voice?"

"That's exactly what I'm saying."

"Well, yours isn't so great, either."

"But I'm not singing."

"God, you're a pain in the butt."

"It's a talent, Libby."

"A talent you've been cultivating since the day you were born, Bernie."

Bernie snorted.

A few minutes after that, Bernie saw a faint light in front of them. "Look, Libby," she said as she picked up speed. "We're coming to the end."

Libby's heartfelt "Thank God" floated out into the air. The tunnel took a jog to the right, and they came to another ladder. They climbed up and found themselves in a large concrete pipe. They could see a faint light coming from one end, and they crawled toward it and emerged a few minutes later. They sat there, taking deep breaths of fresh air, enjoying the tang of the river, the smell of honeysuckle in the air, and the flickering light from the streetlamp above them. Their hands, feet, arms, and legs were caked with dirt, and their knees were bloody from crawling over the earth-gravel mixture.

Bernie looked around. Never had the world seemed lovelier. "We're at the culvert," she announced. "We're at the place where we saw Ivan's car." She stood up. Suddenly everything clicked. "I'll bet you anything this pipe goes to the bank vault. Or close to it."

Libby raised an eyebrow.

"No. Seriously," Bernie said. "The bank vault must be higher. I bet whoever fixed the tunnel realized that. The pipe must be new. So they decided to take advantage of it. I bet if we followed the pipe, we'd find it ends near the bank."

Libby stopped dabbing at the trickle of blood running

down her knee with the bottom of her Bermuda shorts for a minute and looked. "Makes sense."

Bernie spoke. "Someone should check it out."

"Not me," Libby answered.

Bernie was about to reply when she heard a rustle and looked up.

Marcy was standing there with a gun in her hand. "Children, children," she said, "let's not bicker."

Chapter 39

Marcy grinned. "Surprised?" she asked.

"Very," Bernie allowed.

"I never thought—" Libby began, but Marcy cut her off.

"You and your sister never thought at all. I have to say it was fun watching you two run around like chickens with their heads cut off, but I guess all good things must end," Marcy replied as she threw a pair of handcuffs at Bernie. "Put these on."

"And if I don't?" Bernie said, catching the handcuffs in midair. She noted they were old and had a couple of rust spots on them.

Marcy's grin grew bigger. "Simple. Then I'll shoot your sister."

"Go ahead," Bernie said, doing her best imitation of nonchalance. "You'll be doing me a favor."

"Is that right?" Marcy said.

"Absolutely," Bernie answered.

"Fine." Marcy released the safety on her Glock. "If you insist."

Bernie held up her hands. "Whoa. Whoa. Whoa. Take it easy. I was kidding."

"I figured," Marcy told her.

"You know, it would be better for you if you let us go," Libby said.

Marcy laughed. "Funny lady. And why is that?"

"Because my dad already knows what you're planning," Libby lied. "He knows about the tunnel and the robbery. If you let us go, you'll be in a better position to make a deal with the DA."

"You should take my sister's advice," Bernie chimed in. "The police are probably on their way now."

"Sure they are," Marcy mocked.

"I left my dad a note telling him where we were going," Bernie said. "He doesn't sleep well in the heat. Wakes up at least two or three times a night, and when he does and we're not there, he'll read my note and call the police."

"I'll take that chance," Marcy replied. "We'll be gone by then, and so will you." She waved the Glock at them. "Of course," she added after a moment's reflection, "I suppose if worst comes to worst, we can always use you as hostages."

"Who is we?" Libby asked.

"You'll find out soon enough," Marcy replied.

"The robbery is what this has been about all this time, isn't it?" Bernie asked Marcy. "You wanted to get everyone out of the doggie day-care space so you could build the tunnel."

Marcy corrected her. "*Repair* the tunnel. Now, put the cuffs on."

"I don't get it," Bernie said. "You don't seem like someone who would be involved in something like this."

"Love made her do it," Liam replied as he popped out behind Marcy and kissed her on the cheek. She took a step back.

"I told you we should have finished up two days ago," Marcy said. Bernie decided she sounded really pissed. "Then we'd be out of here by now."

"You worry too much, Marcy," Liam replied.

"And you don't worry enough," Marcy countered.

Liam checked the time on his phone. Then he turned to Bernie and told her to do what Marcy had said and put the cuffs on.

"So Jennie was right," Bernie said to him. "She said you were behind this whole thing."

"Involved," Liam said, checking the time again. "I'm involved. I'm hardly the one in charge." He scowled.

"Don't worry," Marcy said to him. "We're still ahead of the game."

"To do what?" Libby asked.

"To get into the vault, Libby," Bernie replied as Liam shook his head. "What else?"

"I told you two to mind your own business," he said. "I told you to keep out of this, but you guys wouldn't listen."

"Neither would Jennie," Marcy added. "Anyone else would have found another place to open her doggie day-care business, but not Jennie. Oh no. She had to have that one." She waved her Glock in Bernie's direction. "I haven't heard a click yet."

"A click?" Bernie repeated, acting puzzled.

"The handcuffs, if you please," Marcy said.

"They're on my wrists," Bernie pointed out.

"But they're not locked."

"Details, details," Bernie told her.

"Close them."

Bernie shrugged and did as she was told. "Oh, well, it was worth a try."

"You always carry those around?" Libby asked.

"As a matter of fact, I do," Marcy replied. "At least one

pair and sometimes two. You never know when they'll come in handy."

"Seller of flowers, bank robber, dominatrix. That's quite an impressive résumé you've got going on," Libby observed.

"Yes," Liam said. "She's a woman of many parts."

"Evidently," Bernie agreed. "Now, Marcy, tell me this. How did you guys know about the tunnel?"

Liam answered. "We didn't," he said. "Tom did."

"And now Tom is dead," Bernie said.

"Indeed, he is," Liam agreed. Bernie decided he looked sad.

"Wasn't he a friend of yours?" Libby asked.

"What happened?" Bernie asked.

"None of your business," Marcy told them. Then she turned to Liam and said, "I'll be back in a couple of minutes, and then we'll finish things up." And she handed Liam the gun, dug another pair of handcuffs out of the front pocket of the backpack she was wearing, tossed them to him, and told him to watch Bernie and Libby and secure them both.

"She the boss of the operation?" Bernie asked when Marcy was out of sight.

"Hardly," Liam replied. "She's a come-along."

"A come-along?" Bernie repeated.

"That's what I said," Liam replied.

"I don't think she sees it that way," Bernie told him. "Doesn't that bother you?"

"Not in the least," Liam told her. He tossed the handcuffs to Libby. "Now it's your turn. Put them on."

Libby raised her hand to catch them, but they flew over her head and landed in the brushy area in back of the culvert.

"Sorry," Libby said, "but that was a bad throw."

"No," Liam said. "It was a bad catch."

"Tsk, tsk, tsk," Bernie said, putting in her two cents. "You're going to be in trouble when Marcy comes back and finds you lost her handcuffs. You're already behind schedule."

"Shut up," Liam snarled.

And suddenly Bernie knew. "That's it," she said. "You're about to double-cross your friends, aren't you? They're about to pull off this job, and you're going to beat them to it, right? Only we turned up and messed everything up, didn't we?"

"Maybe I'll just shoot you now and get back on schedule," Liam told her.

"You could," Bernie said, "but you probably should confer with Marcy about her plans for us. You don't want to make her any more annoyed than she already is. After all, she does have the gun."

"Don't worry, Liam," she went on. "We'll help you look for the cuffs, won't we, Libby?"

"Oh definitely," Libby said. For a moment, she thought about running instead, but she discarded the idea. The only way she'd make it would be if Liam was a very bad shot, and she wasn't willing to take that chance.

Liam jumped down and waved the gun in Libby and Bernie's direction. "Get going," he said.

"Aren't you going to look?" Libby asked.

"No, I'm going to watch you look," Liam told her.

"You could handcuff us to each other and save yourself the trouble," Bernie suggested.

"Move," Liam growled.

Bernie shrugged. "I'm just trying to be helpful."

Liam snorted.

"So how did you guys figure out this robbery?" Bernie asked Liam as she and Libby combed the ground for the cuffs. The longer she could keep Liam talking, the better.

That meant they had that much more time to figure out a way to get out of there. Or for her dad to show up. Either way would work. All she could say was thank heavens she'd left that note.

"The truth?" Liam asked.

"Yeah," Bernie answered. "The truth."

"If I can make your last minutes on earth happier? Sure. Why not? Bannon's uncle was involved in the heist," Liam said. "No, I'm not making this up. It's true. He was involved. He drove one of the getaway cars, and he told Tommy about it, so Tommy decided to come here and check it out, too. So we decided to come along."

"Who is we?" Bernie asked, looking up from the ground.

"Me, Ivan, and Tommy." Liam corrected himself. "Me and Tommy came first. Ivan came here a little later."

"It sounds as if you've known each other for a while," Libby observed.

"Oh yeah." Liam smiled at the thought. "We went to high school together. We were surf buddies."

"I thought Renee brought Ivan here," Bernie said.

"She did. But one of the reasons he went with her was that he missed us. He just wanted to hang with us, you know. At first, Ivan didn't want to have anything to do with this." Liam indicated the bank with his free hand. "But then he changed his mind. He got real interested in the money. I think being at Renee's beck and call did it." Liam chuckled. "I mean, it didn't seem a bad gig to me, but, hey, to each their own, I always say."

"So you came here with a plan?" Bernie reiterated.

"Naw, not really," Liam said. "It was more of a goof. Like some crazy treasure hunt. Something to do. We just wanted to check out the tunnel, and then Ruffo caught us and Marcy breaking into the place—we were trying to figure out where the tunnel started—and things got more se-rious."

"Two dead people serious," Bernie said.

"Yes, indeed," Liam said. He shook his head and sighed. "Things definitely got out of control."

"So how come you killed your friend?" Bernie asked him.

"I didn't," Liam cried.

"So who did?" Libby asked.

Liam started to say something, then changed his mind.

"You know," Bernie told him, "if you turn state's evi-dence and tell the DA who did, I'm sure he'd go easy on you."

Liam shook his head. "I can't do that."

Libby was about to ask him why he couldn't when she spotted the handcuffs in the dim light. She gave an imper-ceptible nod to Bernie, then indicated the spot with a flick of her eyes. Bernie raised both eyebrows to indicate she didn't know what Libby was talking about. Libby nodded more emphatically. Bernie shook her head. Liam was just about to ask Bernie and Libby what the hell was going on when two brown blurs careened into him, knocking the Glock out of his hand.

Bernie and Libby both froze for a second; then they both ran for the gun, almost colliding with Googie.

"I got it," he said, scooping the Glock off the ground and pointing it at Liam while Bertha and Ernie continued licking him to death.

Then, before either Bernie or Libby could say anything, Jennie ran up and kicked Liam in the stomach.

"You son of a bitch," she cried. "I knew it was you." And she kicked him again.

"That's enough," Googie told her as she moved her leg back for a third kick.

"Oh my God. What are you two doing here?" Bernie

asked Jennie and Googie as Libby went to get the hand-cuffs.

"Using our superpowers," Googie said.

Jennie laughed. "I couldn't sleep."

"Seems to be a thing these days," Libby noted.

Jennie laughed again. "I was lying in bed, tossing around, and after a couple of hours, I decided to take a last look at my dream. I'm supposed to turn myself in the day after to-morrow, and I just wanted to say good-bye."

"And I decided to go with her since I was up, anyway," Googie added.

"I know how that goes," Libby remarked as she handed Liam the handcuffs and told him to put them on.

"Then we heard voices," Jennie continued, "which is when George and I decided to check things out. Lucky we did."

"I'll say," Bernie agreed. She heard the wail of a police siren in the distance.

A moment later, the place was swarming with cops. Two minutes after that, Sean parked his car, ran up to his daughters, and gave both of them a big hug.

"Glad I'm an early riser," he said.

"Me too," Bernie replied as she watched a policeman emerge from the brush with Marcy in tow.

"Look what I found," he said.

Chapter 40

Bertha and Ernie's wedding went off without a hitch, which was amazing considering what had happened, but everyone helped. Jennie did the flowers, Googie set up the tables, Sean pitched in as photographer, while Amber did the DJing, one of Googie's friends tended bar, and Libby and Bernie took care of the food.

It's true the decorations were a little sparse, but all the guests agreed that Bertha looked ravishing in her veil before her best dog of honor ate it, and Ernie looked handsome in his black bow tie. Everyone clapped as Jennie and Googie led the wedding party, tails wagging, down the aisle to the grassy yard, where Libby did double duty as an officiant and Bertha and Ernie exchanged small peanut butter–filled Kongs.

"I think things are working out well," Bernie said to Jennie, commenting on the reception, as they watched the guests fill up their plates with dog bone–shaped multigrain crackers and little cranberry-studded goat cheese logs, small pastry-wrapped hot dogs, meatballs, and selections from platters of vegetables and dips arranged to look like golden retrievers.

"I think so, too," Jennie agreed. "The wedding cake looks delicious," she added, referring to the one Bernie and Libby had made for the human guests. That was a triple-tiered genoise flavored with framboise and topped with whipped cream and freshly picked strawberries. The sisters had also made a smaller liverwurst, carrot, and apple cake for the canine guests, all of whom were out in the backyard, chasing each other around and eating home-made dog treats.

"I knew it was that son of a bitch," Jennie said to Bernie as Amber started to play the song "How Much Is That Doggie in the Window?" "At least I got to kick him."

Bernie laughed.

"I just don't get it," Jennie went on as she flicked a cracker crumb off her black-and-white-checked shift.

"Get what?" Bernie asked.

"Why Fred Senior killed Tom and Denise."

"It was his son, Fred Junior, who did," Sean said, coming up behind Bernie and Jennie. "And to answer your question, it's greed, the root cause of all evil." He turned to Bernie. "You want to tell the story?"

She shook her head. "You tell it. You were the one that figured it out, anyway."

"Not really. I got it half right. You got the other half."

"Too bad we didn't put them both together earlier," Bernie noted.

"Yes, it was," Sean allowed. "There were just a lot of players."

"Yes, there were," Bernie agreed. Then she moved off to refill the cheese platters and to make sure they weren't running out of wine, leaving Sean to tell the tale.

"You know about the tunnel, right?" Sean asked Jennie.

Jennie nodded. "I overheard Liam talking when Googie and I and the pups snuck up on him."

"And that Ruffo discovered Marcy and the Three Ami-gos"—as Sean had come to think of Ivan, Tom, and Liam—"in his place?"

"Yeah," Jennie said. "He walked in when they'd just found the tunnel."

Sean took a sip of the seltzer he was holding. "Too bad they didn't know Ruffo had a couple of spy cams set up."

"So what happened?" Jennie asked.

Sean responded, "What happened was that in exchange for not calling the police, the Amigos offered to cut Ruffo in on the deal. That was good luck for Ruffo, because he needed the money. A lot of money, having shorted some stocks when he shouldn't have." Sean made a tsk-tsking noise. "Which is what happens when you think you know more than you do. Anyway, Ruffo was about to lose his house and the strip mall, which was why he decided to take the Amigos up on their offer. Unfortunately for him, he'd already signed a lease with you for your doggie day-care place, and he couldn't get out of it. At least not without paying you a substantial penalty, which he couldn't do, because he was flat broke."

"So he decided to try to make me leave," Jennie said, connecting the dots.

Sean nodded. "Exactly. Only you didn't."

"So he came up with another plan." Jennie wrinkled her nose. "But killing Tom and framing me for the murder? Wasn't that a little . . . ?"

"Extreme," Libby said, coming to a stop. She'd been on her way to get another crudités platter.

"Yes," Jennie said.

"Only Ruffo had nothing to do with that," Sean said.

"I don't understand," Jennie told him.

Sean took another sip of his seltzer. "Okay, this is where it gets complicated. Remember Ivan?"

"Of course I remember Ivan," Jennie responded. "What about him?"

"Well, Renee caught him as he was coming back one night from a work session with the other two Amigos."

"This was before she asked us to follow him, right?" Libby asked to clarify the matter.

Sean nodded. "Right. Renee was going to throw him out of her house because she thought he was seeing someone . . ."

"But he is," Libby objected.

Sean raised his hand in a "Wait a minute" motion. "True, but he wasn't then. At any rate, he spilled his guts and told Renee what he was up to. Now, she owed money to the Gangemis, so she told Fred Senior, who in turn told Fred Junior, who went to have a chat with Ruffo and the rest of the crew. So now everyone was working for the Gangemis."

"Including Ruffo?" Jennie asked, wanting to make sure.

"Yes, including Ruffo." Sean took another sip of seltzer. "Oh, did I forget to tell you that Ruffo had borrowed a rather sizable amount from the Gangemis, as well? Now, at this juncture, Bannon decided he wanted a bigger share of the profits. According to Liam, they were practically digging the tunnel for free. And so Bannon went to Fred Senior to"—Sean did air quotes—"negotiate."

"And Fred Senior had him killed?" Jennie asked.

"No," Sean replied. "Fred Junior did."

"Why?" Jennie asked.

This time Libby answered. "Because he didn't like someone telling him what to do."

Jennie swallowed. "He sounds nuts."

Sean took over the story again. "He is nuts. Three guys have disappeared around him in the past five years." Sean frowned. "I don't think his dad wants to admit it, though.

It would be a hard thing to do," he added, thinking of what he would do if he were in that situation.

"And Denise?" Jennie asked.

"She figured out what happened after Tom died. That's when she made her big mistake and decided to try to go for the gold, as it were," Sean said. "So she went to Fred . . ." Sean's voice trailed off. "Why she thought the outcome would be different from what had happened to Tom is beyond me."

"How did she figure it out?" Jennie inquired.

"Evidently, Tom had been hinting around about what he was involved in. Then when she went to his place to look for him, she found a page of schematics and put two and two together. In any case, Fred took care of her, as well." Sean took another sip of seltzer. "Permanently. Problem solved."

"How much did the original robbery net?" Jennie asked.

"Five million—give or take." Sean turned to Libby. "Which would be worth what now, Libby?"

"One hundred million maybe," Libby estimated.

Jennie whistled.

"And that is the saddest bit of all," Sean said. "This time there was nowhere near that amount of money in the vault. People aren't saving that much these days, and they don't use cash or own that much jewelry, for that matter. The crew would have been better off hacking into the bank." He shrugged. "Times change, and so do the crimes people commit."

"I bet Marcy is sorry she hooked up with Liam," Jennie said.

"I bet she is, too," Sean agreed.

"So did they arrest everyone?" Jennie asked.

"Yup," Clyde said as he joined the group. "We rounded everyone up. Well, everyone except for Fred Senior. Fred

Junior claims his dad didn't know anything that was going on, a claim the DA seems to have bought."

"I heard the decision not to prosecute Fred Senior was part of a plea deal Fred Junior made with the DA," Sean said.

Clyde nodded. "That's what I heard, too."

"You sound glad," Jennie said.

"I am," Sean said. "Seeing his kid go to jail is punishment enough."

"And Ruffo and Renee?" Jennie asked. "What's going to happen to them?"

"Ruffo is turning state's evidence," Clyde told her.

"And Renee is getting a slap on the wrist, a year of home confinement, for exercising extremely poor judgment," Sean said.

" 'Extremely poor judgment' is one way to put it," Libby commented. "Well, I guess we can take one thing away from this," she said.

"Which is?" Sean asked.

"Always work alone if you're going to do something like this. I've heard that too many cooks spoil the broth, but this is ridiculous."

Sean was about to agree when Bernie yelled, "Jennie, Libby, help me."

Jennie, Libby, and Sean turned just in time to see Bernie running after Bertha. Then they saw why. The golden had the bottom half of the wedding cake firmly clamped in her mouth.

"Get her," Bernie cried as Bertha headed into the backyard.

But no one could. They were all busy laughing.

Recipes

When you read these recipes, think summer, think fresh ripe peaches and raspberries, think barbecues and picnics, think neighborhood get-togethers.

This first recipe comes from my friend and neighbor Ruth Stein. It was passed down from her grandma Gerda to her mother, Henny Waldeck, and makes an unusual and pleasant close to an evening meal.

COLD CHERRY SOUP

One 15.25-ounce can sour cherries
1 cup granulated sugar
2 tablespoons tapioca
1 large egg yolk
1 large egg white
Freshly squeezed lemon juice (optional)
Ground cinnamon for dusting

Place the cherries and their juice, sugar, and tapioca in a medium saucepan. Fill the can from the cherries with water, add the water to the cherries, and allow them to steep for 5 minutes.

Next, bring the cherry mixture to a boil over medium-high heat, stirring constantly. It will thicken a little bit as it cooks. Once it reaches a boil, turn off the heat. Set the cherry mixture aside.

Lightly beat the egg yolk in a medium bowl. Add a teaspoon of the reserved cherry mixture and stir constantly so that the egg yolk doesn't curdle. Gradually stir in the rest of the cherry mixture. Taste the soup, and if it is too sweet, add a little lemon juice.

In a medium bowl, beat the egg white with an electric mixer on medium-high speed until stiff peaks form. Using a teaspoon, place mounds of the beaten egg white atop the soup.* Sprinkle with a little cinnamon. Chill the soup in the refrigerator for several hours, or until it is cold.

Serves 4

---

*I chill the soup first and then beat the egg white and spoon mounds atop the soup right before serving.

The next two recipes come from my oldest friend, Linda Kleinman, who introduced me to French cooking and Julia Child. The first recipe, poached peaches with sauce cardinal (raspberry puree) and crème Chantilly, makes the perfect summer dessert, especially when stone fruits and berries are in season; while the second recipe, pears poached in red wine, is perfect in fall and winter.

POACHED PEACHES WITH SAUCE CARDINAL AND CRÈME CHANTILLY

Poaching the Peaches
6 cups water
2 cups granulated sugar
8 large firm peaches, peeled, halved, and stoned
One 4-inch piece vanilla bean or 3 tablespoons vanilla
    extract

In a heavy 3- to 4-quart saucepan, bring the water and sugar to a boil over high heat and cook, stirring, until the sugar dissolves. Boil the syrup for 10 more minutes, and then reduce the heat to as low as possible. Add the peach halves and the vanilla and poach, uncovered, at a low simmer for 10 to 20 minutes, or until the peaches are barely tender when pierced with the tip of a sharp knife. Allow the peaches and syrup to cool and then refrigerate until they are cold.

Preparing the Sauce Cardinal
Two 10-ounce packages frozen raspberries, defrosted and
    drained
2 tablespoons superfine sugar
1 tablespoon kirsch

With the back of a large spoon, pass the raspberries through a fine sieve into a medium mixing bowl. Stir the sugar and kirsch into the raspberry puree. Cover tightly and refrigerate.

Preparing the Crème Chantilly
¾ cup chilled heavy cream
2 tablespoons superfine sugar
1 tablespoon vanilla extract

With a wire whisk or an electric mixer on medium-high speed, whip the cream in a chilled medium mixing bowl until it begins to thicken. Add the sugar and the vanilla, and continue whipping the cream until it forms soft peaks that are firm enough to hold when the whisk or mixer is held above the bowl.

Assembling the Dessert
To assemble, transfer the chilled peach halves with a slotted spoon to individual dessert bowls or arrange them attractively on a large platter. (Discard the syrup or save it to use for poaching fruit again.)

Spoon the reserved sauce cardinal over the peaches and then decorate with the reserved crème Chantilly. If you wish, garnish the dessert with fresh raspberries and/or chopped pistachios. Serve at once.

Serves 8

PEARS POACHED IN RED WINE

2 cups dry red wine
1 cup granulated sugar
2 tablespoons freshly squeezed lemon juice
One 2-inch stick cinnamon or ½ teaspoon ground
   cinnamon
3 large ripe but firm pears (or 6 small pears), peeled,
   cored, and halved

In a 12-inch enamel, stainless-steel, or glass saucepan, bring the wine, sugar, lemon juice, and cinnamon to a boil over medium heat and cook, stirring, until the sugar has dissolved. Reduce the heat to low, add the pear halves, and cover the saucepan. Cook the pears at a very low simmer for 15 to 20 minutes, or until they are soft but not mushy. Test this with the tip of a sharp knife. Cool the pears in the syrup until they are warm.

To serve, remove the cinnamon stick (if used), and with a slotted spoon, arrange the warm pear halves in dessert bowls. Spoon some syrup over them and serve at once. The pears are also delicious chilled.

Serves 6

I have to thank my friend and neighbor Apryl Grover for the next two recipes: wild rice salad and mango, avocado, and shrimp salad. Tasty and easy to make, they are perfect to bring to cookouts or other get-togethers.

WILD RICE SALAD

Preparing the Dressing
¼ cup rice vinegar
1 tablespoon Dijon mustard
2 medium cloves garlic, peeled and minced
½ teaspoon salt, or to taste
½ teaspoon ground black pepper, or to taste
¼ teaspoon granulated sugar

Stir together all the dressing ingredients in a small bowl and set aside.

Preparing the Salad
1 cup uncooked wild rice
4 cups chicken stock
Juice of ½ small lemon
1 pound cooked chicken or turkey breast (optional)
4 ounces fresh sugar snap peas, stem end and string removed, cut in two
1 medium red bell pepper, seeded, deribbed, and diced
3 green onions (both green and white parts), stems removed and minced
2 ripe medium avocados, halved, pitted, peeled, and diced
1 cup dried cranberries
½ cup pine nuts

Rinse the wild rice in a fine-mesh strainer with cold water and drain well. Pour the chicken stock into a medium saucepan, bring it to a boil over medium heat, and add the rice. Reduce the heat and simmer, stirring occasionally, for 45 minutes, or until the grains start to open and are tender. Drain off any excess liquid and transfer the rice to a medium serving bowl. (The bowl should be large if you are incorporating chicken or turkey into the salad.) Allow the rice to cool for 10 minutes.

Next, add the lemon juice to the rice and stir. Fold in the chicken, sugar snap peas, red pepper, and green onions. Cover and refrigerate for at least 2 hours.

To serve, toss the rice salad with the reserved dressing, and then garnish the salad with the diced avocado, cranberries, and pine nuts. Serve at once. Voilà!

Serves 4 to 6

MANGO, AVOCADO, AND SHRIMP SALAD

Preparing the Dressing
¼ cup freshly squeezed lime juice
2 tablespoons olive oil
1 clove garlic, peeled and left whole
Fresh cilantro, minced, to taste (optional)
Dash of hot sauce

Combine all the dressing ingredients in a small bowl, stir well, and set aside.

Preparing the Salad
¾ pound cooked shrimp
3 small mangoes, peeled, pitted, and diced
2 ripe medium avocados, halved, pitted, peeled, and diced
1 medium red bell pepper, seeded, deribbed, and diced
2 green onions (both green and white parts), stems
   removed and minced

Arrange all the salad ingredients on salad plates.
Remove the garlic clove from the reserved dressing, garnish each salad with dressing, and serve at once.

Serves 4

My last recipe is from my new friend and neighbor, Glynda Dancy-Edwards, a cook, dog trainer, and all-around handy person. This cookie recipe makes a lot of cookies, cookies that are perfect to take on a road trip, enjoy at a picnic, or give away as presents.

GRANDMA DANCY'S SOFT MOLASSES COOKIES

1 cup granulated sugar
2 sticks (8 ounces) unsalted butter, melted
2 large eggs
7 cups sifted flour
¾ tablespoon ground cinnamon
1 teaspoon ground ginger
½ teaspoon salt
¼ teaspoon ground nutmeg
1 cup molasses
1 cup boiling water
1 tablespoon red or white vinegar

Preheat the oven to 375°. Line 3 baking sheets with parchment paper.

In a large bowl, whisk together the sugar and butter until creamy. Add the eggs and whisk until well incorporated. Set aside.

In a separate large bowl, mix together the flour, cinnamon, ginger, salt, and nutmeg. Slowly add the flour-spice mixture to the reserved sugar-butter mixture and mix with a spatula or wooden spoon until combined. Set the dough aside.

In a medium bowl, combine the molasses, boiling water, and vinegar and stir until well blended. Add the molasses mixture to the reserved dough and mix until fully incorporated. Let the dough stand, uncovered, for 5 minutes.

Drop 1 to 2 tablespoons cookie dough 2 inches apart on the parchment-lined baking sheets. Each baking sheet should hold at least 12 cookies. Bake for 7 to 8 minutes, or until the edges of the cookies are golden brown.

Store the cookies in an airtight container for up to a week.

Yields about 3 dozen cookies